Pigs get Slaughtered

Copyright ©2024 A.D. Vaughan
Cover by A.D. Vaughan
All rights reserved.

No part of this publication may be reproduced, distributed or transmitted in any form or by any means without the prior written permission of the publisher, except in the case of brief quotations embodied in reviews and certain other non-commercial uses permitted by UK copyright law.

ISBN: 9798871901557

*To Naomi
Noah and Louis*

Pigs get Slaughtered

A Novel

by

A.D. Vaughan

Prologue

Emma had begun to find herself a bit of a routine. When you're working day after day at a client's office, it's easy to feel like you're the outsider, like you don't really belong there. She'd got into the habit of buying a sandwich and a coffee at the Pret A Manger around the corner. Just something to make her feel a little more part of the set-up.

"Are you having your usual?" said the woman behind the counter.

"Yes, I think I'm ready for it," she replied, with a smile.

The woman poured out the coffee and passed it over with a bag containing the cucumber and tuna sandwich. Emma thanked her and took it back up to the office.

She usually ate with the accounts staff, sitting around the central desk space. The auditors had a separate room that she could use, but it felt a bit sad to be stuck in there on her own. They didn't mind another girl sitting with them. It was a chance to share the office gossip with someone who hadn't heard it all a thousand times before.

"Hey Emma, have you heard the latest?"

"No, tell me more," she replied.

Christine, the credit controller, gave her the whole story; the fall out from the office night out. She knew enough about the main characters now to feign interest. It was a bit like tuning in to a soap opera. It gave the staff a chance to imagine that there was more to their working day than the mundane reality. For Emma, it just killed a bit of time before she needed to get back to work.

She headed back into the small office that the company had reserved for the audit team. It was a bit pokey, but they'd managed to squeeze three desks into it. There were two of them working on the job full time but Emma was on her own today. The audit manager would drop in from time to time to check up on things or meet with the company Finance Director.

Most people would imagine it's pretty boring being an auditor. It probably is for most people. All that number crunching and checking of balances. Emma didn't mind it though. She liked the challenge of understanding how the business worked; following the money through the system and piecing together the puzzle. Then, when it was all done, she could move on to the next job.

There was always a sense of relief that she could leave it all behind; that she wasn't stuck there like all the regular office workers. You were never around long enough to fall out with anyone, so you always left on good terms. They'd usually say they'd meet up for lunch sometime, but it never happened. The firm didn't like them to fraternise with the clients.

Emma was getting to the point where she was ready to leave this place behind. It had been pretty good while it lasted and one of her easier assignments. The company was run from a head office in India but they seemed to have all the right systems in place. She couldn't remember a job where everything seemed so straight forward. She just needed to reconcile the remaining cash accounts and she'd be done.

She spent the early afternoon pulling all the documents together and testing the control procedures with one of the Admin staff. When they needed any copies, the company let them use the photocopier at the end of the hall.

Someone had sellotaped an A4 sheet to the cover. 'Out of order.' *That's all I need*, she thought.
    "Oh, the guy's coming to look at it tomorrow." said Pamela. Pamela was the office manager.

"Oh right. Is there another one I can use?"

"Well, there's one upstairs but you won't be able to use your card with that one." She gave her a conspiratorial look and lowered her voice. "There's a copier in the F.D.'s office. Just use that one. He won't mind." Emma could see the door to his office was open behind her.

"Okay, thanks. It's only a couple of prints."

There was no one in the office but she glanced up and down the hall anyway. He seemed to spend a lot of his time in the CEO's office from what she could tell. The copier was just inside the door; it wouldn't take a moment.

As she opened the cover of the machine, she stopped. There was a sheet of paper face down on the glass. She turned it over and saw that it was a blank piece of headed paper. It had the name of the company's bankers, Santander, along the top; just like the bank statements she'd been looking through this afternoon. It made her pause for a second. She was still wondering about it while she made her copies; still searching for a plausible explanation as she closed the cover and stepped out into the hall.

She saw him out of the corner of her eye; the F.D. emerging from the CEO's office at the very same moment. Had he seen her? She didn't think so. When she glanced back over her shoulder, he was still talking in the doorway. She'd got away with it; but wait, had she put the headed paper back in the copier? She couldn't remember. As she reached the Accounts department, she snatched another furtive glance. He was coming back down the hall. Too late now.

Emma got back to the pokey office and sat down in front of her laptop. There must be a perfectly simple explanation, she told herself. There were probably countless reasons why he'd have copies of the bank's headed paper. It left a nagging doubt though; one that stayed with her for the rest of the afternoon. She should probably say something; at least just query it. Maybe she'd catch a word with the CEO later.

It was dark when she came out of the building. She had to make her way down a narrow pedestrianised street towards Guy's Hospital. The car park was at the back; a bit of a seedy place, but handy for the office.

She was glad she'd mentioned it in the end. It would have been wrong not to say anything. He said he'd raise it with him and that she'd done the right thing. The more she thought about it, the more suspicious it became. She'd double check the balances with the bank tomorrow. That would rule out any possibility of fraud.

As she headed off, she could see the top of The Shard shining above the buildings lining the road. The pub on the corner was busy with the after-work crowd. Someone opened the door and let out the sound of friendly chatter; the warm glow of the interior spilled out onto the street. It marked the end of the active street frontage before the shops and restaurants gave way to drab flats and the empty business premises beyond.

She picked up the pace a little to make it quickly past the shadowy doorways. The street sounds gradually ebbed away and it was just her and the old man walking his dog up ahead. He turned at the corner, leaving her to complete the last stretch on her own. She could see the NCP car park ahead; the faint glow from the stairwell entrance.

It would be hard to imagine a more unwelcoming structure. The dark gloomy exterior with minimal lighting, looming over the street. She pushed open the single swing door that lead into the stark concrete staircase. The smell of urine was immediately noticeable. Emma never took the elevator. The idea of being stuck in there was a little more than she could contemplate. She preferred to take the stairs.

The sound of her footsteps reverberated up the stairwell. The sharp click of her heels sounded unnaturally loud in the confined space. As she reached the second floor, she heard the swing door close with a dull thud. Someone else had joined her on the staircase; a more gritty and shuffling footstep. It made her hurry up the remaining two flights. The place gave her the creeps.

She was glad to get out of the stairwell and onto the parking deck. She'd always try to find a space on the street side if she could; the lighting was better on that side. Then she remembered; there were no free spaces this morning. She was over in the far corner.

As she walked around, the lights of a departing vehicle briefly illuminated the corner where she was parked. She could make out the front of her car next to an over-sized SUV. It was only when she got to the driver's side, that she could see it had been parked far too close. A large wing mirror was blocking her from getting to the driver's door. She stood there for a moment feeling irritated. She wondered if she should put a note under his windscreen wiper; give him a piece of her mind.

She decided it wasn't worth the effort. She could walk around the car and squeeze into the driver's door from the other side. There was plenty of room to pass along the side of her car. She just needed to step over the concrete kerb at the back; the one that prevents cars reversing too far.

Had she tripped over the kerb? She wasn't sure. She must have bumped her head on something. She felt momentarily dazed. Somebody had caught her and stopped her from falling over. They lifted her back onto her feet; then lifted her up higher. It all seemed to happen so fast.

She could feel herself going over the rail; the cold touch of metal against her thigh. She couldn't understand what was happening. A sudden rush of cold air and the blur of the lights against the night sky. Everything was spinning around her. She didn't know who, or why, but she knew she was falling, falling……..

Chapter 1

The light tinkle of piano keys announced the start of the day. Nothing too demanding, just a gentle nudge to let him know it was time to get up. Alex ignored it for a while, before it began to annoy him. He stretched out an arm to hit the snooze button and drifted back into the the warmth of the duvet. The 10 minute stay of execution before real life took its course. Some days it would disappear in the blink of an eye, but on others, the time took on a strange elasticity that would allow him to drift in and out of consciousness through a series of half dreams. It was one such morning.

Time inevitably returned to its regular continuum and the alarm sounded once again. This time there was no reprieve and he rose to his feet next to the futon bed, rubbing the sleep from his eyes and running the fingers of one hand through his hair. It was six o-clock and the first hint of morning was casting soft shadows around the edge of the curtains. The house was quiet and the only sounds were the occasional rumble of a car passing by on the main road.

Alex turned on the lamp on the side table, illuminating the room. A fairly typical London bed-sit, but a little bigger than most, and with its own bathroom. Two sash windows overlooked the street and there was a small bar kitchen area alongside the bathroom. A desk stood by the window with a wide screen monitor and a small sofa and rug defined the sitting area.

He wandered over to the window and pulled back the curtain to check the lay of the land. The street was quiet and the early sun rise had generated a pale glow over the roof tops on the other side of the street. It had the makings of a nice Spring day.

Alex glanced over at the desk by the window. That would be his place of work for the rest of the day; the monitor, his window onto the world. He'd been a full time private investor for the past three years and an early start to the day came with the territory. The RNSs, the formal announcements issued by public companies, come out at 7am sharp. If you want to trade the news, you need to be up-to-date and ready to go by 8am when the market opens.

There was still plenty of time to get some breakfast from the local shop around the corner. He swapped his T-shirt for a black sweat shirt and pulled on a pair of jeans that were hanging over the chair. As he left the room, he made a conscious effort to shut the door slowly, causing just a dull click as it closed.

There were 2 apartments on each of the 3 floors. He had one on the top floor; quieter than those below and warmer in the winter months, but susceptible to unwelcome interactions with his fellow tenants while negotiating the staircase. It was too early to expect any such bad timing this morning, although Miss Marks, the landlady, had a habit of prowling the staircase at odd hours.

The house stood at the end of a short cul-de-sac off the main road. It was always quiet at this time in the morning. He turned onto the main road and made his way down to the only open shop at this time of the morning. A bundle of blankets stirred in the entrance to the discount store as he passed by.

The exotic smell of Indian spices met him as he entered the shop and a young woman wearing a headscarf greeted his arrival with a cheery smile. He marvelled at how she could summon up the positive energy at this hour and smiled back.

"Something smells good, what's on the menu today?" She ran through the options and he settled for a Chai Latte and vegetable samosa, to go.

He wandered around the shop whilst waiting for the Latte. An old man was sitting at the table in the window reading a paper between sips of his morning tea. Smoke from a cigarette spiralled up from the ashtray on the table. Alex picked up a sliced loaf of bread and a carton of milk from the mini supermarket that occupied the rest of the shop and returned to the counter. A little expensive but that's the price of convenience. He took his change and left the shop, leaning his shoulder against the door whilst holding the cup in one hand and the shopping bag in the other.

The house was still quiet as he stepped back into the hallway and he closed the door carefully to keep it that way. Nobody left the house before seven so he was back in his room before the first of his fellow tenants had begun to stir.

Alex sat down in front of the monitor and turned on the computer. There was still ten or fifteen minutes before the day's announcements were released, so he opened the CNBC stream to catch the early morning business news. They were on a commercial break. A couple in their mid to late fifties were walking hand-in-hand along a deserted sandy beach. The classic image of a happy and early retirement. A deep and smokey voice explained that, with the right people on your side, this could be your future too. The beach scene faded away to reveal an eagle's head in side-profile.
    "Stamford Goldway," said the smokey voice and the words appeared below the logo, "for all your investment needs."

Alex had decided a long time ago that he wasn't about to entrust his future to the professionals. All those fees and add-ons, on top of a below average performance, was never going to cut it. Over the last ten years he'd proved to himself that he could do a lot better.

He'd been introduced to stock market investing at university. A friend had asked him to help write an algorithm to screen for stock market investments he was making. They had some pretty decent results before they ended up over-trading in a downturn. For Alex though, the seed had been sown. He'd always been fascinated by games and problem solving and here he'd found the ultimate game; one that could last for years, was endlessly fascinating and had a very clear and unambiguous way of keeping the score.

He decided to take the plunge and begin investing full time a few years ago. He'd been working for around five years as a software developer for a gaming company. He had one foot on the corporate ladder, except it felt more like one foot firmly on the treadmill. When the company was taken over, he decided to take a redundancy package and consider his options. He could have jumped straight back onto the IT merry-go-round, but instead, decided to take a year off to see if he could turn the hobby into a viable day job. Three years on, and he'd managed to double his capital as well as covering his living expenses.

Alex took a sip of his tea and kept one eye on the clock as it approached 7am. When the time arrived, the RNSs began to be released, appearing automatically in a software program that he'd written to capture and summarize them. He went through them, quickly scan reading to decide whether they merited any further examination.

There wasn't much of interest; the usual mix of non-executive board appointments and share buy-backs. A couple of trading updates looked promising, but on deeper inspection, turned out to be in line with expectations so unlikely to move the share price much. It was beginning to look a bit thin on the ground, before something caught his eye. It was a company called A.I. Simulations, one that Alex had on his watch list. The announcement simply confirmed that the company had signed an initial agreement with a well-known game developer to explore future opportunities for collaboration. It seemed fairly innocuous on the face of it, but Alex immediately saw its significance. The company developed tools for training subway drivers and signal control operators. If this marked a move into the gaming industry, there could be a significant re-rating of the stock.

This was the part of the job that he liked the most. The moment where it felt like he'd unearthed something. The gold prospector who's found the first traces of what might lead to a new seam. The familiar buzz of excitement where he sensed there was an opportunity to be grasped.

Experience had taught him that he needed to suppress the excitement. He needed to be disciplined and think rationally. The one thing about trading the markets is that you have to have a plan. You can't allow yourself to simply react to events as they unfold; you need to be absolutely clear about the price you're going to buy, and if the trade turns bad, the price you will exit. Alex made a note of the prices that he'd commit to on the pad he kept on the desk.

At 8:00am he had the live prices streaming on his monitor. A.I. Simulations opened up five percent, but he waited. He wanted to see it rise above the all-time high a couple of points higher. He could almost feel it straining at the leash but told himself to stick to the plan. The price ticked up a point and then, as it hit his buy price, he made his trade. Over the next half an hour, the price rose a further five percent and Alex bought again, averaging up into the trade.

By mid-morning the price had risen twenty percent on the day and had paused as some profit-taking started. He had to decide whether to take his profits or let it run, the eternal dilemma; stick or twist? The trading volume was still not as high as he would have expected, so in the end, he decided to sell half and remain invested with the rest but with a stop loss five percent below the current price.

He stood up from his computer and stretched his arms above his head to remove the tension and stiffness. He'd made about £1,500, or a little less if he got stopped out on his remaining trade. Not a bad morning at the office.

He always told himself that the daily successes and failures were just noise, but he couldn't help enjoying the moment. It was times like this that he missed the real life office environment. No one to share the small victories with or relive the moments. He could call his girlfriend but she probably wouldn't thank him for interrupting one of her client briefings, and besides, she didn't really approve of his current career choice. What Alex did have though, was his small band of like-minded misfits; his fellow investors who had formed their own community on the investing bulletin boards.

All kinds of humanity inhabit these digital chatrooms, from multi-millionaire professional investors through to get-rich-quick wannabes and outright crazies. Over the years he'd learned to filter out the more extreme elements and had identified a small core of investors who's opinions he respected or who he just plain liked. They tended to follow each other into various investment ideas and swap research on the boards or at the various networking events organized around London.

He logged on to the bulletin board site and checked the A.I. Simulations board. There were a few posts; the usual array of cheer leading and ramping, but who could blame them for a bit of overblown optimism. It cheered everyone up. Alex added his two pennies worth, giving some background on the gaming company that he could recall from his time in the industry.

There was no one he recognized amongst the posters, so he decided to group message the usual crowd, to see if anyone else had caught the move. Most of the replies expressed regret at missing out but a couple had bought in this morning and already sold for a quick gain. He wondered if he should close his own position and glanced at the card taped to the side of his monitor.

"Bulls make money, Bears make money, Pigs get slaughtered."

It was one of those old adages of Wall Street. The idea being that you can make money in the markets by betting prices will go up and you can make money betting that they'll go down, but the greedy, those who ignore risk, will always lose out in the long run. Alex went through the trading position again in his head. He was satisfied that with his stop loss in place, the risk/reward ratio made it worth pursuing.

He got up and tried to clear his mind for a while. So much of the trading day was spent waiting for something to happen. Sometimes, you just have to let things take their course. He took the chance to fetch a roll from the sandwich shop on the high street and some fruit from the stall on the corner. He ate it on the sofa whilst flicking through the latest edition of Time Out on his i-pad.

You have to be cut out for the investment game; have the right psychological make up. Everybody knows what you should do. There are literally thousands of books telling you just what you need to know. The problem is we're all human, and we keep making the same mistakes over and over. Alex had made his fair share when he started out, but he'd tried to turn each mistake into a valuable lesson. He wasn't immune from making more, but he'd developed a disciplined approach to investing that usually protected him from the worst of them.

The current price of his open trade was displayed in the corner of his monitor. By mid-afternoon, it had given back part of its earlier gains and the share price was sitting just above his stop loss. It looked likely that he'd get stopped out, but he felt no regrets. It was simply the price of making the trade. You're never going to win them all.

As he was turning this thought over in his head, the share price on his desktop refreshed. The price had turned and begun to retrace part of its afternoon fall. More interestingly, the volume of trades had suddenly increased significantly. Alex sat back down in front of the monitor and gave it his full attention.

When you've been closely following the markets for years, you get a feel for how they react; like the original traders who bet on the ticker tape in the early days of the stock markets. You get a sense of when someone is looking to accumulate the stock. Alex had that feeling now. He checked the shares on offer and saw that these had mostly dried up. Any further buys would likely see the share price increase. Now was the time to sit tight and try to make the most of his position.

Over the next hour, the price rose sharply, taking the chart into new highs. Alex kept his attention fixed on the price chart and volumes of trades going through. Still the buying remained strong and as it progressed, he moved his stop loss higher to ensure that he locked in a good part of the profit.

Ultimately, the excitement got a little more than he could handle and he exited the position while the demand remained strong. He missed the final advance just before the close but it's never a bad idea to leave something for the next guy. Besides, he'd had one of his best days trading yet, clearing a profit of around £3,000.

He leaned back in his chair and grinned. Is there anything to beat the satisfaction of a successful day's trading? That feeling when a carefully laid plan pays off.

Chapter 2

It was getting dark by the time Alex left the house and unlocked his bike from the railings. The street lights were on and the light from the shops lining the main road gave everything a warm and inviting glow. The evening traffic was backed up along the road as he turned the corner but Alex was able to progress uninterrupted alongside the kerb, much to the annoyance of the long-suffering commuters.

It was only a couple of miles from Wood Green to Palmers Green and he knew pretty much every bump in the road. Alex had grown up around this part of north London and was able to weave from road to pavement at will wherever there was a vehicle blocking his path. It only took him around 10 minutes to complete the journey from his flat to the place that he'd always called home.

Looking at the building as he crossed the road and dismounted, he couldn't decide what it meant to him now. The two upper floors looked a little gloomy and in need of a coat of paint to the render. The restaurant on the ground floor was located on a corner and had two large windows with canopies above. It looked a little neglected and the sign, which read *Taverna Katerina,* could do with a touch up. He'd wanted to get away from here for so long but it seemed like he couldn't. It was his past, and had always threatened to be his future; a future he felt like he desperately needed to change.

He leaned his bike against the lamppost in front of the restaurant and secured it with the chain from his backpack. He glanced at the window of the restaurant and could make out one or two early diners; not exactly a thriving hot spot but it was still early in the evening. Alex walked down the narrow passage at the side of the building that led to the yard at the back of the kitchen. The light above the back door automatically came on as he entered. He walked up the steps and knocked on the narrow glass panes. A young woman opened the door and smiled with a hint of disapproval.

"You just made it. He was about to disown you and cut you off from the will." Alex laughed.

"What, you mean there's something to inherit?" He embraced his sister-in-law warmly and stepped into the kitchen.

It was a good sized kitchen; brushed steel work surfaces and a big extractor fan over the central island where most of the serious business took place. Two chefs were busy preparing the food. One, a tall gangly youth, was mixing the salads and looked up to grin and nod a greeting to Alex. The other, remained focused on preparing kebabs from the marinated lamb and vegetables arranged in bowls in front of him. Without looking up he said:

"Glad you could make it bro. Gordon Gecko is in the building." He glanced up and caught Alex's eye and they both forced a smile.

Jack was a year older than Alex and as kids they'd done everything together. As they got older, it just seemed that life was taking them in different directions. Jack had never imagined that he would do anything other than work in the restaurant. He didn't have the options that Alex had and was never going to go on to further education. What he did have though, was a talent for cooking and the truth is, he was in his element in the kitchen. He'd introduced new ideas for the menu and had a creative talent for combining tastes and textures that would be better suited to a higher class of restaurant than the family taverna.

"You'd better get your skates on, he's chomping at the bit," he said.

Alex ducked into the small office at the back of the kitchen and changed into the suit and tie that he always kept on the hanger. He looked into the small mirror that hung on the wall and adjusted his tie. Did he look like the Maitre d'? Not really. More like the kid going for his first job interview, which is what he'd bought the suit for in the first place. He brushed his hair back with his fingers and smoothed out the wrinkles in his trousers. That would have to do. As he came out of the office, Maya frowned and straightened the collar of his shirt before nodding her approval.

"I'll go and put him out of his misery," she said.

Alex's father, Yiorgos Samaras, known to everyone as George, had one weekly appointment that he could never miss. It was his night with the old guys; playing backgammon above the Greek bakery around the corner from the restaurant. Backgammon was really just the excuse rather than the main event. The excuse to pour the liquor and talk about the old days in Cyprus.

These were the people he'd known since he came over more than twenty years ago. Some of them even originated from the same town of Paphos and they'd supported and relied on each other to make a life for themselves here in London. George had needed that support after Alex and Jack's mother died when they were just eight and nine years old respectively. It had floored him. Without her, he'd been cast adrift, and with two boys that he hadn't the first clue what to do with. He had a cousin that lived in London with her husband and she'd offered to help look after the boys until they got back on their feet. That was the only option he had and so he swapped the long summers and laid back lifestyle of Cyprus for the rainy streets of London.

George Samaras entered the kitchen from the restaurant, gesturing at his watch.

"What time you call this?" he said to Alex in his thick accent. He was a good looking man in his youth but life had begun to take its toll. He had a strong face but now worry lines marked his forehead and his cheeks had become sunken. A greying beard lined the edge of his jaw and matched the colour of his combed back hair.

"I build this business for you guys. You got to learn business is serious." Alex said nothing. "We got two tables booked for 7:30 and one table for 8:00. Remember, you offer them liqueurs, right. We got plenty great liqueurs." He slapped Alex on the shoulder and went to retrieve his coat from the office. A distinct smell of brandy followed in his wake.

He'd been standing in for his Dad every Wednesday evening since he took redundancy and to be honest he really didn't mind doing it. It got him outside of his solitary day job and he could tell himself that he hadn't completely abandoned his family roots. Besides, it gave the old man his weekly dose of nostalgia.

George emerged from the office still pulling his coat over one shoulder. He stopped momentarily at the large cabinet lining the end of the kitchen and transferred a bottle of something into his coat pocket. Maya exchanged a brief look with Jack who shrugged his shoulders and went back to preparing the food. One or two final instructions were relayed, as George made his way out of the back door, and Maya closed it behind him. She looked up at Alex as though expecting him to say something, but he didn't meet her gaze. He didn't want to have the conversation just now.
"I'd better go check on the customers" he said, and leaned against the swing door to the restaurant.

There were three tables occupied and Alex did the rounds, topping up wine glasses and exchanging pleasantries with the customers. He then faded the traditional folk music and put on something a little more contemporary. A little less weekend plate smashing and a bit more in tune with the mid-week relaxing dinner for two vibe.

He looked around the restaurant, the backdrop to his formative years, and everything looked so familiar; like nothing had changed in twenty years. The original fresco on the far wall with the Mediterranean blue sea and white buildings with blue shutters was still there. The blue had faded a little, a bit like his memory of the real thing, gradually becoming foggy and less distinct.

The restaurant needed a make over. It tended to attract a customer of a certain age and they were the kind of customer that had a strict budget in mind when they sat down to eat. The restaurant offered value for money but didn't offer that experience you wanted to tell your friends about and choose for those special nights out. With Jack's contemporary ideas in the kitchen and a more wine bar/bistro approach, they could make something of this place. Of course, they'd never get anything like that past their father, and besides, the place was barely making enough to break even, let alone pay for a make over.

The bookings arrived as arranged and two other couples dropped in over the course of the evening. Alex did his best to encourage them to stretch the budget with after dinner drinks and Greek coffee and all in all, it wasn't a bad nights takings. Maya did most of the serving, whilst Alex looked after the wine and other drinks and the evening passed quickly. When the final customers left, just before 11:00, Alex retracted the canopies and lowered the blinds to the two windows, while Maya cleared the remaining tables. They dimmed the lights and retreated to the kitchen.

"Good feedback on the Souvlaki Jack," said Alex as he entered the kitchen; "and they loved what you did with the feta salad. At this rate, you'll be getting another Michelin star."
"Thanks bro, that makes all the hard work and the crap wages worth it. Now get that cheap suit off and help with the

washing up."

Alex stepped into the office and returned the suit to its usual hanger, before changing back into his regular clothes and rolling his sleeves up. As he emerged into the kitchen, Maya was loading the dishwasher and Jack and Pete, the assistant chef, were clearing the remaining food from the worktops. They saved what they could in sealed plastic boxes to go in the fridge. That just left the mountain of pans and utensils next to the sink, which Alex recognized as the reward for his evenings work.

How long had he spent scrubbing pans over the course of his youth growing up here? Too many years to recount. The long evenings when his friends would be out playing football or hanging around the precinct, he would never get back. He'd come to despise the kitchen back then and everything that it represented. Looking back now, he could begin to see what it must have been like for his Dad. A single parent landed in a foreign country with two kids. He was just trying to survive and it needed all hands on deck.

Alex set about his task and quickly settled into the familiar routine. Everyone knew their job, and like a military operation, they weaved around one another, returning everything to its rightful place and restoring the kitchen to its usual state of preparedness. A final wipe down of the surfaces and everything looked ship shape. Jack collected the credit card slips and cash from the register in the restaurant and paid Pete in cash for his hours. The remaining money and receipts he put in a metal box in the office. It would be accounted for later by George, who took care of all things financial.

Pete collected his jacket from the office and announced his departure.
"Not staying for a drink Pete?" asked Jack.
"Nah, I better get back and feed the dog. He'll be

chewing the furniture." With that, he disappeared out of the back door and closed it behind him.

"How about you bro?" said Jack.

"I'll stay for a quick coffee if you're brewing," replied Alex.

The three of them sat around the main island sipping the hot coffee. It felt like there was something unsaid that Jack and Maya wanted to get out, but in the end Jack just said:

"So, how's the stock market casino treating you?" Alex could sense the scorn that Jack had for his present occupation, so he didn't go out of his way to talk about it.

"It's been pretty good lately, but I don't get over excited about it. There'll be a pay back sooner or later. How's the restaurant making out? Seemed like a decent night tonight." Jack glanced at Maya.

"It's difficult to know the big picture. Dad keeps all the books. It doesn't seem to matter what goes through the till, we always struggle to generate much cash."

"Maybe I should look over the accounts some time. There might be somewhere you can tighten things up."

"Well, good luck with that idea. He's never used anyone else to do the books. You'll be lucky to get near them."

"How's it working out since you moved in upstairs?" asked Alex.

"Better than I was expecting," replied Jack. "We've got the whole of the 2nd floor and he's moved up to the top floor. The commute to work's a lot shorter too."

"Yeah, welcome to my World. At least, you work on a different floor," said Alex with a laugh.

"So, is he always popping down for a cup of sugar, Maya?"

"No, we hear him playing his old record collection but he doesn't bother us. He usually pops down for a coffee before the restaurant opens." She hesitated and then added: "Alex, he....., your Dad I mean......, he seems to be drinking more than he used to. I know he's always liked a drink, but lately, it's become more regular. Judging from the liquor store, he seems to be getting through more than the customers." Alex looked at Jack, but he avoided his gaze and studied his coffee cup.

"Yeah, I thought I could smell booze on him before he went out tonight, and that's before the old guys hit it over the backgammon. Have you talked to him about it Jack?"

"You know the old man, he'd never admit there's a problem."

"Has he been OK at work? I mean, is everything alright?"

"Yeah, nothing unusual. There's the normal problems of paying the bills and balancing the books but that comes with the territory in this business."

"Maybe I will have a word with him about taking on some of the book work. It'll be just one less thing for him to worry about," offered Alex. Jack shrugged his shoulders.

"So how's it going with you and Lisa?" asked Maya, changing the subject. Alex was glad to move on.

"Fine. She's moved into a flat in Hampstead whilst we sort out somewhere together."

"Somewhere together?" said Maya smiling. "You've been talking about that for the last 2 years."

"Yeah I know, but I just need to get enough money together for a decent deposit and still have something left to invest," he replied, somewhat defensively. "It's not like I get a regular salary. I need to keep the expenses down so I can get to where I want to be that much quicker."

"And where is it that you want to be, bro?" asked Jack. Alex looked at him.

"You know what, I really don't know, but I want to have choices. That's what money gives you. It let's you decide your future for yourself, not have it thrust on you like......,"

"Like me, you mean?" said Jack. Alex took in a deep breath.

"No, that's not what I mean Jack. You love this business; you're a natural with food. I just can't see myself here when I'm Dad's age. I guess I just want to discover what's out there."

"Be sure to let us know what you find," said Jack, smiling. Alex cracked a smile too.

"Sorry, I'm getting way too heavy here. Any chance you could work your magic with that pitta bread and the leftovers and I'll be on my way."

Jack retrieved a few things from the fridge while Alex got his stuff together and Maya cleared away the cups.

"We should have a night out with you and Lisa sometime," said Maya.

"Yeah, let's do it. Lisa's got a birthday coming up, so maybe we can do something together." Jack had prepared the take away and handed it, wrapped in foil, to Alex. He took it and stuffed it in his backpack. "Right, I'll be off," he said, as he opened the back door and nodded farewell.

It was a clear night and had got a little colder over the last few hours. He turned up the collar of his jacket as he made his way back through the passage to the main road. As he unlocked his bike and wheeled it over to the crossing, he noticed two figures standing and talking further up the road. They were a little way off, but he could recognize the shadowy outline of his father. Alex was surprised to still see him. He was talking with a taller figure; someone who seemed younger. Alex stood for a moment and just watched them until his dad abruptly walked off down the road. The younger figure remained standing there looking after him.

There was something that struck Alex as strange about the scene. His dad knew most of the locals in the area and would greet anyone and everyone, but this didn't seem like one of those random meetings in the street. He waited a moment to see if the other man would come back towards him, but he didn't. Eventually, he just sauntered off in the opposite direction.

Alex got on his bike and set off home. He thought about it briefly as he cycled back to the flat, before the cool breeze began to clear his head. His mind turned to other things.

Chapter 3

A week could disappear in the blink of an eye. That's the thing about working from home with the same four walls, the same work space and the same routine. One day would pretty much blend into the next, and that's how it had been for the last week or so. Alex had opened the curtains to a dull and overcast day but it wasn't going to spoil his mood. Today was going to be different. Today was a chance to get out there and meet people; gather first hand information and actually feel like he had a real job for a change.

He did most of his research online, but occasionally, there was a chance for him to attend a company's Annual General Meeting (AGM). He'd arranged to attend two meetings of companies he was invested in. It would give him a chance to meet the people who manage and work in the companies and get a real sense of the personalities he was backing. Online research was one thing, but there was no substitute for looking the directors squarely in the eye.

He had everything he needed on his MacBook which he packed into a vinyl bag that he always used. He could pull up the key data or charts during the meetings and check any details that arose in real time. He also had the letters of representation from his broker that would grant him access to the meetings, and he slipped these into the outside pocket of the bag. A quick look around to make sure he'd got everything, and he headed out of the door.

He always liked to wear a suit for these occasions. It avoided any problems of getting into the meetings and created the right impression with anyone he met. The brown leather shoes that he was unaccustomed to wearing, made a satisfying tapping sound on the wood floor as he made his way downstairs.

As he descended the final flight to the entrance hall, he could see the landlady, Ms Marks, sorting the mail that had dropped through the letter box onto the hall floor. She took it upon herself to place the letters into the appropriate compartment of the shelf alongside the front door; a separate compartment for each flat in the house. Just another way for her to keep tabs on the comings and goings of her tenants.

Alex grimaced and cursed his misfortune. He'd had to endure a lecture from her the other day about his girlfriend, Lisa, staying over for a few nights before she moved into her new flat. He generally liked to stay out of her way if he could manage it.

She turned around as she heard him coming down the stairs and the usual frown gave way to a slight look of surprise and what appeared to be a half smile.

"Good morning Mr Samaras. You look like you've got somewhere important to go," she said.
"Just a couple of meetings in the city centre," replied Alex, once again marvelling at the transformational effect of a suit and a decent pair of shoes. He took the envelope that Ms Marks was extending to him and saw that it was a letter from his Tax Accountant. He dropped it into the section of the shelf labelled 3A. "I'll pick that up later," he said.
"It looks like it might rain later," said Ms Marks holding the door for him.
"Hmm, I'll take a chance on it," replied Alex as he forced a smile on his way out.

The first meeting was at 11:00am at the company's brokers in the City. Alex had given himself plenty of time. When he emerged from the underground station, he still had about half an hour to make his way to the offices. He checked the directions on his phone. It was no more than a 10 minute walk away.

It wasn't a part of the city that he knew well but he soon located the offices; an imposing seven-storey building on a corner with the entrance facing the road junction. The brokers had the top two floors.

The doors of the lift opened onto a spacious reception; a design masterclass of hardwoods, tinted glass and ambient lighting. *Clearly, no expense spared on the company's choice of brokers then*, he thought. A smartly dressed young woman immediately appeared at his shoulder to inquire if he was here for the AGM. She relieved him of his letter of representation and led him down a warmly lit corridor to a large conference room.

A welcome slide with the company's logo was projected onto the far wall and chairs were lined up facing a top table, with four chairs for the company representatives. Most of the shareholder chairs had been taken, or were reserved with bags, notepads, etc. The company directors were in conversation with a couple of fund manager types and a few people were helping themselves to the buffet along the side wall. Alex recognized a distinctive over-sized figure busy piling up a substantial part of the finger buffet onto a paper plate. He walked up behind him.

"Matt, you look like you're getting your money's worth."
"Hey, Alex," he replied. "Yeah, the way I look at it is, I'm a shareholder, right. I'm a part-owner of the business, and so by definition, I'm a part-owner of this buffet. I'm only taking what's rightfully mine." Alex chuckled and picked up a small bottle of mineral water. "Come on, I've saved you a seat," said Matt, and they moved over to a couple of chairs near the front.

Alex first met Matt at a Private Investors social event. He stood out as he always did: large and with an unruly mop of light brown frizzy hair. He could never be accused of over dressing for any occasion, but this rough exterior covered a formidable intellect. He studied mathematics at City University in London but dropped out in his final year to switch to philosophy, which he then quit half way through the course. With a track record of never completing anything, his job opportunities were somewhat restricted. He found his way into the world of private investing, an occupation that it turned out he was well suited to.

Alex unpacked his laptop and pulled up the company's final results summary that would form the basis for the meeting. The company worked in the area of digital marketing and had delivered impressive results since its public offering about 3 years ago. Matt had brought it to Alex's attention soon after it went public, and it had been a star performer for both of them. The question was: had the current valuation become over stretched or was the company poised for a step change in growth?

The board members had taken their places at the top table; all remarkably young, but perhaps to be expected for a company in the digital space. The meeting was opened, and after a few formalities, the Chairman confidently summarized the year's results.

The results were good and he gave a glowing outline of the company's future prospects. As the founder of the company, he had a complete grasp of the details and laid out a clear strategy for the company's future. A very impressive individual, even if, in his pin stripe suit and open neck shirt, Alex couldn't help seeing the Al Pacino character from Scarface. Next, the Finance Director went through the results in detail and the Chief Operating Officer fleshed out the company's growth strategy. All the right messages and sound bites were delivered, and there was a general air of satisfaction pervading the room, with much nodding of approval.

After a questions and answers session, where the board members seemed to be on top of all the issues, the meeting moved on to the resolutions. The Auditors were reconfirmed and a very generous nil-cost options plan, as part of the company's long term employee incentive scheme, also went through with the minimum of fuss. Alex looked at Matt and rolled his eyes. Another case of Christmas coming early for the company Directors. Having said that, when they were delivering so well for shareholders, it wasn't something that either of them felt like picking a fight over.

The meeting was then brought to a conclusion and the audience were invited to re-visit the buffet. The directors would be around for a further half hour to informally answer any other questions.

"Not sure I'm ready to top slice this one yet," said Alex.

"Me neither," replied Matt. "There's some real momentum building with the share price and a lot of Institutional buying to come I reckon."

"Well, I can confirm that much," said a voice behind them, "but you didn't hear it from me, right." They both turned around and laughed when they saw a familiar face.

"Blimey, the big guns have arrived," said Alex. "You didn't tell me you were coming to this one, Jamie."

"No, I thought I might be able to get in ahead of the bulletin boarders, but I should have known you two would be one step ahead," he replied.

Jamie Sinclair was a legend in the world of private investors. A highly successful private investor, who just happened to be an equally successful manager at a well known hedge fund. Maybe it was his down to earth upbringing on the north side of Edinburgh, but he had none of the elitism that's so often found in the City financial world. He'd just as happily attend a private investor social event as he would a bankers drinks party. He was without doubt, the wealthiest person that Alex knew, and also one of the smartest.

"So Jamie, now the smart money's arrived, can we put this share in the 'fill your boots' category?" said Matt, jokingly.

"Don't get too excited Matty, I've already built a holding with a couple of decent sized off-market trades. I'll probably only add on a pull back but I think we'll all do pretty well out of this one over the next year or so. Listen, do you guys want to get lunch? I've got an interesting idea I want to run by you."

"Yeah, I've got an hour or so before I'm going across town for another AGM," replied Alex. "You coming Matt?"

"Well, I'd love to lower the tone of your business lunch, but I need to get back. I promised my Mum I'd look in on her."

"Well, it looks like it's just me and you Alex," said Jamie.

"I guess we can scrub Burger King and go up market then," joked Alex.

"I know a nice place just around the corner. Come on, I'll expense it," said Jamie.

The three of them emerged from the building onto the pavement under a grey sky and a slight chill in the air.

"Will I see you both at the PI social event next week?" asked Matt.

"Yeah, I'll be there for sure," said Alex.

"I should be able to make it, barring any last minute crisis," added Jamie.

"Great, well fill me in on Jamie's big idea later, Alex."

"Yeah, I'll Facetime you later on," said Alex. With that, Matt headed back to the station and Jamie led Alex around the corner in the direction of the restaurant.

It was a small place occupying the lower ground floor of a Georgian terrace and with iron railings lining the stairway to the entrance. The front of the restaurant was a series of glass panelled doors that could be opened in the summer but allowed the maximum amount of light into the space when closed, as they were today. The tables at the front of the restaurant were occupied so they found themselves seated at a small table along the side wall.

"It's owned by an Armenian guy," explained Jamie "but he serves a fusion of eastern Mediterranean dishes."

"Home from home," said Alex and looked through the menu. They ordered a few side dishes with some Armenian flat bread and shared a half carafe of wine.

"So, how's the market treating you?" asked Jamie.

"Things are going really well, but I'm not kidding myself. We're in a bull market so it's not been difficult to make money over the last six months. I'm just trying to make hay while the sun's out and then do my best to hang on to it when the tide turns." Jamie smiled.

"That's why I think you'd be great at a hedge fund Alex. You see the bigger picture and understand the psychology of this game. There's so many people out there that think they're stock picking geniuses, whereas the game isn't about picking stocks, it's about seeing trends and keeping one step ahead of the crowd."

"I'm guessing that's not the big idea you wanted to share with me," said Alex. Jamie laughed.

"No, but I thought I'd plant the seed while I had the chance."

"Have you heard of a company called Robrex?" he asked.

"No, I don't think so," replied Alex.

"Well, that's probably not surprising. It was a company that sold flooring materials up until a few years ago when it wound down its operations. The remaining shell company was involved in a reverse take over by an Indian IT Services company. They're a very profitable business and now they're looking at expanding. We've been invited to take part in a placing to raise capital for a big acquisition that's going to be transformational. I'm convinced the market hasn't even begun to appreciate the significance of this move." Alex leaned back in his chair.

"So, I get a free lunch **and** a share tip?" he said. Jamie smiled.
"Well, I was hoping you'd take a look at the company for me. We're a little too close to the action and it would be good to have a fresh pair of eyes look it over; make sure we're not missing anything. I can get you into the presentation to Institutional investors next week and if we invest, I'll make sure you get a tranche of the shares at the placing price."
"Can I bring Matt into this?" asked Alex.
"Yeah sure, but remember you're both insiders now, so keep it to yourselves, and no trading until the placing's confirmed."

So this is what it's like to be on the inside, thought Alex. If this deal was as good as Jamie was making out, he could probably make a killing by trading the stock. He wasn't going to of course, but for the first time, he realized how easily access to inside information could be exploited. Just a word in a friend's ear, a nod and a wink and we'll split the profits. *Information really was power,* he thought.

They spent the rest of the lunch talking about shares they were both invested in, or watching. Alex always enjoyed chatting with Jamie. He knew many of the best traders and fund managers in the City. He always had an endless list of stories and anecdotes to entertain and educate in equal measure. Alex could have happily wiled away the whole afternoon but suddenly remembered his other appointment.

"Oh shit, I've got this other AGM in 20 minutes. I'm going to have to run."
"Where is it?" asked Jamie.
"It's the other side of the river, near London Bridge station. I can take the underground and it should be fairly

easy to find," he said, reaching for his bag from under the table.

"Let's jump in a taxi," said Jamie. "I can drop you off there on the way back to my office. It doesn't sound too far out of my way."

"That would be brilliant," said Alex, relaxing a little. "Thanks mate."

They settled up the bill and managed to flag a black cab from outside the restaurant. The taxi ride gave them time to firm up details for the company presentation the following week. After he was dropped off opposite London Bridge underground station, Alex still had 5 minutes to get to the AGM.

The office was just a short walk to an old three-storey stone building on a narrow street behind the main road. The name of the company was on a plate fixed to the wall outside the entrance: W A Castings plc. It was a family run business that Alex had taken a liking to. They had five sites around the country that manufactured high precision alloy castings, as well as holding patents on a number of metal coating technologies. Definitely what you'd describe as 'old school;' it paid a generous dividend and on most measures, would be considered a good value share.

As he entered the building there was that slightly sweet smell of oil and metal that told him he was in the world of manufacturing. A dark tiled floor led to a mahogany reception desk which was unattended. Alex tapped the small brass bell on the counter and after a few seconds a young woman came out through the swing doors behind the desk and smiled.

"Hello, can I help you?"
"I'm here for the AGM," replied Alex.
"Oh." She sounded a little surprised. "The directors are upstairs in the training suite. I'll take you up."

"Do you need to see any ID? I've got a letter of representation from my broker."

"Oh yes, I better take a copy of that."

"Here, you can keep this," he said, handing it over to her. She led him up the stairs to the second floor and along a short corridor with photos of foundry works and castings lining the walls. She indicated an open door with an outstretched hand and stood aside to let him pass.

The room reminded Alex of the programming class he'd attended at the local night school before he started university. The light weight metal tables at the end of the room, the foldable chairs, the vinyl floor tiles with scuff marks. Three men wearing suits stood behind the top table; three generations of the family by the looks of it. A young woman, probably from the PR firm, was holding a company brochure and smiled as he entered. The oldest of the three men looked up and raised his eyebrows in surprise. He broke off his conversation and came over with his hand outstretched.

"Thank you for coming," he said, smiling broadly under his thick moustache. "I'm the Chairman, Bill Atkins. We're just about to start." Alex nodded and returned the smile. He'd already braced himself for the inevitable fact that he was the only shareholder attending and took a seat on the front of the two rows of empty seats.

Alex took out his laptop and busied himself pulling up some spreadsheets that he'd prepared to summarize the company's financials. The PR girl walked over and sat next to him.

"I think it's just us," she said.

"Sorry,...?" said Alex.

"I think we're the only shareholders attending," she explained.

"Oh...., er yeah. Best to stick together. Safety in numbers," he said smiling. She held out her hand with a friendly smile.

"My name's Leonna."

"Hi, I'm Alex."

"Do you come to many of these?" she asked.

"I try to get to them if I can. I had another one this morning. How about you?"

"This is my first. I haven't been investing very long but I thought it would be interesting to come along."

At that moment, the Chairman cleared his throat.

"OK, shall we make a start?" He made a brief introduction in which he set out the history of the company and introduced his fellow directors. As Alex had supposed, they were the three generations of the family; the Chairman and founder of the company; his son, the Finance Director and his grandson, the newly appointed head of Coatings Division. He then introduced the first slide of the presentation. An over-sized slide appeared on the screen behind him with much of the information obscured.

"Oh, that's not right," he said. Alex and Leonna exchanged a glance and suppressed the urge to smile. "It was alright on the other computer," he said. Alex had a pretty good idea of what the problem was and tentatively offered to take a look. The Chairman was more than happy to accept the offer. As he'd thought, the computer's screen resolution didn't match the projector and he quickly made the necessary adjustment and the slide appeared correctly sized on the projector screen.

With normal service resumed, the meeting continued and there was a genuine effort from all the directors to engage with the two shareholders. Alex had the sense that they were delighted to share their enthusiasm for the business with people who were actually interested in learning about it. Leonna asked some searching questions of the FD about future capital expenditure. Alex, on the other hand, was interested to explore the new market opportunities for the company's coating technology with the youngest of the family.

The meeting went on longer than any of them expected, but by the time it was over, they both had a very positive impression of the company. On the face of it, it seemed like an unexciting steady business in a mature industry. In reality, their coating technology had the potential to open up some high-tech markets in the aerospace and medical fields. It felt like a company where managers and shareholders interests were closely aligned.

"Do you fancy a cup of tea?" asked Alex.

"Yeah, I'm ready for one," she replied. They moved over to the side table where there was a large urn, some paper cups and a plate of assorted biscuits.

"I always think you can tell a lot about a company from the refreshments," he said.

"So what do you think this says?" asked Leonna, pouring out two cups of tea.

"This is a company that understands the importance of the efficient use of capital," he said. Leonna laughed.

"Yes, not a chocolate biscuit in sight. How about a jammy dodger?"

"No thanks, I had a good lunch but you go right ahead."

She blew on her tea and tucked a loose strand of brown hair behind her ear. Alex sipped his tea and stole a sideways glance. She was very attractive; beautiful green eyes and almost flawless features, but made little effort to accentuate any of it. It was almost like she was unaware of her own beauty, or maybe it was that she just didn't want to stand out. The navy blue skirt and jacket could have been hand picked to blend in with the crowd.

"So, do you have a day job Leonna?" he asked.

"I work for an accountancy firm. I'm on the graduate trainee program; mainly audit work at the moment." She glanced up at him. "Yes, I know, it's not terribly glamorous but I'm hoping it'll eventually lead to something a bit more exciting."

"And what got you into investing?" he asked.

"I inherited some money from my Grandmother. It's not a lot but I wanted to see if I could grow it into something."

"Would she approve?" asked Alex.

"Probably not," laughed Leonna. "How about you? Have you been investing for a while?"

"About ten years. I'm actually doing it full time at the moment to see if I can make it work," replied Alex. "It's funny. It doesn't matter how long you do this for, you never quite feel like you've cracked it. You're always expecting the unexpected."

"So, what are you expecting with WA Castings?" she asked. "You know, I was quite impressed," he replied. "I'm beginning to think that I'll increase my holding. It's unlikely to blow the lights out but probably a good share to tuck away and forget about. Suitable for Widows and Orphans, I'd say."

"Suitable for Grandmothers as well?" asked Leonna. He laughed.

"Yes, I think so, but don't go mad with Granny's hard-earned."

They chatted about the company for a while and then a little about each other's background. Alex learned that she lived in Kingston, in south west London, sharing a flat with a friend. She'd grown up in that part of the city, a typical middle class suburban upbringing.

Someone started to fold up the chairs and stack them against the side wall and this seemed to signify the time to make a move.

"Are you taking the train back," asked Alex.

"Yes, I'm heading back to London Bridge tube station."

"Me too. Shall we get going?" Alex packed his laptop away and followed Leonna out of the door. She stopped to take a look at a photograph in the corridor. It was a black and white image from around the 1960s. A young man in a three-piece suit was standing with a group of workers in front of the building they were in.

"That must be old Mr. Atkins."

"Yes, I think it is," said Alex. "He's put his whole life into this company and it's still going, stronger than ever. Now all we need is for his grandson to take it to the next level."

"I wonder if it's what his grandson really wanted to do," she said, "or whether he felt he had no choice but to join the family business."

"I imagine he grew up never questioning it," said Alex. "Besides, I can think of worse family businesses to be saddled with," he added with an ironic shrug.

They found their way down to the lobby which was unmanned as before and a glance out of the main door told them that there'd been a change in the weather.

"Oh, it's chucking it down," said Leonna.

"Shall we call a taxi?" asked Alex.

"It's only round the corner. Here, I've got an umbrella," she said, pulling a small retractable model from her bag. "You're welcome to share."

They ducked under the umbrella and walked as quickly as they could manage down the street in the direction of the station. They both fell silent as they suddenly became acutely aware of their close proximity under the small umbrella. It was a rather awkward few minutes, punctuated by the occasional apology as they bumped legs or shoulders. They were both a bit relieved to reach the safety of the station canopy and recover their normal composure.

"I'm taking the Northern line to Kings Cross," said Alex.

"Oh, I'm on the Jubilee line to Waterloo," replied Leonna. There was a moments pause and then she smiled. "It was nice to meet you, Alex," she said, before turning to walk away.

"Oh, hold on, I meant to tell you. There's a private investors meet-up next week. It might give you a chance to meet some interesting people, share ideas, you know."

"OK, that sounds interesting. Where is it?" Alex pulled out a scrap of paper from his pocket and wrote down the name of the pub and the time and passed it over to her. "I'll try to make it if I can," she said slipping the paper into a notebook she kept in her bag. "Well, hope to see you next week," she said before heading off towards the ticket gate.

Alex watched her go through the gate and stood motionless for a minute wondering why he'd felt the desperate need to keep in touch with someone he'd met just a couple of hours earlier. He checked his phone. No messages. He put it back in his pocket and headed off into the station.

Chapter 4

Alex had called Matt after he returned home to tell him about the investment idea he'd discussed with Jamie. They agreed a time later in the week to meet up at Matt's place to talk about it and take a closer look at the company.

It wasn't a long way from his flat to Matt's house in Islington so Alex took the bike. It was only about twenty minutes before he arrived on the high street. The sun was breaking through the clouds that had blanketed the sky throughout the morning and the sunlight glistened off the puddles that remained on the pavement.

There was a sandwich shop that he knew on the main road and he stopped to pick up something for lunch. They had a good selection of healthy options and he picked out a couple of pitta breads stuffed with humus and salad and some falafel. He smiled to himself as he came out of the shop, imagining Matt's reaction. *That'll be a shock to his system*, he thought, as he packed the lunch away in his rucksack.

He turned off the main road and it wasn't far to the tree-lined street where Matt lived. It was a quiet and pleasant road with three-storey terraced houses on one side and a two-storey terrace on the other. Matt had one of the two-storey houses at the bottom of the road, with a low brick wall lining the pavement at the front of the property. Alex pushed open the gate and wheeled his bike inside before propping it up against the bay window.

He rang the bell and waited. After a while, he rang again and waited a little longer. Still no answer. He pulled out his phone and called Matt's mobile. He answered almost immediately.

"Hey Alex, are you coming over?" he said.

"Matt, I'm standing outside your front door," replied Alex.

"Oh sorry mate. I've been temporarily incommunicado. I'll be right with you."

A few seconds later, the front door opened and the unkempt figure of Matt stood before him. He was wearing what would ordinarily be described as loose track suit leggings, but on Matt, they were somewhat more figure-hugging. The relaxed look was completed with a black AC/DC T-shirt and a pair of headphones hung loosely around his neck.

"Come in," he said. "I was just busy averting World War three."

"You mean you've had a hard morning playing 'Call of Duty,'" said Alex, manoeuvring around the pile of free newspapers that littered the hallway around the front door.

"Listen, if you ever need to get in, there's a spare key hidden under the window sill. I lock myself out all the time," said Matt.

He led them through to the living room where a wide screen TV was paused mid-game. The remnants of Matt's breakfast, evening meal and various snacks in between, were strewn around the floor. A large cushion sat in front of the TV.

"I think we've arrived at the nerve centre of the operation," joked Alex.

"Yes, standards have slipped since Mum moved out," Matt replied, while gathering up the plates.

"How is she?"

"Mostly confused," he replied, with a shrug of his shoulders. "She still recognizes me, but she gets me mixed up with her Dad, my Grandad. The main thing is she's somewhere that she can be properly looked after, and it's local so I can visit her pretty much every day."

"Here, grab a seat," Matt said, motioning towards the table in the official dining area. "Fancy a cup of tea," he added, as he headed into the kitchen and started loading the dishwasher.

"Yeah, thanks," said Alex. "I brought some sandwiches if you're still hungry." Alex unloaded his rucksack of the sandwiches and took out his laptop.

"You know, this looks like an interesting company. It's a bit of a one-stop-shop for IT services and with virtually all their staff based in India, their posting some pretty impressive profit margins."

"Yeah, on paper it looks impressive but where's their moat?" replied Matt from the kitchen. "What's to stop the next Indian IT company eating into those margins?"

"You're right, that is the big question. According to Jamie, this acquisition they're planning is a game-changer. It doesn't just beef up their traditional IT services capability; it gets them into digital marketing software too. They can cross-sell all of this to their existing customer base and likely grow their margins. They're moving into a real growth area which could lead to a much higher multiple for the stock."

"Ah, the Holy Grail Syre," said Matt, as he deposited two mugs of tea on the table. "The double whammy of growing profits and a re-rating. Count me in."

Matt lifted the edge of the paper bag to examine the contents of Alex's sandwich offering.

"Do people actually eat this stuff?" he said, reluctantly taking out a folded pitta bread.

"Matt, you'd be surprised what people put in sandwiches these days, besides bacon."

"Well, I'm firmly of the view that there's not much you can do to improve on the bacon butty. It's a bit like the bicycle; you can tinker with it, and come up with the BLT perhaps, but essentially, the concept is pretty much flawless." Matt grimaced as he gingerly took a bite out of the pitta bread and Alex laughed.

"Matt, you actually look like you're in physical pain trying to eat that. I should have known better than to interfere with your natural feeding pattern."

"I'm just not designed for this vegan stuff. It's like feeding lettuce to a lion. Hang on, there's some left over chicken tikka in the fridge," he said, getting up and disappearing into the kitchen. He came back after a minute or so with a plate and began dipping the pitta bread into the curry sauce. "Yeah, not bad. I may just have saved this excuse for a sandwich." Alex shook his head and went back to studying his laptop.

"Right, we'll do the usual analysis," he said, stretching back in his chair. "You focus on the quantitative stuff and I'll look at the quality metrics. Then, when we're done, we'll go over it together and consider the bull and bear points."

"Do you want me to look at the cash flow?" asked Matt, manoeuvring the last of the pitta bread into his mouth.

"No, it's OK. I'll pick that up when I look at the quality of the profits they're posting," replied Alex. "OK, let's get to work."

Alex and Matt had done this kind of analysis together countless times. With his background in maths, it made sense for Matt to crunch the numbers in the published accounts. Alex would assess the quality of the company. This involved looking into the profitability of the business and how sustainable the profits were likely to be. Too often, creative accounting can boost the apparent profits a company is making. An analysis of the cash flow would reveal just how real the profits actually were.

They spent the next couple of hours digging into the published accounts of the company and pulling up whatever else they could find on the Internet about the company.

Matt had his head phones on, connected to his mobile. With the volume cranked up, Alex could make out the heavy metal beat that perfectly synchronized with his nodding head. He would occasionally scribble figures onto a notepad and then later punch the numbers into an old fashioned desktop calculator that he had on the table. He had that touch typing way of using the calculator that came from countless hours of number crunching.

Alex, meanwhile, was lost in his own world with ear plugs in place and Spotify providing the soundtrack. He had a template spreadsheet that he used to do his analysis and after he'd completed that, he searched the Web for whatever else might add to his understanding of the company.

Eventually, when he was done, Alex raised his arms and pushed his elbows back to relieve the stiffness in his back.
"OK, are you more or less ready?" he asked Matt, momentarily forgetting that he was still in his heavy metal world. He motioned for him to take off the headphones. "Are we ready to go through the numbers?" he asked again.
"Yeah, sure. I've got a pretty good handle on it now," replied Matt.

He gave a brief run down on the figures. There were only 2 years of audited accounts for the business but with the broker forecasts, this painted a picture of a company growing revenue and profits at well over 20% a year and on an undemanding price/earnings ratio. The company was carrying a fair amount of debt but this was covered by the assets of the company in the form of the office properties owned in India. All in all, a very healthy picture.

Alex went through his own analysis which showed an impressive operating profit margin of around 15%.
"To be honest, I'm not sure how they manage to maintain that level of profitability but I guess it's down to their low cost base in India," he said.
"What does the cash flow analysis tell us?" asked Matt.
"Well, it seems to support the profits their posting, but I'd

be a bit worried that the margins may come under pressure going forward."

"I guess that's why they're looking at this acquisition," said Matt, "They probably want to differentiate themselves from the competition."

"What do you make of the IT Services they're offering at the moment?" he asked.

"I can't see anything that plenty of other companies couldn't muscle in on," said Alex. "It's the usual mix of support services, security features, etc. Nothing out of the ordinary. It's going to be interesting hearing how this acquisition target might change things."

They discussed the positive and negative points of the company from an investment perspective and overall, both had a positive impression of the company.

"You know what, I think I'd seriously consider taking a stake in this company without Jamie's game-changer," said Alex.

"Yeah, I know what you mean, but it's always nice to have a margin of safety," replied Matt. "Jamie's going to let us buy in at the placing price so if the share price moves up on the announcement, we can be in profit before we even need to decide to buy."

"Yeah, we can either flip the shares for a quick profit or hold for a big re-rating, with the margin of safety built in," said Alex. "We'll have a better idea after tomorrow's presentation. You're coming, right?"

"Do I have to dress up for it?" asked Matt.

"Well, we're supposed to be high-powered hedge fund analysts so you might want to dust off your suit," replied Alex.

"I'm not sure I can still get in it but I'll dig it out and see. What time are we meeting?"

"I said we'd see Jamie at his office at 10am. The presentation's at 11am so we can take a taxi together."

"OK, I'll see you there," said Matt. "Are we done with the analysis?"

"Yeah, can you give me your notes and I'll write something up for Jamie," said Alex, as he turned off his laptop and began packing it away with the notes they'd both made.

"Do you fancy doing battle on the X box before you head off?" asked Matt.

"Oh man, I would so like to whip your ass," replied Alex. "Unfortunately, that'll have to wait for another day. I have to get Lisa a birthday present before tonight. We're having a birthday dinner."

"Going somewhere special?" asked Matt.

"No, nowhere special, just my Dad's place. I'm not sure Lisa's crazy about the idea, but I just wanted everyone to be together. We haven't spent a night together for a while."

"Well, give her my best and tell her that she deserves someone better," said Matt.

"Don't worry, she knows that already," said Alex, laughing.

Alex got up from the table and hung his rucksack over one shoulder. He followed Matt through the living room and out to the entrance hall. The sun was still out and the water had dried off the road in front of the house. The trees along the road had that translucent light green colour of leaves just opened and there was the smell of honeysuckle in the air.

"Right, I'll catch you tomorrow for the big event" said Alex, bumping fists with Matt.

"Yeah, have a good one tonight and go easy on the Ouzo," he said.

"Not much chance of that with my old man around," replied Alex, with a rueful smile. He unlocked his bike and manoeuvred it out onto the road, closing the gate behind him. One last nod to Matt, who stood hands in pockets in the doorway, and Alex set off up the road.

Chapter 5

The sound came from a long way off, gradually getting louder as it began to pierce the fog inside his head. It was a few seconds before Alex could make sense of the alarm coming from his phone and finally, reach out to put an end to it. Slowly, he slid his arm under the duvet into the cool part of the bed before realizing that he was alone. No Lisa. Had they argued? Did she storm off from the restaurant? No, he remembered them taking the taxi back together. Something about an early meeting at work. Everything was OK; just a heavy night on the booze.

He tried to piece together the events of the previous evening in his head. He'd met Lisa at the station and they'd taken a taxi to the restaurant. He remembered them sitting at the table and giving her the earrings. She'd liked them and wore them straight away. Then he remembered everyone sitting around a big table. The restaurant had closed and there was Jack and Maya and his Dad. The old man had been drinking and there was an endless series of toasts. He couldn't recall much of the detail but there was a lot of laughing. There was something else too; something that he was forgetting. What was it?

He closed his eyes and tried to remember. After a few seconds he slowly withdrew his hands from beneath the duvet and put them over his face.
"Oh God, the fire," he moaned. He remembered his Dad had been wearing a large paper napkin to protect his white shirt and tie. The thing had caught fire as he insisted on helping Lisa blow out the candles on her birthday cake. He was so plastered he hadn't realized until it had singed his beard and taken the shine off his white shirt. Jack had ended up throwing most of a jug of water over him to put out the

flames. Alex cringed at the recollection but couldn't suppress a chuckle at the absurdity of it. It would be one of those stories they'd laugh about for years. He wasn't entirely sure that Lisa would welcome the reminder but she'd taken it pretty well on the night.

He pulled himself out of bed and stretched his arms wide. His head was throbbing and his throat parched. He shuffled over to the sink and filled a mug of water, gulping it down before repeating the process. He could hear the light patter of rain on the window panes and drew back the curtains to reveal a grey start to the day. Droplets of rain raced each other down the glass and puddled on the window sill.

He had the presentation with Jamie and Matt this morning so he'd need to get his head straight before that one. There was still plenty of time. He could leave the flat at 9am and he'd be at Jamie's office within an hour. He went into the bathroom and stepped into the shower; letting the warm water cascade over his head and slowly bring him back to life.

By the time he'd finished, he'd missed the market opening but there was nothing that he was particularly interested in. His mind was more focussed on the meeting later that morning. He sat down at the computer and pulled up the company share price chart.

In theory, the market shouldn't be aware of the upcoming placing, but in reality, inside information has a habit of leaking out. A glance at the chart, showed that the share price had been creeping up over the last few days. That was a good sign that the reaction to the placing would be positive. Better still, they wouldn't need to chase the price up. Jamie had promised them shares at the placing price.

Alex was feeling good about this whole deal. For once, it felt like he was on the inside, alongside the professionals. He even looked the part as he headed out of the room; fully suited up and with a typed copy of his research tucked into the side pocket of his laptop case. There was no need to creep down the stairs at this time in the morning. Most of the house had already left for work and the place was more or less empty.

As he reached the hallway at the bottom of the stairs, he looked for his umbrella and noticed that it was missing from the stand. That's the problem with buying a cheap umbrella; it's always the first one to get 'borrowed.'

There were two left. One was a light-weight model, the sort that ladies balance on their shoulders on hot summer days. The other, a large golf umbrella with a leather bound handle. Circumstances dictated there was only one practical option and he pulled the over-sized umbrella from the stand. The moment coincided precisely with the door to Ms. Mark's flat opening and the landlady herself appearing in the doorway.

"Oh, good morning Mr. Samaras. Horrible weather this morning," she said. She glanced at the umbrella he was holding and then at the stand next to him. "....but I can see you're well equipped," she added, with a slight raising of one eyebrow.
"Yes, I......," replied Alex, motioning with the umbrella and forcing a smile. She knew, of course, and she knew that he knew that she knew.
"Well,...." she said with a triumphant smile, "I'd better not hold you from your appointment. Good day Mr. Samaras." With that, she headed up the stairs and Alex swiftly made his exit from the scene of the crime.

It was quicker to take a bus to Jamie's office in Canary Wharf. He could catch one from the High Street. The wet weather made the journey a bit longer than scheduled, but he still had plenty of time as he descended the stairs of the bus on their arrival in Docklands. Even on a miserable wet day, he couldn't help but be impressed at the scale of the place. He was in the hub of one of the key financial centres of the world and the architecture was designed to let you know it. Walking in the shadow of the monolithic office buildings, the indelible impression was one of reliability, security and permanence.

Jamie's office was a short walk from the bus stop. A large glass canopy marked the entrance to the building and led to the three-storey high lobby inside. Everything was of a scale that made you understand that you were small fry and had arrived at the top table. Whether you would get a seat at the table however, was governed by the three immaculately presented receptionists behind the long desk that lined the wall facing the entrance.

Alex picked the friendly looking one on the left, and announced that he had a 10 o-clock with Jamie Sinclair at Redmead Capital. She asked him if he had a business card and he passed over one of the cards that he'd had made for such occasions. He'd designed it himself and was quite proud of it. It described him as an 'Independent Stock Analyst' and he'd had it printed on the heaviest card he could get. When it comes to business cards, weight is everything, and this one passed the test with flying colours. She directed him to the lifts and told him it was the 15th floor.

Jamie's company had one half of the floor and a glass door led through to the company's reception. He announced his arrival at the reception area and after a short wait, Jamie came out to meet him and led him through to his office. Alex had been there once before, so it was no surprise to see the Fender Stratocaster propped up on its stand in the corner; likewise, the pictures of guitar heroes lining the walls.

Jamie handed Alex a brochure from his desk.
    "Have a read of this, it's the prospectus for the placing."
He motioned for Alex to take a seat on the sofa. Alex flicked

through the document; scan reading the marketing spiel to get to the numbers that really mattered. It was clear that the acquisition would add to the company's bottom line straight away. At the placing price, they'd be acquiring revenue and profit at a significantly lower multiple than the company's own shares were trading at.

"This all looks good," said Alex. "Just based on the numbers here, it looks a great deal. The interesting thing for me though is the synergies that it opens up. It'll be interesting to hear what they have to say about that in the meeting."

"Yeah, we're on the same page there," said Jamie. "I think it's the opportunity for cross-selling of their marketing software that could turbo-charge this one. It's a vast market and a great opportunity to transform their recurring revenues."

"Yeah, and at a very tidy profit margin too," added Alex.

"Listen, we better get moving," said Jamie. "Is Matt not coming to the meeting?"

"He's on his way by taxi. He should be here in about 5 minutes."

"OK, we'll see him outside the office. We can take the taxi to the meeting. Just give me a couple of minutes to sort out a few things," said Jamie, as a ducked out of the door.

Alex got up and wandered over to the window. Things were looking a little brighter on the street. He stood behind the desk and imagined for a moment that it was his desk, that it was his office. This was about as high up the ladder as you could get. Yet, here he was, just about to set off into the city with Jamie to close the next big deal. It all seemed a bit unreal. Why was he letting them in on something like this? They were friends on some level for sure, but this was something different. This was business.

Alex wandered out from behind the desk and began looking

at the photographs on the walls. They were all black and white. Hendricks, Clapton, Stevie Ray Vaughan and the three Kings; BB, Albert and Freddie. Definitely more blues than rock. Then there was a group of young guys, college students probably. He recognized a youthful Jamie on guitar playing a pub or some other small venue. Alex smiled to himself.

"Spot the odd one out," said Jamie from behind him. "I can get you a signed copy if you'd like."

"No thanks," replied Alex. "I don't think I'm quite ready to become a Jamie Sinclair groupie just yet. Shall we get going?"

They headed out to the lift and down to the lobby. It wasn't long before Matt's taxi pulled up and they joined him in the back. The meeting was to be held at the company's broker's office. They were cutting it fine, but they arrived with a few minutes to spare.

The building was on a narrow street, enclosed on both sides by grey stone facades of Georgian architecture. Classic old school financial district. Jamie announced their arrival at the ground floor reception and they were escorted to the 3rd floor conference room.

There were already about 20 suits chatting in small groups; some standing and others sitting. Jamie exchanged greetings with a few acquaintances and they were shown to their seats. A copy of the prospectus had been placed on each of the chairs. Alex got a pen out and flicked through the document highlighting the main points that he'd taken from his earlier read-through. He passed it over to Matt.

"Just take a look at the bits I've marked. I had a read of it at Jamie's office," he said.

Matt busied himself with the document and Alex leaned back in his chair.

"So, who else is here Jamie?" he asked.

"Oh, the usual suspects," he replied. Their broker pitched the placing to all the major small cap funds and those that showed an interest were invited to the presentation. If we decide to take a stake, we'll negotiate with them over how much we can get."

"It's a good chance to see the management up close today," said Alex. "Do you do much of a background check on them?"

"We're a bit limited in the due diligence that we can do for overseas companies. We get a Dun and Bradstreet report and try to speak to customers to get a feel for the company, but at the end of the day, we're relying on the documents signed off by their brokers and the auditors."

"You can be sure those documents will include all the usual disclaimers," added Alex.

"You're not wrong there," said Jamie.

The company directors were beginning to take their seats at the front of the room and a woman holding a microphone came out to announce that the presentation would start shortly. Everyone took their seats and a man of about 40, stood up and took the microphone. He was stylishly dressed in a well-tailored suit and open neck shirt, with black hair and immaculately trimmed designer stubble. There was an unmistakable air of confidence that surrounded him, and as first impressions go, they don't come much better.

He introduced himself as Sandeep Gupta, the CEO. He spoke with an Indian accent but in perfect, well educated English. He proceeded to give an outline of the company over a backdrop of images and videos showing the company's head office in Mumbai. He talked through the company's growth strategy and its global aspirations before introducing the company that they were looking to acquire. Everything came across as coherent and logical, and it was difficult to be anything other than greatly impressed.

The CEO then handed over to the Finance Director who went through the figures in the prospectus. He was competent, all be it lacking the charisma of the CEO. The company's broker talked through the placing offer and the timings for completion and then invited questions from the audience.

There were various questions, mostly regarding the growth strategy and international expansion. The questions struck Alex as rather lame and just set the CEO up to further emphasise the upside. It felt like the whole room had already given it the thumbs up without even considering the execution risk. He raised his hand to ask a question and directed it to the FD.
"How do you plan to transition the servicing of the acquired customers by your existing management team? And have you made any allowance for losing business during this process?"

The FD was a little hesitant. He talked about the quality of their management team and that they would be looking to retain key management staff from the acquired company. His answer began to drift off a little before the CEO interrupted. He made the point that customers were on a rolling one year contract and that this would give the company time to build relationships. He would be personally visiting all the major customers to help cement those relationships. The positive vibe in the room was restored and the rest of the meeting passed off to everyone's satisfaction.

As the meeting began to break up, Jamie grabbed a word with the brokers and Alex and Matt compared notes.

"I'm struggling to find much that I don't like about this deal," said Matt.
"I reckon you can speak for just about everyone in this room too," added Alex. "With that CEO in charge, you get the feeling this company's really going places."
"Too good to be true do you think?"

"Well it sure ticks all the boxes. We don't have to commit just yet. We can see what the market reaction is to the announcement first."

"Yeah, if only all investing was this simple," laughed Matt. "We're in the money before we've even started."

Jamie rejoined them and they prepared to leave. He had that self satisfied look on his face that suggested things were going to plan. They took the stairs down to the lobby and Jamie suggested they have a debrief. There was a Cafe Nero just around the corner and they reconvened around a small table.

"Well, you guys are going to have to give me a bloody good reason not to take a stake in this placing," said Jamie, taking a sip of his double espresso. Alex looked at Matt and shook his head with a wry smile.

"It's not often you see what looks like such a 'no-brainer' with everything pointing in the right direction," he said. "The only question mark for me is the company being based overseas, but I don't think even that would stop me investing. I'd maybe just be a little more cautious about position size and keep a closer eye on things."

"How about you Matt?" asked Jamie.

"Everything that Alex said, apart from the bit about caution. I'd most likely mortgage the house, sell a kidney and invest the lot, but that's probably why he's better at this game than I am." Jamie laughed.

"I think we all pretty much agree that it's an investment opportunity," he said. "I spoke to the broker at the end of the meeting and I think he'll get us a decent slice of the cake. It's almost certain to be over-subscribed and we'll probably look to top up after it's announced to the market. They'll be firming up the placing this afternoon and they'll be an announcement tomorrow morning."

"How much can we buy from you?" asked Matt.

"I'll put aside 15,000 shares for each of you. The placing price is £1-40p so you can decide how much you want to take. I'd like to get it settled within about a week." Alex and Matt looked at each other and nodded.

"Sure, that sounds great. Thanks for including the little guys," said Alex.

"Yeah, we usually just get to pick up the crumbs," added Matt.

"It's been good to get a different perspective from you guys," said Jamie, "and of course, I'd be lying if I said I didn't know that by getting you two on board, it'd spread the word with private investors."

"There, you see Alex. I knew it. We've been used and abused again," joked Matt.

"Well, we've got the Private Investors Meet-up tomorrow night. What better chance to get the word out?" said Alex. "Are you coming Jamie?"

"Yeah hopefully, but you could do me a favour by waiting a couple of days until we've built our position. I don't want private investors driving the price up before then if we can avoid it."

"OK sure," said Alex.

"Right, I better get back," said Jamie, rising from the table. "Can I drop either of you at the station?"

"No thanks, I think I'm going to grab some lunch here before I go. Are you going to join me Matt?"

"Yeah, I'm starving, but there's nothing here that's going to do the job. Come on, there's a place around the corner that does all day cooked breakfast," he replied, jumping to his feet.

They squeezed their way out between the tables and the rapidly expanding lunch queue and made their way out to the pavement. Jamie raised a hand to summon an approaching taxi and the driver dutifully pulled over to the kerb.

"Right, I'll catch you guys tomorrow for a few beers," he said, before climbing into the back of the taxi.

As the taxi pulled off, Matt motioned with his head in the direction of his lunch venue.

"Come on let's have a debrief of the debrief over a Full English." Alex smiled and slapped him on the back.

"Lead the way big man."

Chapter 6

The movement of the train rocked his head gently from side to side; that familiar rattle and rush of sound as they entered each station. The unique feel of the London Underground that's somewhere between a train and a ride on a roller coaster. Alex had found a space next to the doors and could lean up against the glass at the end of the bench seat. There was a damp muggy atmosphere in the carriage. Water was dripping around his feet from the umbrellas of the passengers standing in rows along the length of the carriage. Condensation ran down the inside of the windows and transformed the station billboards into elaborate watercolours.

It was just after 7pm and he was on his way to the Private Investor's Meet-up. It was being held at a pub on the river near Hammersmith. He'd been there before and it would have been perfect to sit outside with a drink if it wasn't tipping it down. He pulled out his mobile, and to kill a little time he reviewed the days events. As Jamie had predicted, the announcement on the placing had come out first thing in the morning. The RNS had popped up in Alex's daily news capture program.

> *Robrex plc (the Company) announces that it has entered into an agreement to acquire the business and assets of K.P. Digital Ltd for a total consideration of £9.8 million.*
> *The Company also confirms that it has received commitments from Institutional Investors to raise gross proceeds of £11.2 million by way of issue of 8 million ordinary shares at a placing price of £1-40.*

There were some other details about the acquired company

and how it was expected to be immediately earnings enhancing; all information that Alex was familiar with from the meeting the day before. *They certainly didn't waste any time getting it over the line*, he thought. They raised £11.2 million and paid £9.8 million, so that leaves £1.4 million for the middle men. *Nice work if you can get it.*

The news had been greeted positively by the market. The share price had advanced to £1-84 at the close, probably encouraged by Jamie's buying to beef up his holding. Alex did the maths in his head. If he bought the full 15,000 shares from Jamie, he could sell in the market straight away and bag a handy profit of about £6,000, after trading costs. He'd try to have a quiet chat with Matt later in the pub to decide what to do.

He looked through his other holdings to kill some time. He became so immersed in trying to make sense of the annual results of one of his long-term investments, that he almost missed his stop. He just caught the announcement as the doors were about to close and managed to duck out onto the platform.

It was rush hour and the station was heaving with dripping commuters. The exit from the station was grid-locked as people grappled with umbrellas, reorganized bags or simply debated whether to run for it. Alex apologetically squeezed his way out to the pavement and set off under cover of his recently reacquired umbrella.

It was a few minutes walk down to the river, but once he'd got past the main road, it was a little quieter. He soon reached the footpath leading to the riverside. The twin stone towers of Hammersmith Bridge greeted him as he joined the riverside walkway. The lights illuminated against the slate grey sky and casting rippling reflections into the river. It was a short walk from there to the pub, and the glow from the windows as he approached was a welcome sight.

Alex leaned against the heavy swing doors at the entrance and they opened into a warm bustling interior. A familiar voice greeted him from near the entrance.

"Alex, over here." It was Phil Carmen. Every networking group needs someone like Phil; an enabler; a conduit for bringing people together. The kind of guy who will tirelessly arrange the events, make the introductions and turn it in to more than just a bunch of guys having a drink down the pub.

"Let me introduce you to Russell," he said, shepherding Alex towards a high table next to a pillar. "Russell used to work in the city," he added, "and I think you know Daniel." Alex nodded a greeting to Daniel and shook hands with his new acquaintance.

They were talking about the prospects of a company that Alex was familiar with. An old favourite of the bulletin board crowd. He'd sold out a little while ago and had begun to be wary of these popular shares that everyone seemed to hold. All that group think and everyone backing up each other's opinion. It was bound to end in tears. He didn't say as much but tried to play devil's advocate where he could.

In between his contributions, his gaze wandered around the room. He spotted Jamie over by the bar, holding court to a group of admirers and Matt was in animated discussion with a couple of the regulars that Alex knew well. He couldn't see Leonna. He didn't know why he'd expected her to be there. It's not like they'd really arranged anything. He felt strangely deflated though.

He made his excuses to the small group and motioned that he was going to get a drink at the bar. He carefully weaved his way between the groups of customers standing in small circles, anchored to a table or some other defensible fixture. As he approached the bar, he caught Jamie's eye and Jamie beckoned him over to join the select group. Alex pointed to the bar and made that familiar drinking gesture to show he was getting a drink in first. He found a space at the bar and soon had a welcome pint of London Pride placed before him.

He took a long drink before turning around to join Jamie and his entourage. That was when he saw her, standing behind a pillar. She was talking to Simon Butler, a fate that immediately invoked a feeling of sympathy in Alex. Simon was someone to be avoided at events like this. He was a man with a theory, and one that he had taken upon himself to share with evangelical zeal: High yield. That was more or less it. Select a group of shares paying a good sized and well covered dividend and with a strong balance sheet and hold forever. Just reinvest all those lovely dividends and let compounding work its magic. The trouble as Alex saw it, was that it was a theory that could get you locked into companies that were no longer growing, and in some cases could be in structural decline. No amount of dividends were going to make up for the capital losses in that case.

Alex walked over in their direction. Simon was in full flow, sharing the finer details of his methods with his latest disciple. For her part, Leonna was showing commendable effort to maintain interest, but as she noticed Alex approaching, there was a barely disguised look of relief on her face.

"Oh, hi Alex," she said. "I wasn't sure if you were coming. Er, we were just talking about, umm...."

"I was telling Leonna how to set up a High Yield Portfolio," said Simon.

"Well, if anyone knows how to do that, it's you," said Alex.

"Yes, I suppose it is my forte," he replied with a look of self-satisfaction.

"You know, I think Jamie was looking for you earlier. Did you catch up with him?" asked Alex.

"No, no I didn't. I wonder what that's about," said Simon. "He probably needs my advice on something. I'd better go and see to it," he said, and after promising Leonna that he would complete her education later, he went off in search of Jamie.

After he'd moved out of earshot, Alex and Leonna looked at each other and laughed.

"You see. I told you these meet-ups were a bundle of laughs," said Alex.

"I've only got myself to blame," she said. "I struck up a conversation with him at the bar and then asked him what kind of shares he was invested in. That's the last thing I remember." They both laughed again.

"Hey, let me introduce you to some friends," said Alex and led the way over towards a group standing not far away.

"Guys, do you mind if we crash your cosy little ensemble?" said Alex. Matt turned around holding an open bag of pork scratchings.

"Hey, Alex, I didn't see you come in," he said, shifting to one side to increase the circumference of the circle.

"I just wanted to introduce Leonna here to some elite investors," said Alex. Matt feigned surprise and looked around him.

"I'm sorry mate, it's just us three," he said. Alex laughed.

"Yeah, I know that, but she doesn't," he said. Alex introduced Leonna to Matt, Carlo and Seb.

This was the core of Alex's trusted contacts in the world of private investing. They were all into small cap shares and all were independent thinkers. Carlo was mid-thirties, shaved head and casually dressed. He owned a successful courier business and had been investing for about 10 years. Seb was younger, about Alex's age, and tall. He had that tousled blonde hair in the style favoured by those that went to expensive private schools. He wore a pair of black rimmed glasses which made him look like an intellectual, which he was, having studied Classics at Oxford. He worked for a publishing company.

"Leonna's just beginning her investing journey," said Alex. "We met at an AGM the other day." Matt took a sideways glance at Alex which he made a conscious effort to ignore.

"You know they say it's best to start investing in a downturn so you can learn from all the hard knocks early on," said Carlo, grinning.

"In case you didn't know, we're in a roaring bull market right now," added Matt.

"Right, I'll try to contain my excitement," joked Leonna. "I'm actually pretty cautious usually. I like to focus on the fundamentals."

"Leonna's an accountant," said Alex.

"Well actually, I'm not qualified just yet," interjected Leonna.

"What firm are you with?" asked Seb.

"Here, let me give you my business card," she said and reached into her bag where she kept some cards in an inside pocket. She passed them around to everyone.

Alex turned the card over in his hand and read it. *Thorpe Hadley Jones Accountants* was the firm. He thought he'd heard the name before; not one of the big four of course, but within that second tier group that had a decent reputation. *Leonna A. May   BA (Hons)*. The address was central London, somewhere near the British Museum, he thought.

"Have you entered the shark-infested waters of the bulletin boards yet?" asked Matt.

"I've dipped my toe in just to get a feel for it. Are you going to give me your Usernames so I can look out for you?" she asked.

"Well, I'm *Saladbar*," said Matt. Alex laughed.

"I guess we can say that's ironic, eh Matt?"

"What on earth gave you that idea?" he replied. "Pork scratchings anyone?" he added, passing around the bag.

"Seb goes by the name of *Fortunate Tyke*," said Alex. "Are you really a Tyke Seb? I mean, were you really born in Yorkshire?"

"Yes, I lived in York until I was about 10," he replied.

"And he was born with a silver spoon in his mouth so that makes him a fortunate Tyke," added Carlo with a grin.

"Actually, there's a hidden meaning in there," said Seb. "Fortuna and Tyche are the Roman and Greek goddesses of fortune. Clever eh."

"That explains why you went to Oxford Seb," said Alex.

"I'm known as *Gregorysboy*," said Carlo. "It's a tribute to my better half, the lady formally known as Kate Gregory."

"Was that instead of getting a tattoo?" joked Matt.

"Oh, I've got the tattoo as well," he said. "Do you want to see it?"

"No, really Carlo, we'll just take your word for it," said Alex. "I'm *Deep Diver,*" he added. "I guess because I like to dive deep into analysing shares and also, I was born in Cyprus and when I was a young boy my Dad used to make me dive for scallops in the bay where we lived."

"That's bullshit right?" said Matt.

"That is 100%.........bullshit," replied Alex, grinning.

"Are you going to tell us your username Leonna?" asked Alex.

"Well, I haven't actually registered myself yet. I've just been lurking so far, but I'll be sure to announce it once I've got my account set up."

"I'll invite you to join our chat group where we share investing ideas," added Alex.

"Thanks, that would be great. It might save me from making some schoolgirl errors whilst I'm learning the ropes."

At that moment, Alex felt a hand on his shoulder. He turned his head to meet the ever-cheerful face of Phil Carmen.

"Listen guys, we're going to do a quick share pitch in the room upstairs. Three minutes to pitch your best idea. I've

got three takers but I could do with one more. Can one of you step up?" he asked. There was an awkward silence as everybody looked at each other but nobody stepped forward.
"Alex, you're always good for an 'off the radar' idea," said Phil. Everyone looked at Alex and nodded their encouragement. Backed into a corner, Alex reluctantly agreed. He'd been looking at a company that produced wholefood cereals and nuts and dried fruit snacks. They were developing a direct to consumer online distribution channel which was progressing well.
"Great," said Phil. "We'll be starting in 10 minutes if you want to make your way upstairs."

"You seem to have been handed the short straw Alex," said Leonna. "Do you have anything to talk about?"
"Yeah, I've got something I can pitch," replied Alex. "But, I might need another drink to aid the delivery. Can I get you anything?" Alex took everyone's order and with Leonna's help they passed out the drinks and everyone made their way up the stairs at the back of the pub.

There was a large room above the pub, with exposed beams and stripped floor boards. Foldable chairs had been set out in three rows with four additional chairs set off to one side at the front of the room for the presenters. By the time everyone was seated, there were about thirty people in the room.

Alex didn't do a lot of public speaking. He knew all the things you were supposed to do; the slow pacing from side to side in the manner of Steve Jobs; making sure you're addressing all parts the room. Unfortunately, when it came to his turn, it all seemed to go out of his head. He was just focussed on what he was going to say and getting it out in the right order. Instead of making eye contact across the audience, he found himself addressing his presentation to the familiar faces in the second row, and to one face in particular.

Leonna was looking directly at him and it felt like he was unable to avert his eyes. She too seemed transfixed in his gaze, like she'd been caught in the headlights. He momentarily lost his focus and had to look down to collect his thoughts. When he looked up again, she'd lowered her face self-consciously. He managed to shake himself out of it and finished his presentation, whilst making an effort not to look in her direction. The questions from the audience helped to re-focus his attention and brought to light a competitor to the company that he was unaware of. He made a note to look into it later.

When all the presentations were finished, Phil drew down the curtain on events and reminded everyone of the upcoming investor show that was being held at the O2 venue. There was still an hour before last orders and everyone was invited to return to the pub downstairs.

"Are you staying for another drink?" Alex asked Leonna as they headed down the stairs.
"Well, maybe a quick one. I've got an early training session at work tomorrow morning," she replied. When they got down to the bar, she offered to buy a round and they all managed to find some space to stand at the far end of the bar.

"So what did everyone make of the pitches?" asked Carlo. "Any multi-baggers in there?"
"I liked Alex's wholefood company," said Seb. "It just sounds like a company in the right place at the right time."
"Yeah, if I had a pet rabbit or a hamster, I might be interested," said Matt. Leonna laughed.
" Actually, I might be a customer," she added. " I really like the idea of the online nuts and dried fruit. If they marketed it right, they could become the Hotel Chocolat of the nut world."
"Yeah, they could call it the Maison de Nut," said Matt.
"Actually, I think Leonna's dead right," said Alex. "They need to differentiate themselves from the competition and

going high-end might be the right idea. We should all look into the company and have a Zoom meet to thrash it out." There was a general nodding of agreement and a non committed shrug from Matt. Seb wasted no time in Googling the company and began sharing his mobile screen with Carlo and Matt.

"Have you ever thought of starting your own company, Alex?" asked Leonna.

"I did used to dream about it for a while. I liked the idea of building something. Creating it from nothing and having it last and grow into something worthwhile. I like what I'm doing at the moment, and I know that eventually it'll give me financial security, but I do sometimes wonder if there isn't something missing."

"Well, don't give up on the idea. I think you'd be good at it," she said.

A brief chime came from Leonna's bag and she reached inside to take out her mobile. She read the message and slowly returned it to her bag.

"Is everything OK?" he asked.

"Yes. Yes, everything's fine. It's my boyfriend. He's coming to pick me up. Apparently, it's still raining."

"Oh, right," he said, prompting a pause in the conversation. *Why wouldn't she have a boyfriend,* he asked himself. *Of course she has a boyfriend.*

"He works at the same firm. We met at work."

"Yeah, that's usually the way it happens." Alex forced a smile and their attention gradually returned to the other three who'd moved on from researching nuts to sharing amusing TikTok videos.

While Leonna joined Seb and Carlo around Carlo's mobile phone, Alex managed to have a discrete word with Matt about their special situation with Jamie.

"What do you want to do?" he asked.

"I'm tempted to take the no risk six grand but it just feels like this has got a way to go yet," replied Matt. "What's your take?" "Yeah, we haven't even begun to get a buzz around the stock yet. I think I'm going to ride it out for a bit," said Alex.

"I guess Jamie's going to want our money pretty soon," said Matt.

"Yeah, he said we had about a week, so we probably need to settle with him by Friday. Do you have the cash?"

"I may need to top slice something but yeah, I can raise it," replied Matt.

"You two look like you're plotting something," said Seb, drawing everyone's attention towards Alex and Matt.

"Just something we've been looking at over the last couple of weeks," said Alex. "We can't talk about it just now but as soon as we can, you guys will be the first to know."

"Under cover, eh?" said Carlo. "Can't you give us a hint?"

"Yeah we could Carlo but then we'd have to kill you," said Matt. "CIA, KGB, It's better you don't know." Carlo tapped the side of his nose with his finger,

"I get it," he said grinning.

At that moment, Leonna raised her hand to wave to someone behind them. Alex turned his head to see a tall guy wearing a suit striding towards them. He had a head of wavy reddish blond hair and a slightly protruding jaw line that gave him a self confident look.

"Hi babe," he said, as he arrived at their group.

"Stephen, let me introduce you to everyone," said Leonna. "This is Alex, Matt, Seb and Carlo." He briefly shook hands with everyone.

"So, you're all hobby investors, right?" he said.

"Er, something like that," said Alex, exchanging a glance with Matt.

"Alex and Matt are full time investors," added Leonna.

"Yeah? Do you make any money out of it?" he asked.

"It puts a crust on the table," said Matt, somewhat

sarcastically. "Well babe, we better make a move," said Stephen.

"Don't you want to stay for a drink?" she asked.

"I've got an early start tomorrow. We'd better get going." Leonna reluctantly picked up her bag from the end of the bar and said her goodbyes to everyone.

"Don't forget to mail me in with your chat group Alex," she said.

"I'll do it," he replied with a smile.

They began to make a move before a cheery voice called out from behind them.

"Stephen Westbrook, you have to be kidding me!" Stephen turned around and his face cracked into a wide grin with a look of astonishment.

"Jamie Sinclair. What on earth.......?" he said. "I mean what are you doing here?"

"I'm catching up with these guys," said Jamie, nodding in the direction of Alex and his group.

"But, I heard you were some sort of hot-shot hedge fund manager," said Stephen.

"Yeah, and some of my best ideas come from this lot," he said. Stephen turned around to address Leonna.

"I went to school with this guy. Can you believe it? I haven't seen him in ages." Leonna smiled at Jamie.

"Hi, I'm Leonna," she said.

"Yeah, sorry. Leonna's my girlfriend. We work at the same firm." He pulled a business card from the top pocket of his jacket and passed it to Jamie. Jamie studied it closely.

"Junior Partner already," he said, raising an eyebrow. "We always had you down as a high achiever."

"Well, nobody ever doubted you Jamie. Head boy, captain of the rugby team. Need I go on?" said Stephen.

"Look, are you staying for a drink?" asked Jamie.

"No, we're going to have to get going, but let's get together sometime. Give me a call and we can meet for lunch."

"Yeah, I'll do that," said Jamie. Leonna turned to say a

final goodbye but Stephen put an arm around her shoulder and ushered her forwards.

"Come on babe, or we'll never get out of here," he said.

"Small World Jamie," said Alex.

"Yeah, I haven't seen him since school. It's not like we were best mates or anything, but I always remember he was a smart guy. Nice pitch you made upstairs by the way," he added.

"Yeah, we're going to do a bit more research on it but I'll let you know if I decide to take the plunge," replied Alex. "Hey, are you done building your position in the Indian IT company?"

"Yeah, we've built a decent size holding so that'll be it, at least for now. You can spread the word if you like."

"Did you hear that Matt?" said Alex. "We've been given the all clear on Jamie's top secret project."

"So we finally get to hear what all this is about," interrupted Carlo.

"Yeah, but it'll cost you," said Matt. "Get the drinks in mate and we'll tell you all about it."

Chapter 7

Alex had a seat on one side of a long table near to the window. There was a socket for his mobile phone on the underside of the table and he had his laptop open in front of him. Sometimes he just liked to get out of his room; swap the usual four walls for a change of scenery. The Starbucks on the high street was handy, and gave him free Wi-Fi and a half decent cup of coffee. It felt like he had somewhere to go even on a day when he didn't.

Now that he'd decided to buy and hold the shares in Jamie's Indian IT company, he needed to get more involved in the conversation around the investment. Robrex had it's own discussion board but it was pretty quiet. There'd been one or two posts following the announcement of the acquisition but they were pretty unsophisticated; just a couple of lines drawing attention to the RNS and expressing positive sentiments.

Alex decided to summarize the analysis work that he'd done with Matt and he wrote it up into a comprehensive post. He usually tried to avoid being too upbeat with his posts, but in this case, it was difficult to be anything other than positive on the company's prospects. He posted it to the board and copied a link into his investor chat group.

Over the next couple of hours, the post generated a fair bit of interest and seemed to stimulate some new buyers in the stock. The price edged up throughout the afternoon and some familiar names popped up on the board. Carlo and Seb had taken a position at the open, on the back of last night's discussion. They were joined by some other respected posters: 'Crazy88' and 'SkyeHigh,' who added their own positive comments. There were a few new names too, notably, 'Ya Man Noel,' who'd been posting on the board for a few months. He had some useful insight into the company and made some good contributions to the discussion.

By mid afternoon, the price had crept above £2.00 and Alex was happy with his days work. He was getting ready to go home when his phone rang. He could see it was a call from Maya.

"Hi Maya, everything OK?" he asked.
"Not exactly," she replied. "Your Dad's a bit the worse for wear. I don't think he's going to be able to work tonight. Is there any chance you could stand in for him? I know it's late notice and everything."
"Yeah sure. You mean....., has he been drinking?" he said, lowering his voice.
"Yes, I popped upstairs to look in on him and found him asleep on the sofa. He's been through the best part of a bottle of brandy this afternoon. He's never done anything like this before."

Alex fell silent, with the phone a little way from his ear. He'd been half expecting it. The inevitable next step in the process to....., well, he wasn't sure where.

"Alex?" said Maya, breaking the silence.
"Yeah, sorry. Listen, thanks for keeping an eye on him. I'll be over early evening before opening."
"Thanks Alex. You're a saviour."

They ended the call and Alex leaned back in his chair. It felt like a pillar in his life had shifted slightly on its foundations. Things that he'd taken for granted and relied upon were a little less solid; the future seemed suddenly more hazy and indistinct.

He called Lisa. It went straight through to her answer machine. Why did it always seem to do that lately? He'd been planning to ride over and make dinner for them both at her flat. He left a message to say that he needed to work at the restaurant. He kept it short, just saying that his Dad was ill and promised to come over at the weekend.

It was still light as he arrived outside the restaurant. He went around the back and Jack opened the door with a half-hearted smile.

"Sorry to land this on you bro. The Captain of the ship has taken to his cabin and it's all hands on deck." He seemed tired. The usual levity was all a bit forced and he looked like he had the world on his shoulders.

"You know I'll always help out if you need me," said Alex. Jack nodded without saying anything and closed the door.

Pete was busy getting things out of the fridge and cutting up the meat on a large cutting board. He looked up with a grin. His mood never seemed to change; always affable and content with his lot.

The door from the hall opened and Maya appeared in the middle of tying her hair up and fixing it with a decorative clip.

"Oh, hi Alex, you're here," she said. "Don't worry, he's fine. I just made him more comfortable on the sofa."

"Thanks Maya. I don't know what we'd do without you," he said with genuine feeling. "I'll just go and check up on him. I won't be a minute."

He went out into the hall with its familiar musty smell and headed up the stairs. The textured wall paper had started to peel away from the wall where it met the staircase and the paper lantern that marked the landing had begun to turn an off-white colour. Too many years of neglect.

As he reached the top floor, he could see the glow coming

from the half open door to the sitting room. He slowly pushed the door open and could make out the figure of his father lying on the sofa with a blanket covering him. A small table light highlighted his face and cast shadows across the sunken cheeks and lines on his forehead. He looked older than his 58 years.

Alex put his hand on his father's shoulder, and for a moment his pattern of breathing stuttered slightly before gradually resuming its usual rhythm. He looked around the room. A pile of vinyl records were stacked up on the floor next to the record player. A classical guitar leaned against the wall, the one Alex had first learned to play with. There was an armchair that matched the sofa occupying one corner of the room and a clothes stand with drying laundry in the other.

A bookshelf stood against the far wall with framed photographs. A photo of Alex's Mum stood on the top with a crucifix attached to the wall above it. It was the picture that had been used at her funeral. It had stood on the coffin in the cold dark stone church. She was young and beautiful, sitting on a low wall with the sea behind her.

He looked down at his father, his head resting on a pillow at the end of the sofa, and was struck by a sense of how vulnerable he looked. He'd always been the rock of the family, the protector and the provider. Lying there, he seemed almost child-like. He rearranged the blanket so that it covered his Dad's shoulder, just for want of something to do, then walked back to the door, drawing it quietly closed behind him.

It had been a while since Alex had done a Friday night and he was surprised at how busy the restaurant got. By eight o-clock, the place was almost full and the kitchen was struggling to keep up with the orders. He and Maya were combining the serving with helping to plate up starters and deserts in the kitchen. Even with everyone lending a hand, they could barely keep on top of things and it was a relief when the orders began to subside after nine and they could all shift back to their regular routine.

"Wow, is it always like this on a Friday?"
"Yep, ever since Sophia left," said Maya.
"Didn't she want to stay?"
"No, it's not that. Jack said we had to let her go to make ends meet."
"But, with what we've pulled in tonight, you could easily afford another pair of hands." Maya shrugged her shoulders.
"I don't know Alex. Your Dad and Jack manage all that. Maybe you can have a word with Jack," she said, looking at him hopefully.

Perhaps he should get more involved. He'd been neglecting it, he knew that.
"Maybe I'll catch a word with him later," he said, absently nodding to himself.

The diners were coming towards the end of their meals and it was time for Alex to do his rounds with the liqueurs. He went back into the kitchen to see what he could find. He was putting the drinks and glasses onto a tray as Maya came through into the kitchen.
"A couple of late diners," she said, and rattled off the order. "Can you take their drinks order Alex?" she added, before ripping off the order ticket and fixing it to the shelf above the serving counter.

Alex took his tray and returned to the restaurant. He glanced over to the newly occupied table by the window. It was a couple. A smartly dressed man with his back to Alex and an attractive, if rather sullen looking, woman opposite. Alex put the tray down on the sideboard and retrieved his order pad.

"Well, you said you were hungry...," he heard the man

say. There was something in the voice that sounded familiar. Alex slowly moved his head to a point where he could catch a sideways glance at the couple. It was only a side view, but he recognised him immediately. It was the CEO from the funding presentation he'd attended with Matt and Jamie; the Indian company, Robrex.

Alex suddenly felt rather self conscious. It was like a spotlight had been turned on him. He'd asked a question at the presentation but he was just one of a whole group of suits. Surely he wouldn't be recognised; not in this situation. He walked over to the table but made a point of keeping his face a little lower than usual; trying to be as inconspicuous as possible.

"Can I take your drink orders?" he said. The man barely looked up, but reached for the drinks menu and scanned the contents.
"Are you having a glass of something darling?" he said to the woman.
"Yes, but something light; white wine perhaps." He ordered a glass of Chardonnay and a bottle of mineral water and passed the menu back to Alex. There was no reaction; nothing to indicate any recognition. Alex was happy to slip away from the table and attend to the order.

He returned the menu to the shelf and began flicking through his order pad, pretended to busy himself whilst he stole a glance back at them. They looked like they were married, like they'd got to the stage when you don't have to try too hard. Both content to do their own thing, just checking in with each other on odd occasions. She was looking in her bag for something and he was sending a text message or email on his mobile. They were both well-dressed, affluent and a cut above the average customer at the restaurant.

Alex fetched the drinks from the kitchen, which he placed on a tray and returned to the restaurant. He looked up and noticed that the woman was now alone at the table. He stopped for an instant, then saw out of the corner of his eye, the door to the restrooms swinging gently closed. *Good timing*, he thought. He'd be able to deliver the drinks and avoid any further close encounters. He walked up to the table and the woman looked up and smiled. One of those smiles that disappears as fast as it arrives, but ticks the box in terms of social politeness.

Alex placed the glass of wine in front of her and the bottle of mineral water to one side to allow room for the food when it arrived. There was just space for the other glass next to the CEO's phone which he'd left on the table. As he placed the glass down, it nudged the phone which instantly revived itself from 'sleep mode.'

The screen came to life, causing Alex to hesitate for a second. He recognized the web page immediately from the banner that ran across the top of the screen. The name of the company, Robrex, was printed underneath with the stock market ticker. It was the bulletin board that he and his friends shared their ideas on. It momentarily distracted him but he quickly regained his composure and cleared his throat.
"Will there be anything else?" he asked.
"No thank you, that's everything," she said, looking up from a diary that she was studying.

Alex retreated back to his usual refuge near to the kitchen doors and took a second to gather his thoughts. It just seemed a bit unexpected. Why would the CEO of a public company bother with the ramblings of private investors on a popular website? Most of the bulletin boards were filled with meaningless chatter about the daily share price movements. Surely, a company CEO had better things to do with his time. Then again, was it really so strange? Maybe even business leaders are curious to know what the man on the street thinks of their performance. He went back into the kitchen but couldn't shake it from his mind.

There wasn't much more to do after that, other than wait for the customers to finish up and settle their bills. Alex usually took care of the payments, but he made a point of asking Maya if she could deal with the couple by the window, who were the last to leave. He made an excuse that he needed to fetch some petty cash from the office and by the time he came back to the restaurant, they were just leaving.

They closed up the front of the restaurant and retreated back to the kitchen. After they'd cleaned up in the kitchen, Jack went out to collect the cash and credit card slips from the till and took them through to the small office. Alex took the opportunity to follow him in to fetch his jacket.

"I had no idea it got that busy on a Friday these days. You must be doing something right," he said.
"Yeah, we're running to stand still," replied Jack, wearily.
"Can't you take someone else on to help with the serving? It'll make life easier for everyone over the weekend."
"The trouble is, they expect to be paid," said Jack. "We have too many overheads as it is."
"But surely, with what you pulled in tonight.....," began Alex.
"Look Alex, I'm telling you, we just can't afford it right now." Jack could barely disguise the irritation in his voice. Alex said nothing for a moment to let things subside.
"Jack, you need to let me know if there's anything wrong." He paused what he was doing and for a moment, it looked like he was about to say something, before deciding against it. He put the cash and receipts into the cash box and closed the lid.
"Don't worry, I can deal with it." Alex wondered if he should push back but decided this was probably not the time.

They came out of the office and Alex picked up his backpack. Maya looked up from wiping the work surfaces.

"Are you going already?"

"Yeah, it's been a long week. I think I'll make a move." She walked around the central island and gave him a hug.

"Thanks Alex, you really helped us out tonight."

"No problem. I'm always here to lend a hand if you need me." He pulled his backpack over his shoulder and walked over to the back door. Jack followed him and held it open.

"Thanks bro, we owe you one." Alex paused at the top of the steps.

"Remember, if there's anything I can do; well, you know....." Jack nodded and Alex headed down into the yard. Jack began to close the door but then seemed to change his mind before ducking outside and drawing the door closed behind him. Alex stopped and turned around as he walked slowly down to join him.

"There is something," he said, hesitantly. "It's only short term; a temporary thing to get us through the next few weeks. It's just a cash flow problem we've got."

"Oh right," said Alex. He wasn't expecting it, although he knew what it took for Jack to ask. He did his best to make light of it. "Yeah sure. How much do you need?"

"Could you stretch to five grand? I mean, just to get us through this. Things will pick up over the summer and I can pay you back within a couple of months."

"Yeah no problem. I'll transfer it over tomorrow." He needed to settle up with Jamie to the tune of twenty grand but he had enough in his trading account to send Jack the other five.

There was a look of relief on Jack's face, mixed with an awkward sense of embarrassment.

"Right, that'll be great. Thanks a lot bro," he said, unable to look him in the eye. Alex thought about pressing him to get a better understanding of what was going on, but in the end, he thought better of it and just nodded.

"I'll see you next week then," he said, and turned towards the gate. As he went through into the passageway, he glanced back at Jack who hadn't moved from where he stood. His mind had already moved on to whatever it was that was preoccupying him. Alex closed the gate and headed off home.

Chapter 8

Over the next few days, things began to hot up. Alex had begun to increasingly focus his attention onto Jamie's Indian stock, Robrex, and the momentum had really started to build. The previously quiet bulletin board had now caught the attention of the first movers. These names in turn brought along their followers and so the demand for the stock rose inexorably. The share price had surged up to 285p, more than twice the placing price of just a couple of weeks earlier. The chart suggested that if it could break 300p, it would climb a lot higher.

It should have been the perfect scenario. Alex had done the research and it all made sense. Plenty of other respected investors felt exactly the same way and the share price action was telling him he was dead right. In spite of it all though, he just couldn't feel comfortable with the investment. There was a nagging feeling that just wouldn't go away; something that he couldn't quite put his finger on. Maybe, it was the encounter with the CEO in the restaurant or the fact that everything was happening so quickly.

When he felt like this, there was only one thing to do. He needed to get out of the flat and clear his head. It was a nice day and there was nothing to keep him at home, so why not take the bike for a spin and get a change of scenery? He changed into his cycling gear and filled up a water bottle. He used the kind of cycling shoes which had cleats built into the sole and locked into the pedals. He carried these down to the front door to avoid taking the shine off Ms. Mark's floorboards,

He stepped outside into the bright sunshine and slipped on the shoes before slotting the drink bottle into its carrier. He'd already decided the route he was going to take. There was a good circular run that would take him off the main roads. It was about 35 miles, so he'd be back at the flat within a couple of hours.

As he pushed down on the pedals to get underway and felt the first rush of cool air across his face, it instantly lifted his mood. That feeling of effortless speed as he flicked through the gears along the approach to Alexandra Palace. The open views down into the park and to the city beyond; it gave him that feeling of escapism and anticipation of the open road ahead.

He had a lot on his mind. It wasn't just his latest investment; there was the stuff going on with his Dad and the restaurant. He'd transferred the money over to Jack and got a short message back with assurances that it was just a short term stopgap. He just felt uncomfortable with the whole situation.

He didn't mind supporting the business, and he was used to having his money at risk, but he usually understood the extent of the risk he was taking. With the restaurant, he realized that he had no idea what financial state it was in. He had no way of understanding what it was going to take to keep it afloat. He was beginning to regret not taking a more active role, but he knew that it was a conscious decision. He'd been trying to put distance between himself and the family business and now there wasn't much he could do other than wait and see how things turned out. He tried to put it out of his mind.

He'd left the suburbs of London behind and was now cycling along roads bound by hedgerows on each side. He could see over the top of the hedges to the open fields beyond and it felt like he'd left the city far behind, even though he'd only travelled a few miles. His mind returned to the subject that had been occupying it all morning, the investment in Robrex.

So far, everything had gone according to plan, in fact, it couldn't have gone any better. He was sitting on a twenty grand profit with the prospect of more to come. He'd done his research and the fundamentals of the business all added up. There was nothing that he could identify which should give him cause for concern, and yet, he couldn't shake off the nagging doubts.

He was still searching for what it was that he was missing as he approached a small village, nestled next to a copse of trees. The branches threw shadows across the road and he passed intermittently from bright sunshine to cool shade; the sun flickering like a strobe light through the trees. It was at that point that he finally saw what it was that had been bothering him. He'd been looking for the piece that didn't fit. Suddenly, he realized that what was making him uneasy wasn't the missing piece but the fact that there was no missing piece; no loose ends. All the figures were just as they should be. The revenue and profit growing at consistently high rates and cash conversion just as it should be. The costs in the business grew in line with rising revenue but never by too much to interfere with the consistent growth in profits. It was a perfect picture of a successful growth company. Almost as though it had been designed that way.

Alex pulled over outside a small shop in the village. It was the end of a row of cottages and stood next to the local pub which was set back from the road. He propped his bike against the side of the shop, took out the drink bottle and walked over to one of the picnic tables outside the pub. There was no one else outside, so he took a seat at one of the tables and quenched his thirst.

Alex felt like he'd resolved something in his mind. He now understood what had been bothering him but he still wasn't sure what it meant or what he should do about it. Was it a case of creative accounting, that just massaged the figures to paint the best picture, or was it something more serious, a fabrication of those figures? Either way, he resolved to speak to Jamie about his concerns and come to some sort of decision. With that decided, he felt a lot better, like he had a way forward.

He took out his mobile from the back pocket of his cycling top and checked his route on the app that he used for the purpose. He was around half way through the ride and had made good time. He'd take it easy on the way back and enjoy the scenery a little.

He felt something brush against his leg and looking down, noticed that he'd been joined by a ginger and white cat. The cat hopped onto the bench seat next to him and rubbed the underside of its chin against his arm. He took the hint and stroked its head gently.

"So, what do you think, Tigger? Am I just worrying about nothing or should I trust my gut instinct with this one?" They say the object of investing is to learn to ignore your gut and stick to rational data-based decisions, but Alex had his gut to thank on more than one occasion over his investment career. The cat said nothing and rubbed its ear against the side of the table in a non-committal sort of way. It stretched its hind legs and strode dismissively along the bench with its tail up before pausing at the end. It sniffed the air a couple of times before deftly dismounting and walking off across the car park.

Alex took another drink from his bottle and decided it was time to make a move himself. He walked back over to his bike and felt the tyres. They were sufficiently inflated and there were no obvious signs of wear. He made sure the quick-release skewers were tightened and gave the wheels a quick spin to ensure they were aligned correctly. He then got in the saddle and headed off through the small village and out into the countryside beyond.

He maintained a nice easy pace on the way back and it was still mid-afternoon by the time he turned into the cul-de-sac and drew up outside the house. He secured the bike in its usual place against the railings and made his way into the hallway. A letter had been placed in his post box, so he picked it up before heading up the stairs.

It was only after a few steps that he realized from the heavy tapping sound that he'd forgotten to remove his shoes when he came in. He paused momentarily before deciding there was greater risk in going back. Better to put as much distance as possible between himself and Ms. Marks apartment at this stage.

Alex stepped carefully onwards, sacrificing speed for a lighter weight of step. As he turned at the top of the first flight of steps, he could hear someone approaching from the floor above. He paused as the footsteps got closer. *Surely it couldn't be*, he thought. The first sight of Ms. Marks sensible brown leather shoes confirmed his worst fears. She stopped abruptly, unaccustomed as she was to encountering her tenants in Lycra

"Oh, you've been out on your bicycle Mr Samaras," she said. "Nice day for it, I'm sure," she added, moving aside to allow Alex to pass.
"Yes, beautiful day," he replied. Alex didn't move and briefly, there was an awkward stand-off, before he, inexplicably, decided to open the letter he was holding. "Ah..," he said, as if it was exactly the news he was expecting. He motioned with the letter for Ms. Marks to carry on whilst he studied the details and she passed by with a curious frown on her face.

As she turned onto the next flight of stairs, she looked back over her shoulder to see Alex still engrossed in the bank statement he was holding. He looked up and nodded to her with a smile. By the time he heard the door of Ms. Marks apartment close, he'd folded up the letter and returned it to its envelope. *'You idiot,'* he said to himself, as he proceeded up the stairs and entered his flat.

He took a quick shower and got changed. It was a little before 4pm, so there was time to catch the last of the market before trading finished at 4:30pm. He pulled up a summary of his holdings on his PC and could quickly see that there had been no significant moves. The Robrex price was continuing to edge upwards though; threatening to break the psychological 300p barrier. If it went over 300p, there would likely be a spike in volume as traders pushed it higher; a perfect opportunity to offload shares into the market. If he called Jamie to let him know his concerns, there might still be time to liquidate his holding before the close.

He didn't like to call him during trading hours as he was invariably busy, but as he held his and Matt's shares in the company account, he didn't have much of a choice. He called his mobile number but it went straight through to answer machine. Alex wasn't sure if he wanted to leave a message but in the end just said:

"Hi Jamie, I just wanted a word with you about Robrex if you have a minute." He wasn't expecting a call back until later but within a couple of minutes, Jamie got back to him.

"Alex, what's up?"
"Hi, Jamie. Thanks for getting back," replied Alex. "Listen, it's about the Robrex situation. I've been doing a lot of thinking about it and I'm just not comfortable with the figures. I'm just not sure I can trust the numbers, especially with it being a foreign company and the reverse take over and everything.

"Alex, relax," said Jamie. "I had the same concerns myself but I've got the inside track on the company now. Do you remember the guy from the Investors Meet Up the other day? The one that I went to school with, with the cute girlfriend. Well, I met him for lunch last week and it only turns out that his firm are doing the audit for Robrex. He's given it me off the record. The company's kosha. They've checked everything. Alex, this one's got a lot further to run. Don't get cold feet on me."

Alex laughed. It felt like some of the tension he was feeling inside had suddenly released.

"I'm just wondering how I manage to make any money at this game when you guys are the only ones with the full picture."

"It's all about getting an edge on the market Alex. No stone left unturned. Hey listen, we're having this guy Stephen and his girlfriend over for dinner on Saturday. It'd be great if you and Lisa could come along too. How about it?" Alex hesitated as he tried to picture the scene.

"Er, I'll need to speak to Lisa. Can I get back to you?"

"Yeah sure, but can you let me know by tomorrow?"

"Yeah I'll give you a call," said Alex. Jamie made his excuses as there were things that he needed to get back to and they ended the call.

Alex leaned back on the sofa and smiled to himself. The guy never ceased to amaze him. He had all the answers, while everyone else was just groping around in the dark. He wasn't sure about the ethics of sounding out the Auditors 'off the record', but he guessed that was an inevitable part of the old boys network. It felt like a weight had been taken off his shoulders.

He got up from the sofa and walked over to the window. The sun was lower in the sky and it cast a warm hue across the street outside. Alex took out the wireless ear plugs from his pocket and put them in. He selected an up beat compilation from his mobile and returned to stretch out on the sofa. Things felt a lot better.

Chapter 9

Alex had called Lisa about Jamie's dinner invite and it hadn't taken much to persuade her. She'd met Jamie before at a drinks event that Alex had taken her to and she knew all about his background. The natural networker in her recognized an opportunity to extend her contacts and, who knows, maybe even get Alex to realize more of his potential.

He'd arranged to see her at her new place. They'd take a taxi from there to Jamie's house in Notting Hill. He'd seen Jamie's house from the outside when they shared a taxi home once, but hadn't been inside. He remembered an impressive three-storey town house on a tree-lined avenue. The sort of place that would cost you anywhere between five and ten million. Then throw in another 500K to fit it out just the way you'd like it. It was a different world to the one Alex lived in. Still, he couldn't help feeling curious to experience it, even if it was just for one night.

He emerged from the station in the centre of Hampstead and paused to get his bearings. He'd always taken his bike to Lisa's new flat up to now, but he didn't want to risk his smart but casual attire to a razor thin bike seat and an oily chain. No, tonight deserved a step up in class. He checked his position on his mobile and identified the general direction of her place. Satisfied that he had a reasonable bearing on his destination, he set off down a side street opposite the station.

It was a nice walk along the narrow streets of leafy Hampstead; a completely different vibe to the bustling pavements of his usual neighbourhood. Well maintained houses of London brick and white render lined the roads and shining new cars of German origin occupied the spaces between the street trees. *Yes, this was where you came to after you'd made it*, he thought. He understood why Lisa had moved here.

It was a pleasant road where she lived. You could glimpse the trees on the edge of the heath above the roof line at the end of the road. Lisa's place was in a terrace of three-storey Victorian houses. She had an apartment on the second floor with a tall window overlooking the road. A hedge lined the pavement along the front of the house and a low gate led to the front door.

He pressed the button marked Flat 2-1. After a few seconds, Lisa's voice answered.
"Hi, come up. I'm nearly ready." She released the lock on the front door and Alex was able to push it open. He went up the stairs to the second floor and the door to Lisa's flat was ajar so he just let himself in and closed the door behind him. "I'll be out in a minute. I'm just doing my hair. Can you call a taxi?" came Lisa's voice from the bathroom.
"Sure. We're OK for time so don't panic," replied Alex, and walked over to the sofa and pulled out his mobile. "Is ten minutes OK?" he called out to Lisa.
"Yes, I'll be done in five," she replied. Alex ordered the taxi and returned the mobile to his back pocket.

She'd done a nice job with the flat. The skirting board was painted matt black which accentuated the honey coloured floorboards. Black and white prints on the walls kept everything understated and sophisticated. Lisa had a great eye for detail and style. That was obvious when she stepped out of the bathroom. Even by her standards, she'd gone the extra mile. Her blond hair was swept back on one side and she wore a short leather skirt with a sleeveless top that showed off her figure.

"How do I look?" she asked.
"Pretty stunning," said Alex, in all honesty. "I think you're ready for your photo shoot," he added, getting up from

the sofa.

"You look nice too," she said , coming over to give him a peck on the cheek, being careful not to ruin her make up.

"Shall we go downstairs? The taxi will be here any minute." Lisa picked up the short suede jacket off the chair and they headed out of the door.

They only had a minute or so to wait before the taxi arrived and as they got in the back, Alex gave the driver the address.

"Oh good, you got something to take with us," said Lisa, noticing the bottle-sized carrier bag that Alex was holding.

"Yeah, it's a nice bottle of Rioja," said Alex. "It's probably not going to make much of an impression on Jamie's wine cellar but it's one of the best bottles we serve in the restaurant,"

"That good, huh?" said Lisa, giving Alex a sideways glance.

"You think I should have pushed the boat out?" said Alex.

"Well, it doesn't hurt to make an impression," she replied. He realized he'd fallen short of Lisa's best laid plans so changed the subject.

"The other couple are a guy Jamie used to go to school with and his girlfriend. I met her at one of our Private Investor meet-ups last week." He thought it was best not to mention the fact that he'd invited her.

"And what does he do?" asked Lisa.

"He's an accountant," said Alex. "They both work at the same firm. Jamie seems to think he's being fast-tracked to the top." Lisa raised an eyebrow.

"Well, this sounds like it could be an interesting evening."

It was about a fifteen minute drive to Notting Hill and Alex remembered the road as they drove up; the bend in the road where Jamie had been dropped off. It was even more impressive in the daylight. The white facades of the houses with their grand portico entrances and the mature trees arching their branches over the road.

Jamie's house was set back from the road behind cast iron railings punctuated by two white columns that marked the driveway entrance. Alex indicated to the driver where to pull over and he settled the fare while Lisa got out of the car.
"Very nice," she said, looking up and down the street. Seeing her standing there, Alex couldn't help thinking that this was where she belonged. Some people are just made for this kind of lifestyle and this was Lisa in her element.

They walked into the driveway, passed the Range Rover and up the steps to the gloss black front door. Alex pressed the brass door bell and after a short wait, Jamie opened the door.
"Hi Alex," he said, shaking him warmly by the hand. "And Lisa, it's so great to see you again," he added, giving her a hug and a kiss on the cheek. The thing with Jamie was, you actually felt that he meant it. He was that sort of person; the kind that everybody warms to straight away.

"Welcome to our humble abode," he said, ushering them into the hallway. An elegant staircase with ornate cast iron balustrade swept down one side and an impressive chandelier hung from the high ceiling.
"You've got to be joking, right?" said Alex.
"Well, Joanne's managed to pull it into shape," he responded, just as his wife appeared in the hallway.
"You must be Alex," she said in a warm Scottish accent and giving him a hug. "Jamie's told me a lot about you."
"And Lisa, you look fabulous. I love your hair by the way," she added, leading her through into the reception room.

Alex followed them in and looked around him at the beautifully appointed sitting room, the trappings of a successful career in the City. When he and Matt were chatting and joking in the pub with Jamie, it was easy to imagine they were all the same; bonded by their shared passion for taking on the market. Standing there in Jamie's sitting room, he had the sudden feeling that they were a million miles apart. Jamie was leading a lifestyle that he couldn't even imagine. It just seemed so far removed from the world that he inhabited.

Lisa and Joanne had hit it off instantly, with their shared love of interior design. Joanne was showing her an abstract canvas that hung next to the fireplace.
"Champagne girls?" asked Jamie and they both smiled and nodded their approval. He put his arm around Alex's shoulder. "Come on Alex, let's get a beer from the kitchen."

Jamie led the way down the hallway to a large kitchen with a tall bay window overlooking the garden at the end. He pulled a couple of beers from the fridge and set them on the marble island counter. He slid a bottle opener across to Alex and retrieved a bottle of champagne from the rack next to the fridge.

"So, are you feeling a bit more relaxed about our friends at Robrex?" he asked. Alex passed him an open bottle of Corona.
"Well, it doesn't hurt to get your 'inside track' on the company," he said. Jamie smiled.
"Yeah, it might be best not to mention it to Stephen tonight. He was a bit reluctant to talk off the record, but I managed to get him to walk the fine line over a nice lunch and a couple of bottles of claret." Alex laughed.
"That's what's known as oiling the wheels, I suppose. Is that how it works in the City then?" he asked.
"That's how it works in business Alex. You have to learn to take every opportunity that's open to you." Alex knew he was right. He also knew that the idealist in him would always come up short when it came to working the system.

"Here, take those beers and I'll bring the champagne, said Jamie, as he took a handful of glasses from one of the kitchen cabinets. They made their way back to the sitting room where the two girls were now on the sofa pouring over a lifestyle magazine. "Lisa, don't start giving her ideas," said Jamie, placing the champagne and glasses on the low table in front of the sofa.

"Don't worry darling, it's only a walk-in closet we were looking at," said Joanne.

"It's not the closet I'm worried about. It's what you plan to fill it with," replied Jamie as he poured out four glasses of champagne. They all laughed and clinked glasses to get the evening under way. At that moment, the door bell sounded. "That'll be Stephen," said Jamie, putting his glass down and heading out to the doorway.

Alex could hear the sound of laughter from the hallway, the kind that comes with the banter of old school friends, usually with a fair degree of back slapping. Jamie led the new arrivals through to the sitting room. Stephen was clutching a bottle of champagne in each hand and raised them by way of a greeting.

"Fresh supplies," he said, putting them on the table with the other bottle. Behind him came Leonna. If Alex had seen her in the street he probably wouldn't have recognized her, but he'd certainly have given her a second look. She'd put her hair up and the ubiquitous business suit had been replaced by a well-fitting short black dress. She looked beautiful, if a little nervous. She caught his eye and smiled before Jamie did the introductions.

Once everyone was comfortably seated with a glass of champagne, it gave Lisa the opportunity to take centre stage. Alex had to admit, she was good at it. The PR executive in her, skilfully orchestrated the small talk and before long, the ice was well and truly melted. She had that ability to make everyone feel good about themselves and what they said, really matter. She also had some good stories, and could be a shameless name dropper, which always kept the conversation interesting.

With everything moving along smoothly, Joanne got up from the sofa and announced that dinner should be ready soon.

"I'll just go and see to things," she said. "Oh, and no, I'm not a domestic goddess. We got the caterers in." It was a light hearted moment, but it answered a question that had been puzzling Alex. Why the complete lack of cooking activity in the kitchen when he and Jamie had fetched the drinks?

"Joanne almost had a nervous breakdown the last time she cooked for guests," said Jamie. "We've decided to leave it to the professionals these days."

"Leonna's a genius in the kitchen," said Stephen, patting her rather patronizingly on the knee. "She can knock up a culinary masterpiece and makes it look effortless. She'll make me the perfect wife some day," he added, laughing.

"Yeah? What do you like to cook?" asked Alex, to rescue her from the awkward moment.

"Oh, pretty much anything," she said. "I just love to shop for fresh ingredients. Then I think about what I'm going to make as I'm doing it. It's my creative outlet, I suppose."

"Alex's family are in the restaurant business," said Lisa, framing it in such a way that it could be anything from a top-end Michelin star restaurant to a successful chain of trendy bistros. Certainly not a north London taverna in need of a loan from Alex to keep the doors open.

"Oh, do you cook?" asked Leonna.

"Yes, I like to try different things, mostly Mediterranean, but my brother's the one with the talent in our family."

Joanne reappeared in the doorway to summon everyone to the dining room and they all made their way through there. The room was another design masterclass. A long modern oak table with a sixties-inspired cluster of hanging light shades formed the centre piece. A pair of large mirrors hung on the wall behind the table, reflecting the artwork hanging from the opposite wall. The table was laid out with an assortment of beautifully presented appetizers that had miraculously appeared from somewhere.

They all took their seats as instructed by Joanne. Alex found himself seated between Joanne and Leonna. Lisa was on the other side of the table between Stephen and Jamie. Jamie topped up everyone's glass with champagne and uncorked a bottle of red that he and Stephen both agreed was more than worthy of the occasion. Alex made a mental note to drink slowly.

The food was excellent and the conversation flowed along with the wine. There was a fair amount of reminiscing of old school days from Jamie and Stephen, They'd both attended Gordonstoun, the renowned public school in the north of Scotland. It seemed that Jamie had been destined for success from an early age and had captained the rugby and cricket teams.

"You were into athletics weren't you Stephen?" he asked.

"Yes, that's right. I always preferred the individual sports where you could control your own destiny. I represented the school at Modern Pentathlon."

"What does that include?" asked Lisa.

"It's five disciplines: fencing, swimming, riding, shooting and running. Not the most practical sport. I've moved on to triathlon now."

"So, you've swapped the horse for a bike?" said Alex.

"Yeah, and if anyone gets in his way, he shoots them," added Jamie with a grin. Stephen didn't strike Alex as the kind of person who took himself too light heartedly and his expression gave away a certain feeling of annoyance at being the butt of the joke. Leonna seemed to notice it too and quickly changed the subject.

"So, how are your investments faring, Alex? Do you have any tips for me?" she asked.

"I think the best tip I can give you is to do your own research," he replied. "I always swore that I'd never give out any tips because they'd be bound to work out badly. I only did it once, after I invested in a company that I was absolutely convinced was going to be a multi-bagger. I was so excited about this company that I couldn't help sharing it with a friend. It turned into my single biggest losing investment. I held it all the way down and sold out for a 95% loss."

"What was it Mark Twain said?" asked Jamie. 'It ain't what you don't know that gets you into trouble, it's what you know for sure that just ain't so.' Absolute certainty's not a healthy place to be in the markets."

"Oh, I don't know; Isn't that what the under-achievers tell themselves," said Stephen, looking directly at Alex. "Anyone who's really made something of themselves has taken a big risk at some time or another." Alex knew he was trying to needle him and he made a conscious effort not to rise to the bait.

"What, you mean, bet the farm just once?" he said.

"Well, yes. You have to be prepared to put it all on the line if you want to rise above mediocrity."

"The trouble is, if you've done it once, you'll do it again, and you only have to be wrong once," said Alex, looking back defiantly.

"Well, I'm firmly with Alex on this one," interjected Jamie. "You've got to be able to manage risk and live to fight another day. I keep telling Alex he'll make a great hedge fund manager one day." Lisa looked up at Alex, waiting for him to respond. When he remained silent she felt that she had to say something.

"Well, I'm sure Alex would welcome the opportunity to get a foot on the ladder," she said. Jamie looked expectantly towards Alex but he didn't meet his gaze.

"It's just not the right time at the moment," he said. Lisa pursed her lips and looked away, barely concealing her annoyance. It wasn't the first time she'd thought that Alex was almost incapable of grasping the opportunity that was right in front of him.

It was a welcome relief for Alex that Joanne decided it was time for the coffee and she got up to fetch the pot that had been quietly brewing in the corner. After that, the conversation broke up into one-to-one chats around the table and Alex found himself paired with Leonna.

"It can be difficult finding your place in the world," she said. "What do you mean?" asked Alex.

"I mean it's not easy to find what it is you want to do with your life. I ask myself all the time whether I really want to spend the rest of my life as an accountant." Alex realized that she could see right through him. It felt almost like a relief to know that someone understood what he'd been trying to conceal, not least from himself.

"It's not that I don't enjoy what I'm doing. I do. I don't think I'll ever stop investing. It's just that I need something that's more than simply the accumulation of capital. Do you know what I mean?" Leonna smiled.

"Yes, I know what you mean. You want to end world poverty and find a cure for cancer." They both laughed.

"No, not exactly," said Alex. "I'll probably settle for a small business."

They chatted easily for a while, talking about work and what they were doing in their free time. A lot of what she was doing, seemed to involve tagging along with whatever Stephen was doing. He was helping her with her professional exams and there didn't seem time for much else at the moment. Alex suggested they have another meet up with Matt, Carlo and Seb sometime, and she seemed genuinely enthusiastic, until she caught Stephen's eye. He seemed to have one ear on their conversation whilst talking to Joanne.

Leonna hesitated and back-tracked a little, saying that she'd have to see if there was time with all her study and everything. After that, the conversation became a little awkward and soon after, Stephen announced that it was probably time for them to make a move.

It seemed the right time to call it a night, and so Alex and Lisa made their excuses too. Stephen had pre-booked a taxi which was waiting outside for them. Lisa and Alex decided they'd walk around the corner to get one from the main road. It was a clear night and it had turned quite cold. Fortunately, they didn't have to wait long before an available taxi pulled over for them.

Lisa was unusually quiet on the journey home and Alex made an effort to break the silence.

"Jamie's really lucky to have such an amazing house. I could get used to living in a place like that."

"Well it didn't happen by accident Alex," she replied, somewhat dismissively. "People like Jamie know what they want from life and they have the drive and ambition to make it happen. You could learn a lot from him, and he practically offered you a job tonight." Alex took a deep breath and let it out slowly.

"Well, maybe I'll take him up on it some day, but I'm just not ready to commit to it right now."

"Alex, you're 28 years old. When are you planning to move on with your life?" she said, turning her head away and looking out of the window. Alex didn't have an answer for her and the car fell silent once more.

"Where do you want me to drop you?" asked the driver as they turned into Lisa's road.

"Anywhere here will be fine," said Alex, reaching for his wallet. "Alex, I think I'll get an early night. I'll probably drop into work tomorrow morning, so you might as well take the taxi home," said Lisa.

"Er,..... right," he said as Lisa stepped out of the taxi and closed the door with barely a backward glance. Alex sat motionless for a few seconds.

"Where to mate?" asked the driver. Alex took a moment to get his thoughts straight.

"I'll get out here," he said, and settled the fare.

Lisa was looking in her bag for the door key as Alex jogged up to the house.

"Lisa, let's not end the night like this," he said. She looked up as she noticed him and sighed.

"Alex, not tonight, OK."

"Well, let's go inside and talk for a bit." She looked down at her bag and began unconsciously playing with her keys. There was a pause, as though she was collecting her thoughts, thinking of the right words, the right way to put it. Alex felt that heavy sinking feeling in his stomach, the one where you know it's coming.

"Alex,.....it just feels like you and I are heading in different directions; like we're on different paths, you know. It seems like we're both investing so much time and energy, and maybe it's in something that's not supposed to be. I think I want to take a break."

There it was. She wanted to take a break. It was about as final as you could get in the circumstances. He stood there wondering what he could say to change her mind, wondering if she even wanted him to try or whether he even wanted her to change her mind. In the end he said:

"So that's it then?" She slowly nodded her head.

"I hope you find what you're looking for Alex," she said, and turned to open the door. He watched her step inside the hallway and the final eye contact before she quietly closed the door.

He remained standing there as the light in her room came on and she drew the curtains. That felt like it. The final gesture; the parting of the ways. He forced himself to move, and walked out on to the pavement. He started to walk towards the station and then decided he'd go the other way, towards the heath. He needed some space, somewhere to think and process everything. It was going to be a long walk.

Chapter 10

The last of the customers had settled up their bill and were making their way out of the restaurant. George was on hand to see them to the door. He followed them out onto the pavement, sharing a joke, before they headed off down the street.

He withdrew the canopies at the front of the restaurant and looked up and down the street. It was quiet, apart from the occasional passing car. An old-style Jaguar was parked across the road with it's lights on. He'd noticed it when he came outside; looking like it was about to set off. It hadn't moved though. He had the rather unnerving feeling that the shadowy figure at the wheel was looking over at him.

He walked back into the restaurant and locked the door. The car was still there when he pulled down the blinds and dimmed the lights. He collected together the liqueur bottles onto a tray and took them through to the kitchen.

"Okay, we finished tonight. Good job everybody," he said. Jack and Pete had started on clearing up the work surfaces and Maya was piling up the plates next to the sink.
"Go and take a rest Dad. We'll clear up in here," said Jack, looking up from what he was doing. George walked over to the drinks store and replaced the bottles in the cupboard.
"Yeah, maybe I'll go sit down for a minute," he replied. He took out a tumbler from the cupboard and poured himself a generous glass of Metaxa brandy. He thought about returning the bottle to the cupboard, but after holding it up to examine what was remaining, decided to take it with him. He disappeared out of the kitchen door on his way up to his apartment.

Maya looked up at Jack and caught his eye. They were both thinking the same thing, but there wasn't much to be said. She took a cloth and headed towards the swing doors.

"I'll go and tidy up in the restaurant."

There was always a good atmosphere in the kitchen at the end of the day. A sense of satisfaction at a job well done; a job that not many people have the skills to pull off. It was long hours and low pay, but at the end of it all, there was the camaraderie; the knowledge that you've gone into the trenches together one more time and come out the other side.

"I like what we did with the starter tonight. Stuffing the tomato with cream cheese makes a nice contrast," said Jack. He always liked to have a debrief of the night's offering. "We need to prepare that in advance though, and then we can just add it to the starter as we're plating it up." Pete nodded his head.

"It might work better with a toasted crusty bread rather than the pitta. What do you think?" Jack smiled.

"I think you're dead right. If you weren't already the second best chef in this place, I'd promote you." They both laughed and carried on clearing up the leftover ingredients.

Jack had his hands full with containers that he was moving to the fridge, when there was a sharp knock on the back door. He looked up, a little surprised to have anyone call round at such a late hour.

"Do you want to see who that is?" he said to Pete. Jack continued to store away the leftovers but kept one eye on the back door. He could just make out a low voice from the steps outside the door but couldn't hear what was said. Pete drew the door partially closed.

"There's a couple of guys say they have a meeting with your Dad," he said. Jack had a feeling he knew what it was about.

"I'll have a word with them. Just finish up in here and if

Maya asks, tell her I'll be back in a minute."

He walked over to the door and reluctantly, pulled it open. It was no surprise to see the figure standing at the top of the steps. The pronounced jaw line and slightly sunken cheeks; the hooded eyelids and manicured hair. Ordinarily, he might have been considered good looking. There was something about the eyes though, and the hint of a sneer that played across his face.

"The old man tucked up in bed is he?" he said, casually taking a draw from his cigarette.
"I think it's better if I deal with things now," replied Jack. "Like I said the other day, there's only so much we can do with the money that's coming in."
"Well, maybe we need to look at some kind of business solution then. Are you going to invite us in?" Jack glanced behind him.
"We can talk out here just for a minute. I need to get back and finish up in the kitchen."

He stepped out of the door and closed it behind him. That was the first time he'd been able to get a good look at the other one. Thick set with closely cropped reddish blond hair and a few days of stubble around his chin. He wore jeans and a black puffer jacket. It wasn't difficult to understand his role in the partnership.

The two men walked casually back into the yard and Jack followed them down the steps. He ushered them over to one side by the gate so they wouldn't be seen from the window.

"I thought you understood the position we're in," he said. "We can pay the regular monthly amount, as we discussed, and when we're able to, we'll add something to it. Things will pick up in the summer. We just need a bit of breathing room." The brains of the outfit looked back at him without expression. He wasn't in any hurry. He took another draw on his cigarette and paused, as though he was giving consideration to what Jack was saying.

"Okay, I understand you need a bit of time to sort things out. We're not going to be unreasonable, but we need to know that our money's secure. We need to know that we're going to get back all that we're owed."

"Look, we're giving you all that we have. There's nothing more we can do," said Jack. The man looked back at him with the same unhurried demeanour.

"I'm not looking for more. I just want security for the loan." He glanced up at the building behind Jack. "You own the freehold on the property, right?"

"Well yeah, but that's got nothing to do with my Dad's loan."

"The way I see it is, your Dad owes us money. We need to know that he's going to pay us back. You see, it makes us nervous if we think he might welch on his side of the deal. If he puts up the property as security, we'll feel less nervous. That will be a good thing for everybody," he said, looking Jack directly in the eye to make his point.

Jack wasn't about to cave in to some kind of strong arm tactic. He look defiantly back at him.

"That's not going to happen," he said. "My Dad took out a loan with you guys. That was his mistake. We're not about to make things worse by chucking in the roof over our heads."

"Well, maybe you should talk it over with the old man; make sure he understands the situation."

"No, I don't need to. It's not going to happen," said Jack, firmly. The man continued to look him in the eye but said nothing. Finally, he sucked on his lower lip and looked down at the ground, as though he'd become resigned to the situation.

"Well, I guess there's nothing more to be said then." He offered an outstretched hand. *Sometimes, you just have to stand up to these guys,* thought Jack. He shook his hand but as he released his grip, the other man's grip suddenly tightened. He felt himself yanked violently forwards. He could see it coming, but there was nothing he could do to stop it. The accomplice had stepped forward and delivered a brutal blow to the side of his face. With Jack's arm held down, he was completely defenceless on that side.

He could feel the crack of bone. The vision in his right eye becoming obscured as the blood entered the eye socket; like a curtain drawing across his field of vision. The two men dragged him through the gate into the passageway and dumped him on the ground. A heavy boot thumped into his side; more splintering of bone and a searing pain ripped through his chest. The blows continued to pound in, each one accompanied by more agonizing pain.

It was difficult to know when it had stopped. The pain hadn't let up but the impacts that left him struggling to breath seemed to have abated. He could make out a voice through the dull haze in his head.
"Right, have we made our position completely clear then?" The voice was breathless from the exertion. "Now I suggest you have a re-think." That was all he heard before one final crunching boot to the head and he passed into unconsciousness.

Chapter 11

The alarm came and went and Alex turned over and buried his head in the pillow. He wasn't yet ready to face the day; to face the new reality. It felt better to maintain a state of suspended animation, where life stood still and what had happened remained unacknowledged. It had been a long time since he'd stayed in bed this long.

Eventually, he summoned the energy to pull himself from the duvet and rose to his feet next to the bed. He walked over to the kitchen and filled a glass with water. He drank it in three or four long gulps and re-filled the glass. He picked up his mobile which he'd left on the counter the night before. The battery had run down to zero with all the GPS use he'd given it and he'd forgotten to put it on the charger when he arrived home.

He'd ended up walking the whole way, turning everything over in his head and trying to make sense of how things had reached this point. There were no easy answers. After finishing off the bottle of wine from the fridge, he'd just crashed out in bed.

He plugged in his phone to the cable on the desk and began picking up the clothes that he'd discarded on and around the sofa. He filled the kettle and flicked the switch to start it boiling. A little bell sound came from his phone, the one that tells you there's a text message. Then came the short chime that lets you know there's a voice message.

Alex took a mug off the shelf and dropped a tea bag into it from the jar on the counter. *Was it a message from Lisa?* he asked himself; a call to tell him that it had all been a mistake, that they could make it work if they both wanted it? He knew deep down that it wasn't her style, but he held off checking whilst he made the tea. It prolonged the possible, however remote that seemed. It kept alive hope, before it could be crushed by the inevitable and mundane reality.

Alex sipped his tea and wandered over to the desk to pick up his phone. It was a message from Maya. In fact, there'd been several missed calls from her. They were all asking him to call her urgently. The last one said, *'Call me. I'm at the hospital.'* It was sent the previous night. Alex didn't bother listening to the voice message, he just hit the call button and waited anxiously for the connection. The possibilities raced through his mind. What was it? A fall, a heart attack? With all he'd been drinking lately, anything was possible.

Maya answered the phone.
"Alex, I've been calling you all night."
"Yeah, I'm sorry. My phone ran out of juice and I forgot to charge it last night. How is he? What happened?"
"They've got him under sedation but he's taken a terrible beating," she said, breaking into sobs.
"What?" he said. He could feel the anger swell up inside him. "Who the hell would do that to a harmless old guy?"
"Alex,....," she said, "didn't you listen to my message? It's not your Dad, it's Jack." She broke down into tears again. Alex couldn't find his words for a moment while he processed what she was saying.
"Jack?" he said. "Oh God, I'm sorry Maya. I just called as soon as I saw your text message. Listen, where are you? I'll come straight over." Maya gave him the name of the hospital and the ward that Jack was in and Alex promised her that he was on his way.

He grabbed some clothes out of the drawers alongside the bed and pulled a shirt off the rail that stood next to them. After quickly changing, he stuffed a few things into his backpack, grabbed the keys off the counter and went out of the door.

It was a bright day outside and the street was busy with the Sunday shoppers, out in the mid-day sun. Alex knew he'd be able to pick up a taxi from outside the station so he walked off quickly in that direction. He began to turn things over in his mind, searching for some kind of explanation. *What was Jack doing getting involved in this sort of thing?* He certainly wasn't the type to back down when challenged. He'd stood up for Alex on more than one occasion when they were younger, but he wouldn't go looking for trouble. It just didn't make any sense. Besides, where would he even go to get mixed up in this?

There were a couple of taxis parked outside the station and not the usual queue that you could expect on a week day. The driver in the first car had his cap pulled down over his eyes and seemed to be catching up on some lost sleep. Alex tapped on the window to get his attention and then climbed into the back seat.

Chase Farm Hospital was up near Enfield, and with the roads being pretty clear, it didn't take long to get there. The driver dropped him off near the entrance. It was a large complex with a landscaped frontage along the main building. It felt more like an airport departure building than a hospital, but it was easy to navigate and he quickly found his way to the in-patients reception. He showed his ID, filled in the forms and was given a visitors tag and directions to Jack's ward.

He called Maya to tell her he'd arrived and she said she'd meet him at the lift. She was standing there when the doors opened and looked glad to see him. She was still wearing the clothes she used for work which surprised him a little. He gave her a hug and it felt like she needed it.
"Are you OK?" She nodded and managed a half smile.
"Come on, it's this way," she said.

They walked past an unmanned reception desk and along a

brightly lit corridor. It had that familiar smell, the mix of antiseptic and disinfectant that took Alex immediately back to his childhood. The visits to his mother in hospital; the times that he didn't want to go, didn't want to see her there or accept that she would never come out.

Maya led him through an open doorway into a room with four beds, one in each corner. Jack was in one of the beds by the window. He looked to be asleep and had a bandage wrapped around his head and covering one eye. There was a swelling around his cheek bone and what looked like stitches below his lower lip.

"What on earth happened?" asked Alex. Maya drew the light weight curtain around the bed, enclosing their quarter of the room, and lowered her voice.

"I don't know exactly. It was at the restaurant, after we'd closed last night. I was tidying up the tables but Pete said that a couple of guys came to the back door. Jack went outside to speak to them and when he didn't come back, I went out to look for him. I found him in the passage, off the street," she said, putting her hand over her mouth and holding back the tears. Alex put his arm around her.

"He's safe now Maya," he said. "What did the doctors say?"

"They say he's suffered concussion. His eye socket is fractured and he's lost two teeth. He's also got two broken ribs and bruising around his chest. There was some internal bleeding but they say it should be OK."

"Do you have any idea who these guys were?" he asked.

"No, I tried to ask Jack in the ambulance but he wasn't making any sense and I really don't want to think about it right now."

"Yeah, I know. Listen Maya, you look like you could do with a break. Have you eaten anything?"

"Not since last night," she replied.

"Why don't you go and grab something and I'll keep an eye on Jack." She hesitated and glanced at Jack in the bed.

"OK, I could just take half an hour I suppose." She picked up her bag from the chair. "Thanks Alex. Just call me if the doctor comes around, right?"

"Don't worry. I'll look after things," he said. Maya nodded and slipped out between the curtains.

Alex sat down on the chair and looked over at Jack. He was a bit of a sorry sight. He needed to get to the bottom of this; find out exactly what was going on. Jack had asked for money the other day. He couldn't help thinking it must be tied up with what happened last night. Did he owe money to someone? It didn't seem like the kind of situation he'd get himself into. Jack was an independent type; self reliant, and he didn't exactly have expensive tastes. It just didn't add up.

He tossed ideas about in his head for a while but it didn't get him any closer to an understanding. He hadn't seen that Jack had turned his head over on the pillow. He was looking at Alex with his one good eye and managed a wry grin when he finally noticed. Alex sat up in his chair.

"Hey Jack, you're back with us. You look terrible by the way." Jack gave a strained laugh and then grimaced with the pain.

"That's why......, I decided on this cosmetic surgery," he quipped. Alex smiled. It felt like a positive sign that, even in this dire situation, they could make light of things.

"Do you need a drink or anything?" he asked. Jack shook his head. "Maya's just gone for something to eat. She should be back soon." There was a pause whilst Alex wondered if this was the right time to talk about it. He knew that when Maya returned, Jack would be reluctant to say anything. It needed to be now.

"Jack, you have to tell me what this is all about. I'll do whatever I can to help, but you need to let me know what's going on." Jack turned his head away on the pillow. "Do you owe someone money?" He shook his head. "So, what is it?"

"It's not me," he replied. He turned his head back to look at Alex. "It's Dad.....It's the restaurant. He borrowed some money......, a lot of money......, from the wrong people."

"How long have you known about this?"

"The other day....., when he got drunk. I asked him about the takings...., from the restaurant." Jack shifted his body to try to get more comfortable and winced with the pain. "He's been paying the interest....., rolling over whatever he couldn't pay."

"Is that why you asked for the five grand the other day?" Jack nodded.

"They want all cash now. They want...... the restaurant as security."

Alex nodded his head slowly. So that was it then. His Dad was up to his neck with the loan sharks and there would be no easy way out of it. They were in trouble.

"How much does he owe?" Jack shook his head.

"I don't know exactly. He said he borrowed forty grand....., but I guess there's a load of unpaid interest on top of that. They want fifteen grand a month." Alex took a deep breath and looked up at the ceiling. They were in big trouble.

"Who are these guys Jack?"

"I'm not sure......, linked to some group in Islington, I think. They're not the sort that take exams and have letters after their names."

"Yeah, I'd guessed that much," said Alex. "There must be some written contract though, something that sets out the conditions and interest payments. Even the loan sharks have paperwork don't they?"

"Yeah, I suppose there's something. You know Dad....., he keeps everything to himself."

"Right, I need to talk to him before we do anything else. Do you have a contact number for the loan sharks?"

"Dad gave me a number......, a guy called Denny. It's on my phone, wherever that is."

Alex looked around but there was nothing visible on the window sill or the side table. He opened the lockable cupboard under the table and found it with Jack's watch and a pile of loose change. He checked the contacts list and found the number for 'Denny.' He copied it into his phone and gave it the name, 'Shark.'

As he returned the phone to his pocket, he heard footsteps approaching. Maya opened the curtain with a look of surprise to see Jack awake in the bed. She looked at Alex with an unspoken question.

"He's fine Maya," said Alex. "We've just been having a chat for the last 10 or 15 minutes." She smiled with a mixture of emotion and relief and went around to sit on the edge of the bed. She put her head on the pillow next to Jack's and whispered something to him.

"I know this probably isn't the best time to talk about it, but what's happening with the restaurant tonight?" asked Alex. Maya looked up and then back at Jack.

"We're closed tonight," she said. "I told Pete not to come in and that I'd let him know when we'd be open."

"I think you need to re-open as soon as possible," said Alex, exchanging a meaningful glance with Jack. "I can work in the restaurant until Jack's back on his feet."

"Who's going to be doing the cooking?" asked Maya.

"We can get Dad to do it. It's not like he hasn't been head cook in years gone by. It's probably not going win you any new customers, but it won't be for long. I'll come over early tomorrow and we can open at the usual time." Maya looked at Jack and he nodded.

"Okay, thanks Alex. I'll call Pete and let him know.

Maya was going to stay for the rest of the afternoon. She wasn't ready to leave Jack on his own and she wanted to speak with the doctor again anyway. Alex decided he should make a move . It would give them some time together to talk about things and besides it was a bit of squeeze for the three of them. He made his excuses and ducked out through the curtain.

What a difference a day makes, he thought as he walked back along the corridor. This time yesterday everything seemed pretty simple. Nothing much to worry about other than the vagaries of the stock market and what he had planned for the weekend. Now it seemed like his whole world had been turned upside down.

He cursed himself for not being more involved with the running of the restaurant. Well, if he didn't find some way out of the current situation, there wouldn't be a restaurant to speak of. *Would that be so bad?* he asked himself. Jack could easily find another job; probably get hired as a sous chef in a top restaurant. The pay would be a lot better and he'd have good prospects. He was kidding himself of course. The restaurant was everything that their father had worked for. It was more than just a business, it was who they were.

He walked out of the main entrance and headed off towards the high street. It had become a little overcast and a cool breeze had begun to blow. He needed to clear his head. He put in his ear plugs and cranked up the volume.

Chapter 12

Alex arrived early at the restaurant. He wanted to talk to his Dad on his own and get to the bottom of it all. He'd expected to find him upstairs and they'd be able to talk in private, but when Maya opened the back door, he could see him over her shoulder in the kitchen. He was wearing the chef's apron and busying himself rearranging pots, pans and utensils. Alex looked back at Maya and she rolled her eyes.

"He's been turning the place upside down; trying to get everything back to how it used to be," she said in a low voice. She stepped aside to let Alex in. He looked around the kitchen and could see that the usual efficient order of the place had been disturbed. He shrugged his shoulders. *Whatever gets the job done,* he thought. It would only be for a week or so.

"Ah, good you here Alex," said his father. "You can help with the meat. We need to go buy fresh meat."

"Yeah, I can help you with that Dad, but I need to speak with you first."

"We talk on the way," he replied, whilst taking off the apron and hanging it on the wall. Alex gave an exasperated sigh. He'd been here too many times before and sometimes it just wasn't worth arguing with him. He was in that mood where he would just throw himself into the work. If you were working, then there was no time to worry about all the other stuff; no time for careful consideration or forethought, just get on and plough your way through it. Hard work would put things right, and if it didn't, well then just work harder.

George picked up his jacket from the chair and marched out of the door that Maya still held open. Alex held back a little as his dad went down the steps and into the yard. It gave him the chance to catch a word with Maya.

"How's Jack?"

"He's feeling much better," she said with a smile. "I saw him this morning and the doctor said they were going to do some more tests. If everything's OK, he could be back home by the end of the week."

"That's great," said Alex, giving her arm a squeeze. "Has my Dad said anything about it?"

"No, not really. He asks about Jack but he hasn't said anything about who could have done it. I told him we should call the police but he doesn't want to get them involved." Alex nodded.

"Let me talk to him about it," he said. With that, he headed down the steps and followed his father down the passage.

They bought their meat from a Greek butcher that his Dad had known for years. It was only about a mile or so away but they'd take the van. They'd be able to select just what they wanted and bring it straight back. The van was parked in a narrow lane at the back of the property and as they approached it, Alex put out his hand.

"Let me drive Dad. I don't get much chance to drive these days." His father handed him the keys and Alex opened the door of the van. The truth was, he was more concerned about whether his Dad had been drinking rather than practice behind the wheel. Anyway, it might be easier for his Dad to talk if someone else was driving.

Alex turned the key in the ignition and put the van into gear, before having second thoughts and turning the engine off. They both sat there without speaking for a while before Alex broke the silence.

"Dad, I spoke to Jack about what happened. He told me it was about the money that's owed." His father didn't respond but just looked out of the side window, appearing deep in his own thoughts. "They came to the restaurant wanting to get security for the loan. They want you to put up the restaurant as collateral. Do you understand?"

George looked down at his hands which moved restlessly, seemingly unable to settle in one position. After a moment, he clasped them together and looked up, staring blankly in front of him.

"I understand I made a big mistake. These people, they will never let me be free until they have everything."

"Who are they?"

"A friend of Demetrius introduced me this guy. He tells me they give easy loans; easy repayment. He's from the north, Turkish. I should never trust such a man." he said.

"Did you sign a contract?"

"Yes, I have a contract, a contract that ties my hands and just keeps taking from me," he replied, with bitterness.

"You need to let me see it when we go back to the restaurant. Why didn't you tell me if you needed money? Maybe I could have helped, or at least given you advice." His father shook his head.

"This is not your business Alex. You have your computers and your investments." Alex could sense the disapproval, but he wasn't about to be brushed off.

"Look Dad, Jack is in hospital and you could lose everything. That **is** my business whether you like or not. We need to work together on this." His father remained silent. It didn't feel like he wanted to argue. "We'll go through the contract when we get back," said Alex as he started the car engine to signal that was the end of the discussion.

It was only a short drive to the meat supplier, a large butcher on the high street. They selected what they needed and Alex brought it out in two carrier bags whilst his father discussed things with the owner. Nothing appeared to be signed or paid for, but they seemed to part on good terms. His father joined him, giving him a slap on the back.

"Come on, let's go," he said.

"Did you pay him?" asked Alex as they walked to the van.

"He put it on the account."

"So you settle the account at the end of the month, right?" His father waved his hand to make light of it.

"He's an old friend," he said, as though that explained everything. Alex was beginning to understand how things worked with the restaurant and how things had got to the state they were in.

By the time they got back to the restaurant, Pete had arrived. He opened the back door for them, already wearing his white double breasted jacket and pants. There was no sign of Maya.

"Okay Pete, I explain what we cooking tonight," said George, reaching for his apron.

"No, wait a minute Dad. We need to talk first," said Alex. His father paused and reluctantly returned the apron to its hook on the wall. "Can you show me what we talked about? Is it in the office?" His father nodded, and walked over to the door that led into the small office. Alex got Pete started on preparing the meat and followed him in.

There was a box on the floor next to the desk. It was full of scraps of paper, receipts and other documents; all weighed down by the metal cash box, that acted like some over-sized paper weight. His father put the cash box on the desk and began leafing through the papers in search of the contract. Alex shook his head, understanding for the first time the truly chaotic nature of the book keeping.

"Is this where you keep everything? In that box?"

"This way, I know where to find everything," he replied, before triumphantly holding up some loosely stapled pieces of paper.

Alex took them off him and examined the front page. It was an unprofessional looking document, simply headed up 'Loan

Agreement.' It had the name of the company, which appeared to be just a trading name, 'D & P Finance,' and an address that was just a PO Box number. There was no mention of any registration with financial bodies or compliance with credit legislation. In all likelihood, it would be illegal, he imagined. That wasn't going to help them though. These people acted outside the law. They made up their own rules, and any retribution would certainly be enforced without going through the normal channels.

He sat down on the chair in front of the desk and spread the papers out in front of him. The main contract was just two pages. The first page included the basic information, entered by hand into a series of boxes. The second page was a list of type-written conditions.

He went through the first page. It noted the names of the two parties and the amount of the loan, £40,000. The interest rate was shown as 7.5% and payable monthly. There was no annualised rate shown, but Alex could work it out in his head. That was interest at 90% per year. It took his breath away. How could his father have entered into something as crazy as this? He doubted whether he'd even thought about the annual rate. He probably imagined that he'd have cleared the loan before then anyway.

Alex checked the start date of the loan. It showed, the contract had been running for around two and a half years. That's a lot of interest, he thought, but Jack had said they were asking for £15,000 a month. That couldn't be just interest, it must include a portion of capital repayment, surely.

He looked at the conditions on the second page. There were details of how the payments were to be made, and that any non-paid interest would be allowed only subject to the agreement of the lender. All non-paid interest payments would be added to the loan outstanding. That all seemed clear enough. He continued down the page and then stopped abruptly. He read it over a couple of times to make sure he'd got it right. No, there was no mistake. It was the killer condition; the total game changer.

'A default charge of 5% of the outstanding loan is payable in the event of any non-payment of interest at the agreed payment date.'

That was it. If you couldn't pay all the interest in any given month, the effective interest rate went up to 12.5%. The rest of the papers that had been stapled to the contract, were each titled, 'Notice of Default.' They recorded instances of non-payment of interest. There must have been 15 or 20 of them.

Alex lent back in the chair and took a deep breath. He looked up at his dad standing next to him, who shrugged his shoulders.
"I know. It's bad huh?"
"Dad, you have no idea how bad," replied Alex. "Do you have a record of what you've paid?"
"Yeah, I write everything in this little book," he said, reaching down to pick up a brown notebook. He handed it to Alex, who opened it and looked through the figures.

It was written in his dad's familiar handwriting. He'd listed each payment next to the date for each month and it all seemed pretty clear. Alex took one of the pens out of the plastic holder on the desk and ripped a page from the back of the notebook. He was going to go through all the payments and see just where they were up to.

He jotted down the monthly payments down one side of the paper and kept a running total of what the outstanding debt should be according to the conditions. The first few payments were for £4,000 so his dad had been paying the interest of £3,000, plus paying back some of the original loan. After 5 months, the loan was reduced to around

£35,000. The next 2 months were underpayments though, and the outstanding loan jumped back up to £42,000. The next 5 months were mostly underpayments, including 2 months running where nothing was paid back at all. It was a fatal mistake. By the year-end, the debt had climbed to a little over £60,000.

The next year, he'd begun by paying £5,000 a month and that just covered the interest payment over the first few months. Alex remembered doing a rough calculation of what he thought the restaurant could make and it had been about £5,000 a month. There was absolutely no room for slippage. Inevitably, the next few months included some underpayments, and by eight months into the second year, the debt was up to about £85,000. That would need monthly payments of over £6,000 just to service the interest.

The repayments returned to £5,000 a month for the rest of the year but it was too late. The death spiral had started and at the end of the second year the outstanding loan had gone over £100,000. The debt from there would grow exponentially and in just the last seven months alone it had reached £200,000. That would need £15,000 a month to just stand still.

Alex puffed out his cheeks and lent back in the chair. Well, there it was; they were pretty much screwed. Was there any way out of this nightmare? He could just about raise 200 grand but it would wipe him out. He'd be back to square one. The other option would be to re-mortgage the restaurant property. There should be sufficient equity in the existing mortgage, and there was a pretty decent business in the restaurant that could support the repayments. He'd run over the figures later. The immediate priority was to stop the debt from rising any further. That meant finding 15 grand a month to buy the time to clear the debt.

"Dad, I need to meet with these people," he said. "Jack

gave me a phone number for someone called Denny. Is he the guy you talk to?" His father nodded his head.

"Maybe I go with you," he said. "These are bad people Alex."

"No, it's better if I deal with this on my own. I'm going to look after these documents, okay?" He slipped them into his backpack. "Dad, you better get started in the kitchen. I'll get changed and open up the restaurant." His father headed back to the kitchen and Alex sat for a while at the desk.

He didn't want to think about the idea of losing the restaurant, or the effect it would have on his dad, but it felt like a real possibility now. Of course, the contract was set up to deliver this scenario. No doubt, they would have been accommodating; actively encouraging his dad to delay repayments and all the time, pulling him deeper and deeper into debt. That was how these guys worked. It left a bitter taste in his mouth.

Well, there was nothing he could do about it right now. There were more pressing matters. They needed to keep the restaurant open for business and money coming in through the till. That might just buy them enough time to come up with a plan. Alex got changed and went out to prepare for opening.

Chapter 13

Alex had bought his breakfast at the local shop. He'd planned to take it back to the flat and eat it there whilst catching up with the early morning news. It was a nice day though, and the two tables at the front of the shop were unoccupied. He could watch the High street come alive through the window.

He sipped on his coffee and vaguely followed the comings and goings out on the street. It was a welcome distraction for a while, but it wasn't long before his thoughts returned to the matters that had given him another restless night. He knew that he had to make the call to the loan sharks, and sooner rather than later. That was something that he'd be happy to put off until a bit later in the morning. The other thing that had been niggling away at his subconscious was a recurring sense of unease with the Robrex investment.

The chat with Jamie had put his mind at rest for a while, but the doubts had begun to resurface. Ironically, it was the increasing interest of investors around the company's stock that felt like a red flag. Too many people buying into the story. The chance encounter with the CEO in the restaurant just served to heighten his unease. If you wanted to manipulate sentiment towards a stock, the bulletin boards would be the perfect place to do it. Now, he knew for a fact that the CEO of Robrex was taking an interest in this area.

He'd looked through all the figures published by the company and there was nothing that suggested it was anything other than a successful growth company. If there was any sort of misrepresentation or manipulation going on, it would only be uncovered by looking deeper into the company. He wasn't going to find it in the accounts. He'd need to research the company from the ground up.

It wouldn't be easy. He'd need to get some first hand feedback from the people that actually dealt with Robrex, ideally their customers. The problem was, he had no way of knowing who these customers were. He'd looked through the latest accounts, but these had no details of the company's largest customers. The Admission Document for the reverse takeover listed some Indian companies that the business traded with, but nothing in the UK that it would be easy to check out.

He needed someone on the inside, someone who'd be able to uncover the information a little closer to home. Jamie had used his contacts with Stephen, who's firm were acting as Auditors. They would surely be able to unearth something. The trouble was, Alex didn't have the old boy network to fall back on like Jamie. He couldn't imagine that Stephen would be willing to stick his neck out for a casual acquaintance but then, ...there was Leonna, he thought. She worked for the same firm and might be able to find out something. It's not like it was anything that could be considered 'sensitive information.' It was just a few names that the company dealt with. The more he thought about it, the more he convinced himself that it was the way forward.

It was probably better to ask her face to face, he decided. It would be difficult to explain everything clearly in an email and he'd rather not leave a record on the company email that might cause her some embarrassment at a later date. That was the official rationale behind his decision, although he knew deep down that the idea of maintaining contact with Leonna was probably a factor too. He'd send her an email, maybe meet for lunch if she was free.

He pulled up her contact details on his phone and wrote out a quick message. It sounded a bit formal so he wrote it again. Then he changed a couple of words so the lunch invite seemed a little more like an after-thought and eventually, pressed the send button.

Alex sipped his tea and took out from the paper bag the wrap that he'd bought for his breakfast. It was an Indian version of what looked like a burrito, with cooked vegetables and small pieces of spiced chicken. It smelt amazing and the taste didn't disappoint either. He finished it off whilst looking through a copy of the local free newspaper that someone had left on the table.

When he'd finished, he walked back to the flat. There was still time to catch the opening of the trading day. As he walked up to the house, he glanced over at his bike, as he always did; just a quick check to make sure everything was okay. He noticed a small piece of folded paper that was sticking up from the handlebars. After he walked over to the bike, he could see that it had been purposely placed between the bell and the small hammer that was attached to it. Alex pulled it out and unfolded the paper. A message was written in neat and rather elaborate handwriting.

> *"Dear Mr. Samaras,*
> *It pains me to bring this matter to your attention, but I feel that I must.*
> *You have, for some time, been parking your bicycle outside the front of the house and attached to the railings. This has a most disagreeable effect on the front aspect of the house and I must ask that from this point forward, you park your bicycle along the side of the house.*
> *I trust that you will comply with this request forthwith.*
> *Yours respectfully,*
> *Elizabeth Marks (Proprietor)"*

Alex had a sudden urge to screw the note up and drop kick it into the nearby skip that was parked at the end of the road and which, incidentally, was having a most disagreeable effect on the front aspect of the house. Instead, he folded it up and replaced it on the bike. He'd just pretend that he hadn't seen it and deal with it later.

When he got back to his flat, he pulled his phone from his back pocket and checked his emails. Leonna had replied already. She'd be happy to meet up for lunch and said she was available today if he'd like. She'd copied a link to a small place near her office and asked if he wanted to meet there at 12:30pm. It was a nice looking Italian near Tottenham Court Road. He sent a reply straight back and told her he'd see her at the restaurant.

He settled down in front of his PC screen to start the day by doing some research into a few ideas he'd been thinking about. It was difficult to give it his full concentration. In the back of his mind was always the phone call to the loan sharks that he had to make. He'd been putting it off; not wanting to make himself the new point of contact in this unfolding horror show. Unfortunately, that was exactly what he needed to be.

He sat back in the chair and looked at his mobile phone on the desk. He went through it in his head, rehearsing what he was going to say and trying to anticipate what they'd demand of him. Eventually, he could put it off no longer and made the call.

The ring tone went on for a long time, to the point where Alex thought he should hang up and check that he had the right number. Then it suddenly connected and a voice just said:
"Yeah?"
"Is that Denny?" asked Alex.
"Who's that?" came the reply.
"Er, this is Alex Samaras, my father George, he owns the

restaurant."

"Oh right, the Greek place?" said the voice on the other line, sounding a little less wary. "So you've got the rest of our money have you?"

"Well, I wanted to meet you to talk about it," said Alex.

"I hope you're not going to waste my time."

"No, I.....I just want to talk about how we can settle this to everyone's satisfaction." There was a long pause.

"Okay, come over to the Angel Tavern in Islington this afternoon. What time can you make it?" Alex wasn't expecting to do this over a drink but maybe it was better to be in a public place.

"I can be there for 2:30."

"Right, I'll be sitting near the back, at the table next to the piano," the voice replied.

"I'll..., see you later," said Alex, before the line went dead.

He placed the phone back on the desk and took a deep breath. He'd taken the first step. He was well and truly involved now. He didn't know if it was for better or worse but at least it felt like he was moving things forward. So, a pleasant lunch with Leonna, followed by a drink with a psychopathic money lender. That was his day sorted out.

By the time he came out of Tottenham Court Road Station, it had turned into a fine day. The street was bustling with the lunchtime office workers and it was a nice walk down Oxford Street towards the restaurant. He just needed to cross over the street and cut through a couple of side roads. As he approached the place, he could see Leonna waiting outside the entrance. She waved and smiled when she caught sight of him and he felt happier at just seeing her.

"They've still got a couple of free tables," she said, and led them inside.

The ground floor was already full with lunchtime diners, but the waitress showed them up to the mezzanine where there was a free table next to the balustrade.

"So, is this your local?" asked Alex.

"No, not really, I usually bring in my own lunch, just whatever I've been making. Yes, I'm the sad character with the plastic Tupperware box at their desk," she said, with a laugh.

"Maybe we should have made it a picnic," he said, and smiled. A waiter came up to the table and took their order.

"Well, are you going to tell me about this new investment idea then? I'm dying to know how it is you think I can help you," said Leonna.

"Yeah, it's a company that Jamie introduced to Matt and I; an Indian company called Robrex plc. Jamie tells me that your firm does the auditing for them." She tilted her head to one side in thought.

"Hmm, I think I might have heard the name. We have so many companies on the books."

"It's an IT company and we all decided to invest. So far, it's been a great success, but I can't get completely comfortable with the investment case. I just have this sense that there's something not right and I want to try to get to the bottom of it." Leonna nodded her head slowly and Alex could guess what she was thinking.

"I know what you're thinking," he said. "Please understand, I'm not looking for any financial details, or to get some kind of inside information. I would never ask for anything like that. I just want to do some digging to make sure that the company is what it portrays itself to be. I'm struggling to find names of the company's UK customers and I wondered if you might be able to help." She thought for a while.

"Yes, I suppose I can have a look around and see what I can find out. I'll probably need to speak to whoever's working on the audit and see if they can dig something up."

"Thanks, I'd really appreciate it. I don't want you to do anything that might get you into trouble, but if the information's easily available, it would be a great help."

"Sure, let me see what I can do," she said.

"So, how did you enjoy the evening at Jamie's the other day?" asked Alex, happy to move the conversation on to something a little less awkward.

"I really enjoyed it. It's not every day that you get to do it in such style."

"Yeah, what a house. I wonder what they'll do when Joanne runs out of rooms to decorate. Buy the house next door, maybe?" Leonna laughed.

"That's probably not out of the question. Stephen seems to think that Jamie's destined for great things in the City," she said.

"Well, I don't know about the City, but everyone I know in the private investor community has a huge amount of respect for him."

"He seems to have a lot of respect for you too. It sounded like you could probably get a job with him if you wanted it." Alex didn't respond. "....but, I suppose you have the family restaurant business," she said.

Alex couldn't suppress an involuntary laugh at the absurdity of it.

"Yes, the family business," he said. "Leonna, it's probably not what you imagine it to be. It's just a restaurant that my Dad started. A restaurant that's going through a bit of a credit crunch at the moment. In fact, straight after this lunch, I have a meeting with a particularly unforgiving creditor."

"Is it anything that you want to talk about?" she asked. Alex gave a sigh.

"There's not much to talk about really. I just need to find a way to re-finance the business and I don't have much time. It's in a difficult spot right now." She looked at him and smiled.

"I think your dad's lucky to have you as a son. You'll find a way to sort this out." He looked up at her, surprised at the unquestioning positivity. He wished he had the same faith in the outcome.

"I just hope you're right. I really don't want to see it go under."

Their orders arrived and the conversation turned to their shared interest in food and cooking. Alex was surprised at how varied and wide-ranging Leonna's knowledge was and the obvious passion she had for creating great food. It was one of those times when two people hit on the common ground and the conversation just moves effortlessly with equal enthusiasm on both sides. Alex didn't want the lunch to end but eventually, Leonna glanced at her watch and said she'd have to get back to the office.

"Let's have lunch again sometime," said Alex, after they'd settled the bill. "Maybe I can introduce you to some Greek food. I know some great places."

"Hmm yeah, that sounds nice," she said. "Perhaps we can do an evening with the four of us. It would be nice to catch up with Lisa again." Alex came back down to earth with a bump.

"Er, yeah, let's work something out," he said, as they began to head down the stairs towards the door.

He didn't want to talk about the break-up with Lisa. Also, he'd begun to realize that he'd allowed his imagination to run a little too far concerning Leonna. They got on well for sure, but the chemistry that he was imagining, was nothing more than her being friendly. By the time they reached the pavement outside the restaurant, Alex had fully reconnected with reality.

"Thanks for meeting me," he said. "Anything you can do to help with the Robrex thing, I'd really appreciate."

"Yes, I'll get back to you as soon as I can," she replied

and smiled. There was a slightly awkward moment when neither of them was sure if a hug was appropriate. In the end, they both just gave a kind of wave and headed off in their respective directions.

Alex walked back towards the station feeling a bit deflated. It felt like the energy he'd got from meeting Leonna was slowly ebbing away. What made him think there was anything special that existed between them? He felt a bit foolish having built up his expectations over something that was just a product of his imagination. He tried to shake it off and forced himself to turn his mind to what was next. It didn't make him feel any better, and certainly wasn't something he was looking forward to.

He got the tube from Tottenham Court Road and found a seat where he could review things. He had a fair idea of what to expect from the meeting with the loan sharks. They'd be sure to try to intimidate him, but he knew that he had to remain as professional as possible. It was business after all. They would always follow the course that was in their financial best interests. He just needed to make them understand that he was the person who could deliver their pay off.

He pulled out the notebook with his dad's payment record and the calculations he'd made himself. He went carefully through the figures to make sure he could recall all the details. There was still an amount of £5,000 to cover the rest of the interest for this month. He'd need to find that to give himself time to set up the refinancing. He needed to convince the loan sharks that reaching a full settlement now was in their best interests. Basically, the loan repayments were just not sustainable and he had to make them understand that they were driving the business to extinction. That would be in nobody's interest.

The pub wasn't far from the station and Alex had checked its location before setting off. It wasn't the kind of place that served the passing traffic on the high street, but was tucked away in an area of low quality businesses and rented housing. The pub was situated on the corner of a nondescript street and had a line of picnic benches squeezed onto the pavement outside, although why anyone would choose to use them, he had no idea. He checked his watch and he was about ten minutes early. He thought for a moment about doing a circuit of the local neighbourhood to kill some time, but then decided he might as well just go inside.

It was one of those places where everyone looks up to see who's come in. There were only a dozen or so people in the whole pub, but they pretty much all gave him the once over before returning to whatever they were doing. Alex instinctively looked to the far end of the pub where he could see the piano up against the wall. The table next to it was empty.

He walked over to the bar and ordered a pint; not because he really wanted one, but it was what almost everyone else was drinking. He looked around while he was waiting. The walls were covered with a peach-coloured wall paper whilst a fitted carpet with a busy pattern ran throughout the pub. It was supposed to give it a warm cosy feel but it just made the place look dated and in desperate need of a make-over. There were round wooden tables scattered throughout, with no more than one or two people at each table. A narrow counter ran around one side of the pub and a heavy looking guy wearing a black sweat shirt occupied a stool there. He was studying the back pages of a tabloid over the remains of a pint. Alex took his drink over to one of the unoccupied stools near the window.

It was about five minutes later, when Alex's appointment arrived in the pub. He looked about 30, with slicked back dark hair and was smartly dressed in a well tailored pin-striped suit. His appearance was completely at odds with the rather shabby pub interior, but from the reaction of the regulars, it seemed like it was somewhere he belonged. He exchanged nodded greetings with a couple of people and stopped at the bar for a brief word with the landlord. He didn't order a drink but walked over to the table by the piano and took a seat.

Alex pretended to be busy checking something on his phone and stole a glance over in the direction of the table. That was when he realized that the man was looking directly at him. He looked back down at his phone but when he glanced up again, he was still looking. He decided it was time to get this over with. He picked up his drink and walked over to the table.

"I'm Alex," he said.
"Take a seat," the man replied. There was no small talk, in fact he didn't say anything at all. Alex had half expected this. It was the part where the guy with all the power just sits there and the nervous interviewee starts filling in the silences. Before you know it you're talking complete gibberish. Alex made an effort to remain calm and thought about what he was going to say.

"I have a proposal," he said. "I want to completely clear the debt and pay you your money. The only way that is possible is if we re-mortgage the restaurant." Alex paused to see if there was a reaction. The man said nothing. "Obviously, we need to agree everything with the mortgage lender and allow time for the money to come through. I think we probably need a couple of months to get everything sorted out. If you could agree to an interest freeze for 2 months, I think we could get you the full amount." There we are, he'd laid it out for him. Alex sat back in his chair and waited for him to say something.

There was a long delay before he spoke, but eventually he leaned forward with his elbows on the table.

"You see, here's the thing," he said. "We're a business, and we don't make a habit of lending out our money for free. Do you understand me?" Alex wanted to tell him what he thought of their business but he kept himself calm. He had to keep it on a business footing.

"I only think it's fair to tell you what the situation is with the restaurant," he said. "The business can't support the interest payments and if we don't find a solution, then it'll end up in administration. Of course that would mean you'd have to pursue your claim through the official administrator. He'd decide the merits of your claim." Alex looked him directly in the eye to make the point. They both knew that wasn't in their interests.

The loan shark rubbed his chin and sat back in his chair. At that point somebody else joined them at the table. It was the guy in the black sweat shirt.

"Oh, this is one of my associates, Terry," he said, as the man took a seat. Terry said nothing but it was difficult for Alex to ignore his presence. The loan shark had taken a lighter out of his pocket and he was turning it over in his fingers as though in deep thought. It was more likely designed to give Alex the chance to become more uncomfortable in his position. Eventually, he said:
"I'm prepared to be reasonable, but first I need the outstanding five grand, and I need it by Friday, in cash. After that, you've got one month to clear the debt before the interest becomes payable again. Is that understood?"

One month would be pushing it, to get everything finalized, but it wasn't as though he was in a strong negotiating position. Alex nodded his head slowly.

"Call me on the mobile when you've got the cash," the loan shark said. "If we don't hear from you we'll always know where to find you," he added. With that, the two men got up from the table and walked off, leaving Alex sitting there alone. He didn't feel like following them out of the door and waited a few minutes.

Had he got what he wanted from the meeting? Well, he had a month's breathing room. It was better than nothing. It would give him the chance to try to set up the remortgage loan. There was still some hope. He took a sip from his pint glass and decided it wasn't worth finishing it. Satisfied that his new business associates had moved on, he got up and walked out of the pub. He was glad to leave it behind him and head off towards the station.

Chapter 14

It had been a long week for Alex. He'd started the process of applying for the re-mortgage, after finally getting the necessary documents from his Dad. He'd had to be a little creative in the application, by outlining how they were planning to renovate the restaurant and plough the money back into the business. He'd even drafted a short business plan with cost estimates that justified the money they were raising. It would have made perfect sense to do it, if they weren't on the hook to the Islington mafia. As it was, it would be money straight down the drain.

Alex had already paid over the £5,000 that bought them another month to finalize everything. He'd had to top slice one of his low conviction investments to raise the cash. The whole business was a bit depressing. He was used to making investment decisions based on the likely return he could make. To be raising money knowing it would be a write off was difficult to come to terms with. He just had to tell himself that it was the necessary cost of exiting a bad financial decision. It was the cost of pressing the re-set button for the restaurant; a way to give his Dad and Jack the chance to make something of it.

The good news was that Jack was now back on his feet and he'd be back in the kitchen tonight. It would be the first night off for Alex in the last week and a half. He could shift his focus back onto the day job and get back into his usual routine.

He'd had a message from Leonna. As luck would have it, her colleague, and flat mate was working on the Robrex audit. She'd come up with some names of customers. There were three names:-

Passwire Inc
Lease Fast Ltd
BYP Holdings Ltd

There were no contact details, so Alex had to do a bit of digging. He was able to find the first two companies with a quick Google search. *Passwire* was a good sized American company that provided money transfer and other financial services. They had a London office and he'd made a note of the address and phone number.
Lease Fast was a car leasing company, with a number of offices around the UK. The head office was a London address so that would be easy to follow up too.
The third name, *BYP Holdings Ltd,* didn't bring up anything, although there were a few similar named companies. Perhaps she'd made a mistake with the name. Anyway, he had a couple of companies that he could look into.

He had a plan to pass himself off as an IT Sales Executive and get to speak to someone in the company's IT department. It would be better to turn up at the company unannounced, rather than try to make an appointment. He still had some old business cards from his days in IT and he could probably talk his way into seeing someone. IT Engineers always like to feel like they're up-to-date with the latest tech developments and he knew enough to at least get them interested.

Both offices were in central London and only about ten minutes apart. It shouldn't take long to stop by at both of them. Alex changed into his suit, ironed a shirt and applied some polish to the only pair of leather shoes he owned. He slipped a few old business cards into the top pocket of his jacket and he was ready to go.

He used the time on the underground to work out his sales pitch. The first company he was going to visit was the finance one. He could put together a pitch about building a stock portfolio management interface for their online platform. He'd done most of the technical stuff himself before, so it wouldn't be difficult to talk over the basic idea. The car lease company might be a little more difficult. He'd just need to make out he was pitching for general IT services and hope he could get in front of someone. What's the worst that could happen? He'd just get shown the door.

He spent the rest of the journey checking over his investments. The Robrex share price had touched £4.00 before edging back to £3.95. It's inexorable climb had taken it to a level where it was now Alex's single largest holding. The irony wasn't lost on him. Here he was questioning whether the company was even legitimate.

The bulletin board had become a place of great joy and self-congratulation. There was no shortage of informed opinion to justify the recent surge in the share price. A few old sages were even predicting that this was just the beginning of a significant re-rating. That's the thing with stock markets. Everyone assumes that the market price represents the true value of the stock. It actually represents the sum total of enthusiasm for that stock at a given point in time. It was fair to say that right now the enthusiasm was running pretty high.

The train pulled in to Blackfriars underground station and Alex got out. The first office wasn't far, just a five minute walk. It was a modern four-storey building occupying a corner site and when he arrived, he stopped at the entrance to study the plaque which listed the occupants. There were four companies, each with their own floor. Passwire Inc had the ground floor; he could see their name on a pair of doors just inside the entrance.

At that moment, a young guy wearing a roll-top sweater and jeans emerged through the doors. Alex seized the opportunity.

"Excuse me, is this the building for Passwire?" he asked.

"Yep, straight through those doors," replied the man, pointing the way.

"IT are based here, right? I'm meeting the manager, er,...oh God, his name's gone," said Alex.

"You mean Dave Callaghan?"

"Yes, Dave," confirmed Alex.

"You might have just missed him. I thought I saw him on his way out."

"That would be just my luck," said Alex. "I'll check with reception. Thanks a lot."

He went through the double doors and approached the reception desk. He smiled at the young lady who greeted him and handed over one of his old business cards.

"Dave Callaghan asked me to drop in and see him if I was passing. We met at a conference."

"Oh, I'm afraid Mr Callaghan's out of the office," she replied.

"Oh, that's a shame," he said. "Could I have a quick word with one of his colleagues? There's something I just want to pass over to Dave."

"Let me see if someone's available," she said, and picked up the phone. After a brief conversation she put the phone down. "Someone will be out in a minute. Please take a seat."

Well that went pretty smoothly, he thought. He took a seat on the sofa and picked up a copy of 'The Economist' from the coffee table. It wasn't long before a tall guy with black-framed glasses emerged from the inner office. Alex got up and introduced himself.

"I talked to Dave about a new interface we're developing to help clients manage their investments. Do you have a few minutes for me to outline where we're up to? I think it's something that would be a good fit for your platform."

"Sure, there's a meeting room free. Do you want to come this way?"

They went along a hallway lined with offices and he was shown into a meeting room at the end. They both took a seat towards the end of the long table near a window that overlooked a central courtyard.

Alex was on familiar territory. He'd done this sort of presentation dozens of times before. He just needed to give an outline of his imaginary project. He knew enough about the company to talk convincingly on its potential for integration within their platform. He just needed to build up a reasonable level of rapport before turning matters to the real purpose of his visit. Eventually, he thought the time was right to drop it casually into the conversation.

"I understand that Robrex do your general IT," he said.
"Robrex?" the man said, sounding surprised.
"You do use Robrex, don't you?" asked Alex.
"Well, yes we do, but not for IT. They manage our call centre. We use a firm in the US for all our IT."
"Oh, I must have got the wrong end of that from Dave," said Alex, a little taken aback. "So, Robrex provide none of your IT services?"
"No, they manage the personnel to man the phones, but all the IT is provided by our American partners."
"Right, I see," said Alex.

So Robrex were doing call centre work. He vaguely remembered some reference to software development for the call centre industry in the admission document, but he wasn't aware of them actually providing the human resources. It was just another question that remained unanswered about the company.

Alex picked up where he'd left off in his pitch, but he'd lost the thread of what he was saying after that. There didn't seem much point anyway in extending the meeting, so he decided to slowly draw things to a close. Having wound it up, he confirmed that he'd contact Dave to see if he wanted to look at things in more detail and thanked his colleague for his time.

As he walked out onto the street, he remained somewhat perplexed by this latest turn of events. Running a call centre and developing and selling software solutions were two very different things. There were plenty of companies offering technical support via call centres in India, but it was a pretty low margin business. A whole different proposition compared to software development, which could be sold as a service and provide good margins and recurring revenues. That was very much a key factor in the investment case for Robrex. Alex added it to the growing list of questions that he had against the company.

He checked his watch. He had plenty of time to get to the next company. It was near Covent Garden. He could go back to the underground station and take a train from there, but it'd be easier to take a taxi. He called an Uber and it dropped him off outside the building.

There was a flight of steps leading up to a large entrance court. A plinth next to the entrance doors supported a name board listing all the companies occupying the building. Fast Lease were on the 8th floor. He entered the foyer and walked over to the lifts on the far side. As he was going up the lift, he still didn't have an idea of what he was going to say. The doors opened on the 8th floor to reveal a glass partition that separated the lifts from the reception area. The company's name was printed across it.

Right, just be confident, like you're expected, he thought. He went through into the reception and approached the front desk.
"The IT Manager please," he said, handing over his card to the receptionist and checking his watch, as though he was on a tight schedule.

"Do you have an appointment?" she asked.

"We met at a conference. He asked me to drop by when I had the chance," said Alex, smiling. She didn't return the smile.

"And who was it you wanted to see?" she asked.

"Er,……the IT Manager," replied Alex. He could see the scepticism written across her face.

"Just a moment Mr Samaras, she said, reading from his business card. She picked up the phone in a manner that suggested this visit wasn't going to last long. She had a short conversation before replacing the phone and to both of their surprise said, "Take a seat please. He'll be right out."

Well, this must be my lucky day, thought Alex, as he sat next to the fig tree. Sometimes you just have to ask. He turned his thoughts to what his sales pitch was going to be. He became so engrossed that he didn't immediately notice the figure that approached him until he heard him say his name. Alex looked up to see a face he hadn't set eyes on since he finished university.

"Hey, Tim," he said. "Are you working here?"

He nodded with a grin.

"Wait, you're not the…….?"

"Yep, I'm the IT Manager," he said and they both laughed. "When I heard the name I thought it must be you, but then, working for a company that died off 3 years ago, that really got me interested."

"Don't worry, I can explain everything," said Alex, laughing.

"Come on, let's go and talk in the meeting space," said Tim and led them over to the table by the window. "Fancy a coffee?" he said, motioning towards the coffee machine.

"Yeah, that'd be nice, thanks." Tim brought over the coffees in plastic cups and set them down on the table.

"So, let me explain," started Alex. "I'm not looking to pitch for IT work. I'm working as a full time stock trader now."

"Yeah, I remember you were writing algorithms for stock picking when we were at Uni."

"Yeah that's right, but today's a bit of under-cover research on a company that I recently invested in. It's a firm that your company deals with, Robrex. I just want to get a little more information from the coal face to better understand what they do and what kind of reputation they have."

"Well, what can I tell you? We haven't had too many problems with them. We've been working with them for as long as I've been here in the company and they seem to do a decent job. We get the usual complaints from some of our less broad-minded customers."

"What do you mean?" asked Alex.

"You know the sort of thing. They want to talk to someone that sounds exactly like them. Forget the fact that they're over-qualified for the job and can solve 99% of the problems in their sleep."

"Oh, you mean they do your call centre work?" said Alex. "Yeah, that's right."

"What about the IT work?" he asked.

"We deal with all our IT in-house."

"So, your only dealings with Robrex are for your call centre then?"

"Yeah, I didn't know they offered any wider IT services. It's not something that we've discussed with them during my time."

So, there it was again. Two customers, and in both cases they were providing exclusively call centre services.

"It just seems strange," said Alex. "The company presents itself as an IT solutions provider and yet they're predominantly a call centre company."

"Maybe the IT is dealt with by another part of the group," said Tim.

Alex, looking up in surprise. "The group? Are there other group companies?"

"Well, I assume so. The company calls itself 'Robrex

Group." Alex shook his head.

"How could I have missed that? I need to do some more digging," he said. It was just raising more questions. It seemed the more he discovered about the company, the more difficult it was to make sense of.

There wasn't much else he could learn from Tim, and they ended up chatting about old times; swapping stories from University and catching up on what various people were doing. Eventually, Tim had to get back to work, so they linked up on social media and promised to meet for a drink sometime.

As he was taking the lift down to the foyer, Alex pulled out the note he'd made of the three companies. There was one left, BYP Holdings. There'd been nothing that showed up on the internet search; no address or contact number; nothing to give him a start in tracking them down. If the name was correct though, there must be a registered address. Every limited company needs to have a bricks and mortar address registered with Companies House, that was for sure.

When he reached the foyer, he took a moment to find the Companies House web site and entered the name in the search box. To his surprise, the company came up, and with it, an address in Croydon. There was very little other information, just the date of incorporation which was only two years previous. Alex copied the post code and put it into Google Maps. The application zoomed into a pretty nondescript area of semi-detached housing; nothing that looked remotely like a commercial business address. It couldn't be right. There must be a mistake with the name.

The only way he'd be able to get to the bottom of it was by contacting the auditors. He could send a text message to Leonna, but she'd probably not get back to him in time to do anything about it today. He decided he needed a quick response and called her mobile number. There was a long wait before she answered the call, and then she spoke in a low voice as though she was trying to avoid being overheard.

"Hello, Leonna May," she said.

"Hi, it's Alex. Sorry to call you in the middle of work," he said. "It's just about the customer names that your friend provided. One of them seems to be a mistake. Maybe there's a spelling error or something. I was wondering if it would be OK to have a quick chat with her to clear it up?" There was a pause and he could sense the hesitation in Leonna's response.

"It might be better if I,....." she started, but then she seemed to change her mind. "Well, I suppose it would be OK. Just let me get the number." After a moment, she relayed a mobile phone number to him. Alex thanked her and promised to let her know the results of his investigation. He called the number straight away and a young woman's voice answered.

"Hello, is that Emma?" he asked.

"Yes, it is," she replied.

"My name's Alex. I'm a friend of Leonna's, Leonna May. You were good enough to let me have some customer names for one of your audit clients."

"Oh yes, Robrex. I'm working there today."

"Is it OK to talk?"

"Yes, you caught me on a coffee run. I'm on my way out of the office."

"Oh great. It's just a question about one of the names you gave me, BYP Holdings Ltd. I'm struggling to find them and I wonder if I might have got the wrong spelling."

"Er, no I don't think so. No, I'm sure that's right, BYP," she said.

"OK, that's strange. By the way, I wasn't aware until today that Robrex do call centre work. Is that a big part of their operations?"

"I couldn't tell you really," she said. "I know the company refers to itself as an IT Solutions Provider but we really focus on the figures rather than the business model."

"Yeah, I understand. Well thanks for your help with the names. It's been really useful."

There was a pause from her end and he was about to hang up, before she continued.

"Leonna tells me that you have some doubts about the company," she said.

"Well yeah, there are a few things that leave me with more questions than answers." It felt like Emma was deciding whether to say something.

"Do you have any doubts yourself?" ventured Alex.

"Well, it may be nothing, but there was something a bit odd this afternoon. I needed to use the company photocopier, but it wasn't working. Someone told me I could use the copier in the Financial Director's office. When I opened the cover there was a blank piece of headed paper that had been left. It had the name of the company's bankers on, but was completely blank."

"That seems rather unusual. Have you raised it with anyone?"

"No, not yet. I'm sure there's a reasonable explanation," she said.

"Well, I guess that's another one to add to my list of questions," said Alex. "Listen, thanks for your help Emma. I really appreciate it."

"No problem. I hope you get to the bottom of it."

"I'm not sure I'm going to spend too much more time trying. Anyway, thanks again," he said, before ending the call.

Alex had pretty much made up his mind by then. There were just too many things that didn't add up to remain invested. He'd speak to Matt and go through everything with him but it felt like this was the end of the road for his involvement with Robrex. He put his phone back in his jacket pocket and set off home.

Chapter 15

Alex had talked it over with Matt the evening before. They'd gone through the whole investment thesis, the pros and cons and all that had come out of the customer visits. Alex had pretty much made up his mind. There were just too many red flags. The niggling gut feeling had become more like a serious case of indigestion. He wanted out.

Matt wasn't quite so sure. He was more of a risk taker than Alex. He still thought it might be worth profiting from the upwards momentum in the share price. It came down to risk versus reward. Was it worth hanging in there to reap more of the upside? In the end, they decided to set up a call with a few of their close friends who were active on the discussion board. It might give them a broader perspective on the investment.

The meeting was set for 10am and Alex still had a few minutes before he needed to log in. He'd jotted down a few notes of the main risks as he saw them. It basically came down to his unease about a company that was based overseas and the difficulty in really being able to understand the business. So much of the investment case was based on information that needed to be taken on trust. Frankly, after yesterday's research, that trust was beginning to wane.

The anecdotal points too, only served to increase his sense of wariness. There was the fact that the CEO was taking an interest in the bulletin board chatter, which didn't inspire confidence, and then there was the episode that Emma had related to him over the phone. If there was any possibility of fraud, then that brought into question the whole financial status of the company.

Alex took his mug of tea over to the computer and logged on to the video conference site. There were already some familiar faces. Seb was sitting at a desk in front of a neatly arranged book shelf whilst Carlo looked like he was in a garage somewhere. Matt welcomed Alex to the meeting.

"I think you know everyone Alex. David, you probably know as 'Crazy88' and we're waiting for Jeremy, otherwise known as 'Skye High.' I invited 'Ya Man Noel' but he's unable to make it due to work commitments. At that moment, another window popped up on the screen revealing a grey haired man with metal framed glasses. It was Jeremy. After another round of greetings from everyone, Matt gave a brief introduction.

"Thanks everyone for making it to this impromptu meeting and sorry to keep you in the dark about what this is about. I think it's safe to say that we're all currently invested in the company Robrex. Alex and I were probably the first to bring the company to the attention of the rest of you, although Noel had been posting on the site for a while before that. So far, we're all very much in the money and there's a general impression amongst most of us that there's more to come. Having said that, Alex has begun to have some concerns about the investment case which he's discussed with me. We both feel that we need to share this with the rest of you and get your feedback. So, let me pass you over to Alex who will now pour cold water over all our hopes and dreams."

"Thanks Matt, I can always rely on you for a good introduction. Now, as Matt said, it's been a profitable investment for all of us so far and I have to say, I was initially impressed with the company and its growth prospects. As time's gone on though, I've just become more and more sceptical of the business. Firstly, let's not forget that this is an overseas based company, and one which came to the market through a reverse take-over. That limits the amount of information that we have access to, in terms of the company's finances and trading history. Yesterday, I met up with a couple of the company's UK customers to try to get some feedback. I was surprised to learn that they both use Robrex for Call Centre support rather than software solutions, which I was led to believe was the company's principal focus. It just made me realize how little I really know about the company's business, and how much I was taking on trust from the company's management.

"I had a lucky escape with one of the Chinese companies that listed on the Junior market a couple of years ago and turned out to be a total fraud. It's so easy to be seduced by the investment story and not question the figures that the company presents. I'm not saying that there's necessarily anything wrong with the numbers that Robrex has put out, but I feel there are just too many questions that remain unanswered for me to stay invested. I'm happy for anyone to persuade me to change my mind, but at this stage I think I'm going to sell up."

"Alex, I think most of us got duped to a certain extent by the Chinese small cap listings," said David. "I wasn't as lucky as you in avoiding the bullet, but Robrex is a different situation. They may be based overseas, but they have UK customers and are audited by a reputable UK accountancy firm. I think that de-risks the investment substantially, and let's not forget that there's a significant amount of Institutional investment in the company. They will have carried out due diligence on the company."

"Well, I'm not sure how thorough that due diligence has been," replied Alex. "When I asked Jamie about it, he said that they were pretty limited in what they carried out. Nothing much more than a Dun and Bradstreet report and face-to-face meetings with the management. I think we give the Institutions more credit than they deserve sometimes."

"I understand what you're saying about the listing,"

added Jeremy, "but at the end of the day we have to rely on the Auditors doing their job or we'd never invest in anything. The real attraction of the investment for me is the recent acquisition. That's the game changer. So, whatever doubts you have over Robrex, it's the acquisition company that matters most."

"Yeah, but how much do we actually know about that company too?" said Alex. "It's another case of us relying on the information that we've been given, but with little opportunity to verify it. What do the rest of you think?"

There was some fairly robust discussion about the merits of the company and the risks of the investment and people were pretty divided in their positions.

"The way I look at this investment," said Carlo, "is that it's already on a high rating. There's a lot of future growth and successful execution baked into the share price right now. There's a risk in investing in the company for that reason alone. For me, it's a momentum play. I want to ride the exuberance to as near to the top as I can before deftly hopping off and pocketing my ill gotten gains."

"The point where fear exceeds greed, you mean?" said Matt.

"Yes, and I'm already riding side saddle," joked Carlo.

"How about you, Seb?" asked Matt.

"I'm a little less cavalier than Carlo. Before today, I was happy to remain invested but hearing Alex's concerns, it's made me re-think the investment. I trust Alex's judgement and if he has genuine concerns, then maybe this is the time to cash in and move on to the next idea. I think it's easy to get fixated on a single company and forget that there are thousands of other opportunities out there. Time to move on I think."

"So, can we just confirm where we all stand on this," said Matt. "Seb, you're a sell right, and I guess you haven't changed your mind either Alex?"

"No, I'm ready to sell up," Alex replied.

"Carlo, you're still precariously perched on your saddle until the first sign of trouble, yeah?"

"Yes, I'll be living life in the fast lane," he replied.

"David, how about you?"

"I think I'm going to stick with it for the time being but I'm keeping a closer eye on things after this."

"And you Jeremy?" asked Matt.

"I'm a firm believer in this stock. I probably won't buy any more until we see the benefits of the acquisition coming through, but I'm in for the long term."

"Well, that's three for and two against," said Matt. "I think I'm going to have to make it three a piece. It's been a great ride, but I think Seb makes a good point. There are plenty of other opportunities out there, so why pick the investment with question marks surrounding it?

"It would be good if you could all keep this to yourselves, at least for the time being. Alex and I have our shares with Jamie's firm and it may take a day or two to arrange the sale. It'd really help if you could avoid spreading too much panic on the bulletin board until we've unloaded."

That pretty much rounded things up, and after a bit of friendly banter, the meeting broke up and the individuals signed out one by one. Eventually, it was just Matt and Alex.

"Well, that was far from unanimous," said Alex. I guess that's what makes a market."

"Yeah, as always it comes down to risk and reward. You don't have to be 100% convinced in an investment, but you need to believe that the odds are in your favour. I'm not sure I feel that any more."

"No, me neither, said Alex. "It just feels like a sense of relief to have made the decision. That's a sure sign that my subconscious is telling me it's the right decision."

"Will you speak to Jamie?" asked Matt.

"Yeah, I'll give him a call straight away and tell him what we've decided."

"Great, I can start looking for a home for the proceeds."

They both signed off and Alex decided he might as well try to get through to Jamie straight away. He picked up his phone and noticed there was a missed call whilst he'd been on the conference call. He opened the phone record and saw it was from Leonna. There was a voice message too. He played the recording and he could sense instantly that something was wrong.

"Alex, it's Leonna. Can you call me please? I need to speak to you ....., erm,.... urgently. It's important. Please call me straight away."

Alex called her straight back and she answered after the first ring tone had barely finished.

"Alex, just a moment," she said, and there was a long pause. Finally, she spoke again. "Alex, something terrible has happened. It's Emma. The Police have been here and everyone's just,......" Her voice began to break before she tried to compose herself.

"Leonna, what's happened?"

"They found her last night. She'd fallen from the multi-storey car park."

"What, is she in hospital?"

"No, she's dead Alex." Leonna could barely get the words out. Alex sat motionless in his chair while he tried to make sense of what she was saying.

"But, I just spoke to her yesterday afternoon."

"I know. The Police will probably be in touch with you. They have her mobile phone."

"Leonna, Emma told me something yesterday...., look, can I meet up with you to talk about this?" There was a pause whilst she thought about it.

"Okay, I can take some time off over lunch," she said. "There's a Starbucks near the station on Tottenham Court

Road. I can meet you upstairs at about 12:30. Listen, I have to go. I'll see you later alright." With that, she ended the call and Alex sat for a few minutes in front of his monitor just trying to take it in and make sense of what he'd just heard.

Dead? It just seemed unreal. Could this have anything to do with the audit she was carrying out? Surely not. If she'd uncovered some kind of fraud, that wouldn't be reason enough for this; for murder, would it?

He stood up and walked over to the window, resting his hands on the window sill and looked down to the street below. He just stared blankly from the window for a while, unable to focus on anything. He imagined her standing on the edge of the multi-storey car park. He suddenly became overcome by a feeling of dizziness, a feeling of toppling over and falling. He had to shut his eyes and take a step backwards into the room. He sat down on the sofa to clear his head and leaned back, looking up at the ceiling. It felt like he was getting into something; something that was way over his head.

It was a relief to get outside and be able to breath the cool Spring air. He'd left plenty of time to make it to the coffee shop. When he came out of the station onto Tottenham Court Road there was still a few minutes before he was due to meet Leonna. He could see the Starbucks on the other side of the street and he crossed over and entered through the large glass doors. He ordered a cappuccino and took it up the stairs to the 2nd floor. He found a seat at a table where he could see the stairs and would spot Leonna when she came in.

She arrived a few minutes after 12:30 and Alex got her attention as she reached the top of the stairs. She came over holding a drink and tried to force a smile. She looked tired. Alex got up and placed a hand on her arm.

"Are you OK?"

"Yes, but I've just had the worst morning of my life," she replied. They both sat down at the small table. Alex gave her time to settle and resisted the urge to ask all kinds of questions. Eventually, she felt able to start.

"I heard first thing this morning. Stephen called me to say that one of the partners had been contacted by the Police. The whole office is in total shock."

"What have the Police said?" asked Alex.

"They talked to some people at the office but they seem to think it was suicide."

"Do they know what time it happened?"

"She was found around 7:30pm. Her car was still there in the car park."

"Leonna, I talked to her at about 4:30pm and there's no way I was talking to someone who was about to commit suicide three hours later."

"You said she told you something."

"Yes, I just wanted to ask her about one of the company names she gave me, and to confirm something about Robrex's business model. She told me that earlier that day, she'd found a blank piece of headed paper for the company's bankers in the FD's photocopier. It just seemed very strange. I got the impression that she was going to query it with them."

"Do you think we should speak to the Police about it?" asked Leonna.

"I don't think they'd take it seriously. We'd need more than that to get anywhere with them."

"Maybe I should do some digging into the company and try to come up with something," she said.

"No, Leonna. I don't think you should get involved. If there's anything going on, it'll be better to keep well away from it. I'm going to speak to Jamie. Matt and I have decided to sell up our holding in the company. I'll try to persuade him to do some proper due diligence on the company."

She nodded vaguely and her gaze shifted and settled on some indeterminate space beyond their table.

"We joined the firm on the same day. We went through the induction programme together and hit it off straight away. A couple of months later, we were sharing a flat together. I just feel like I got her involved in something which has led to this."

"Leonna, you didn't do anything which led to this. We don't know if work has anything to do with this, and even if it did, she was just doing her job; doing what anybody else in the same position would have done. This has nothing to do with you." She let out a long sigh.

"I can't believe she would have tried to kill herself. It just doesn't make sense. She wasn't the kind of person to be down for any length of time. I would have known if there was something wrong."

"Did she talk about the job?"

"Just very general stuff. I think she was enjoying working on the audit. She said it was pretty easy. All the information she needed was there and everything seemed to tally."

"Yeah, everything adding up just as it should. That was the impression I got when I looked into the company. Almost too perfect."

"Leonna, it might be a good idea to take some time off work if you can. This is a massive shock and dealing with grief affects people in different ways. Don't feel like you have to soldier through it. It may be better to just get away for a while and have a change of scenery."

"Yes, maybe that would be the best thing," she said. "Alex, I really appreciate being able to talk with you about this. I tried to talk to Stephen but it's really hit him hard. He was mentoring a number of the trainees and I think he's having problems dealing with it."

"Yeah, I can understand that. You have to deal with all this and then still keep the show on the road. It can't be easy."

They talked some more, and both of them began to open up about personal things; things that they'd left buried for years. Leonna spoke about her father, who'd walked out on the family when she was a young girl, and Alex talked about the loss of his mother in a way he'd never done before. He'd never been able to share his feelings with his Dad or Jack, but now somehow, it felt like the right time and the right person.

When it was time for Leonna to get back to the office, they got up from the table and it felt to Alex like he'd unburdened himself of something, like a weight had been removed from his mind. They walked out onto the street and hugged each other warmly.

"Thanks for being here Alex," she said.

"Yeah, and you too," he replied. "If there's any news from Jamie, I'll let you know, okay. In the meantime, just take care of yourself okay." She smiled weakly and nodded before walking off in the direction of her office.

Alex crossed the road and then paused outside the station. It would be better to have a face-to-face with Jamie to explain everything. If he called him now, he might be able to fix up a meeting while he was still in the city. He pulled up his mobile number and called him. To his surprise, Jamie picked up the call straight away.

"Hey Alex, what's up?"

"Any chance I could meet you either this afternoon or tonight? I really need to have a serious chat about the Robrex situation. There's something that you need to know."

"Er, sure. I'm going to be in a meeting most of the afternoon. Can you drop by the house around 8pm?"

"Yeah, I should be able to do that," said Alex.

"Okay, I'll see you later," he said, and made his apologies.

Alex took a deep breath. It felt like a relief. He just wanted to get this whole Robrex thing behind him now. After tonight he'd be able to move on.

Chapter 16

The British Library was open until 8:00pm and it wasn't too far away. Alex decided he might as well stay in the city centre before going to meet Jamie. He was able to find a seat on the first floor, next to one of the vast pillars that rose up into the cathedral-like space. He'd packed his laptop, so he had everything he needed to keep himself busy.

He tried to work on some new research for a while but it was difficult to stay focused. He just kept coming back to the events of earlier in the day. He wanted to put it all behind him, but he couldn't help thinking about it; searching for answers or explanations. Eventually, he found himself re-reading the Admission Document for Robrex. He'd flicked through much of the document when he first read it, just picking out the important financial details. This time, he took it slower and studied it more carefully.

It started with the key personnel in the company. There were small photos for each of the directors and an outline of their backgrounds. He recognized the CEO, Sandeep Gupta. According to the document, he studied at the University of Delhi and then the Indian Institute of Management (IMM) in Bangalore. The University of Delhi was the top ranked university in India and the IIMs are notoriously difficult to get in to. They're the highly competitive business schools that churn out the future Indian business leaders. Altogether, a highly impressive educational background.

Alex found his details on Linkedin. After leaving business school, he started his own business and appeared to have built his career as a self employed entrepreneur. Why no experience working for a corporation before he started his own business? He'd heard about the IIMs through an Indian friend at University. If you graduated from one of these schools, the Multi-nationals were lining up to offer you a fast track management trainee position. Didn't he want to see the world for a few years, get some experience and establish his business contacts? Or maybe it was just something else that was being asked to be taken on trust.

He decided to do a little more digging. He pulled up the home site for the IIM in Bangalore and, as he'd hoped, there was an alumni page. He needed to register to get access, but after that he could search through all the graduates listed on the site. He found a short list of Guptas, but no Sandeep. That seemed odd. When he double checked again on Linkedin, he noticed that there were no dates relating to his educational history. No way for fellow graduates to question his credentials. It was just another question mark to add to the list.

He'd already made up his mind anyway. There was nothing he was going to find that would change his mind now. He'd give Jamie his decision straight away and be glad to be out of it. When it was time for him to make a move, he packed up his things and headed out onto the street. The station was just across the road and the street was already busy with evening commuters. By the time he reached Notting Hill, the light was beginning to fade and the street lights were on marking the route down to Jamie's house.

As he walked down the tree-lined road, it brought back the memories of the dinner party at Jamie's and the break up with Lisa. It was only a matter of a few weeks ago but somehow it seemed much longer. The initial pain of the separation had already turned into a feeling of acceptance. The sense that one of them at least had had the courage to call time on a relationship that just wasn't going anywhere.

He entered the driveway and walked up the steps to the front door. He rang the bell and a light came on in the hallway.

Jamie opened the door, still wearing his business attire but minus the suit jacket and with his tie loosened.

"Hey, come in Alex. Joanne's out with a girlfriend so it's just you, me and the fridge." Alex grinned and followed Jamie down the hall towards the kitchen.

"Have you eaten?" asked Jamie.

"I grabbed a sandwich earlier."

"Have a look in the fridge. There's some stuff that Maria made yesterday."

"Who's Maria?"

"She comes over and cooks for us during the week." Alex opened the fridge door. A number of plastic containers were stacked up on the shelves, all neatly labelled.

"What do you fancy, pasta, rice or sweet potatoes?"

"I could do pasta, but whatever you want is good," replied Jamie. Alex took out the 'smoked salmon pasta' and lifted the lid. Flakes of smoked salmon in a cream sauce with capers and fresh dill. it looked delicious. He put it in the microwave and set the timer.

Jamie had taken the tops off a couple of Belgian beers and he passed one over to Alex before they sat down at the island counter.

"So, you still have doubts about the Robrex investment?" he said.

"Yes, I've started to question the whole legitimacy of the operation. It's much more than that though." Alex went through the entire thing. The visits to their customers, the shocking news about Emma and his latest research into the CEO.

Jamie was silent for what seemed like a long time. Eventually he looked up at Alex.

"I presume you want out of the investment?"

"Yes, I've talked it over with Matt and we both feel it's just uninvestable with what we know."

"There's something that I should have told you at the

outset," said Jamie. "I just never expected it to come to this. When we bought in to the placing, we signed a 'lock-up' which means that we can't sell any shares until the company announces its next trading update. That's due around the end of the month, in a couple of weeks or so. The brokers didn't want any of the institutions flipping the shares for a quick profit."

"Right, so we're stuck in for at least a couple of weeks then?" said Alex.

"Yes, I'm afraid so."

Alex got up and retrieved the pasta which had been sitting and cooling off in the microwave.

"I'm thinking we need to do a thorough examination of the company with the minimum of delay," said Jamie.

"I think the only way you can really do that is to get someone to look into the company on the ground in India," said Alex, as he brought two plates of pasta and set them on the marble counter. "Do you have someone who can do that in India?"

"There are firms we could use. They'd be basically private investigators but they'd most likely lack the in-depth knowledge to uncover a sophisticated financial scam. There is somebody I think would be able to do a far better job."

"Yeah, who's that?" asked Alex.

"You," said Jamie. Alex paused with a fork full of pasta half way to his mouth.

"Me?", he said, looking taken aback.

"Yeah, why not? You know this case better than anyone and you'll know what you're looking for. I'll pay you of course and you can expense everything."

Alex sat for a moment without saying anything. He'd been thinking he could put all this behind him and now he was stuck in the investment and being asked to get deeper still into the mix. Part of him just wanted to sit it out and wait until he could exit the trade, but there was a part that yearned to get to the bottom of it all. It wasn't just the question of fraud, he needed to find out if this had anything to do with the death of Emma. He owed her that much at least.

"I have an Indian friend from University. He might be able to put me in touch with someone on the ground over there who could help us," said Alex. "Let me speak to him first and then I can get back to you."

"Okay, but you need to make it quick. You'll be able to exit your position easily, but if I'm going to offload the company's holding, we'll need a well thought out plan. You'd need to head out there within the next few days."

Alex would have to agree with his Dad to cover his usual weekly night at the restaurant, but other than that, he was completely flexible.

"I'd really need to find some way to get into their head office and talk to someone; find out what kind of work they're doing."

"Well, you're resourceful Alex. You'll find a way," said Jamie. "Remember though, we need something more than just hearsay or impressions that things are not quite right. We need to be able to back up any accusations with rock solid facts."

"Yeah, that's why I think I need someone who knows the system over there to help me. Hopefully, my mate Ravi can hook me up with someone."

Jamie went through the logistics of Alex's trip and how his PA would book the flights and find a hotel in Mumbai. Everything would be taken care of once he'd confirmed the date he could fly out. Alex began to realize that things seemed to be progressing apace. What had started off as something he was going to think over, had quickly become a matter of when, and not if. Jamie had that way of manipulating you. If he believed in you, you found yourself going out of your way to do whatever he expected of you.

With things apparently more or less settled, Jamie uncorked a nice bottle of white wine and poured a couple of glasses.

"We must have you and Lisa over again soon," he said. "The girls got on like a house on fire last time." Alex shifted uneasily on his chair.

"Yeah, that's probably not going to happen. Lisa and I are having some time apart, as they say." Jamie looked up in surprise.

"Are you giving each other some space, or is it the end of the road?" he asked.

"It's pretty much the end of the road," replied Alex. "It's probably the best thing for both of us in the long run. We just seem to be on different paths."

"Sorry to hear it," said Jamie. "Well, you know what they say about one door closing and another one opening," he added, whilst raising his glass.

"Yeah, let's just hope it's not one of those trap doors," said Alex as they clinked glasses.

They chatted about things over the rest of the bottle of wine, mostly market stuff and their shared passion for music. It was getting late and Alex eventually decided he should make a move. Jamie saw him off at the front door and Alex promised that he'd speak with his Indian contact the next day and let him know how quickly he could get underway.

As he walked off along the street he thought he should give Matt a call. He needed to let him know the latest twist in events.

"Hey, Alex, did everything go OK?" said Matt.

"Well, not exactly as planned. I'm just on my way home from Jamie's house. I told him everything, but there's a snag. He signed a lock-up on the shares which means we're stuck with our Robrex holding until around the end of this month."

"Well, things could be worse," said Matt. "Did you see the move up in the share price this afternoon?"

"No, I've not been keeping an eye on things. Hold on a minute." He quickly opened the portfolio app on his phone and immediately saw that the daily move was highlighted in green, +14.5%. "Wow, what's the cause of that?"

"It was mentioned in one of the Tip Sheets," said Matt. "I'm beginning to wonder if now is really the time to be getting out."

"There's something else." said Alex. "Jamie's asked me to go and check out the company in India. We might have a better idea of the risks we're running after I come back."

"What? You're going to fly out to India?"

"Yeah, I'll probably be going in the next few days. It's important that we keep things under wraps until we know for sure what's going on, so don't tell anyone what we're doing, right."

"Ooh, top secret eh? I shall be the very height of discretion."

"No, seriously Matt, this mustn't go anywhere."

"Yeah, I get it, but keep me briefed on what you find out will you."

"Sure. I might need your help at some point along the way. I'll let you know what the schedule is. Look, I've got to get going. I'll probably give you a call tomorrow."

They ended the call and Alex returned his mobile to his back pocket. Just as he did so, there was a short chime. He'd missed a call whilst he was speaking to Matt. It was a number that he didn't recognize but there was a voice message too. Alex played the message.

"This is Detective Sergeant Harris from the Metropolitan Police. A message for Mr. Alex Samaras. Could you call me back on this number to arrange a time that I could speak to you. It's just a routine matter where you might be able to help us with our investigation. Thank you."

Alex took a deep breath. That was something else he could do without.

Chapter 17

It was a cool start to the day after overnight rain and the sun had finally come out to dry off the streets. Alex had spoken to Ravi first thing and they'd agreed to meet at his office for lunch. He decided to cycle in to town. It would be quicker to take the train but it looked like it was turning into a nice day; a good chance to get on the bike and feel the cool breeze in his face.

He hadn't seen Ravi in a while. He'd been the stand-out student on their course and was hired straight from Uni by Google. He was working as a GIS specialist, developing their Google Earth mapping software. He'd got the dream job, the one with 'Big Tech.' The one with the great office, the share options and the fast track career. The one they'd all dreamed of before the grim reality of 'Small Tech' came calling. Alex had kept in touch and they'd occasionally meet for a beer or grab lunch somewhere.

The office was in a great location, right next to Kings Cross Station, and facing onto a nicely designed open space. Alex got off his bike and wheeled it up to a low metal barrier that he could secure it to. The space was beginning to fill up with office workers making the most of the sunshine. They sat along the edge of the water feature eating their sandwiches or gathered around the tables set out in front of the restaurants.

Alex made his way to the Google building and entered the reception area. No matter how many times he'd been there, the multi-storey height of the central atrium always made him look up in amazement. He took a seat on one of the sofas and sent a quick text message to Ravi to let him know he'd arrived.

A few minutes later a tall young guy with glasses and a neatly trimmed beard came out of the lift. He came over to greet him.

"Hey Alex, how are you doing? I've got you a visitor pass. We'll go to the lounge on the top floor shall we?"

"Yeah, that sounds good. Is that the one that looks like the set from the tele tubbies?" said Alex with a grin. Ravi laughed.

"No, that's the wellness suite on the fifth." They walked over to the lifts together.

"How's it going with the digitization of planet Earth?"

"Oh, you know, there's no end to it. We're working on the time lapse videos. Just when you think you've got on top of the data management, they throw something else at you."

They got out of the lift on the top floor and entered a bright and spacious lounge area. It was a little more sophisticated than some of the other spaces in the building. Still a bit of the Ikea feel but with a little less of the kids play area vibe. The great thing about coming to Google though, was the free food. Ravi led them over to the help-yourself buffet which was heaving with every kind of cold snack, salad and fruit option. Alex filled up a bowl and poured himself some fresh apple juice. They took it over to one of the tables near the window.

"Now I know why you work such long hours Ravi," he said. "Yeah, it's certainly cut my food bill. I have to remind myself sometimes that I have a home to go back to."

"I guess that's the idea," said Alex. "You've got all the food you need, you can work out in the gym, use the games room, why would you ever want to leave?"

"Yeah, I've got my own little Matrix. Who needs real life?" he said with a grin. "Anyway, how's real life treating you Alex?"

"It's giving me a lot to think about," he replied. "You know I told you on the phone about this Indian company that I'm researching. Well, what I didn't mention was that I'm flying out to India to take a look at the company. They're based in Mumbai."

"Wow, I wish I was coming with you."

"Yeah, I wish you were coming with me too. That's why I wanted to talk to you. I wanted to see if you could put me in touch with someone that could help me with the research." Ravi finished chewing on a mouthful of cous cous salad.

"Well. if you want to get corporate information on a company in India, you'll probably need to use a local research agency."

"The trouble is I don't have much time. I just have a window of opportunity to find out what I can myself. I really need someone local who can help me on the ground."

Ravi thought for a while and then a smile slowly crept across his face.

"Actually, there is someone I could introduce you to; my cousin Yash. He lives in Bombay and works for the local government. That might be useful, you know. If you have to go through the usual channels to get corporate details, it can take forever. He should be able to help you navigate your way through the notorious Indian bureaucracy."

"Great, that sounds perfect," said Alex.

"Right, let me email him to make sure he's going to be around. I'll copy you in and you can fix to meet up when you get there. I should warn you, he's a bit of a party animal. He'll probably want to show you the sights while you're there."

"I better polish up my Bollywood dancing technique in that case," said Alex, laughing.

"So, what made you start investing in the Indian market?" asked Ravi.

"I'm not. The company's listed on the UK stock market. I was introduced to it by a friend who's a Hedge Fund manager. He's heavily invested and wants me to do some retrospective due diligence. Better late than never I suppose."

"I guess you have some doubts about the company or you wouldn't be going all the way to India, right?"

"Well, yeah, there are some things that I'm not convinced about. I just want to see for myself if the company is everything that it makes itself out to be."

"You know there isn't the same level of regulation and accountability that you find over here," said Ravi. "A lot of business in India is based on personal relationships and trust in who you're dealing with you. If you don't know the people you're working with, then you need to tread carefully."

"I'll bear that in mind," said Alex.

"Do you think you'll re-locate to India at some point?" he asked.

"Yeah, I'll probably end up going back eventually. I'm already getting the pressure from the family. They think I should be married by now and they have a whole list of suitable candidates.

"Do you want me to do some scouting while I'm over there?" joked Alex.

"No, please don't. Anyone you meet while you're out with Yash will definitely be unsuitable," he said, laughing.

They talked for a while about careers and university days; swapping stories about mutual friends, before it was time for Ravi to get back to work. He assured Alex that he'd make the contact with his cousin and they went their separate ways at the lift.

When Alex came out of the building, the sun was still out and it had turned into a warm day. He made his way over to his bike and removed the lock and stored it in his backpack. He hesitated from setting off as he wanted to call Leonna. He should let her know that he was going to India and that something was being done. He wanted to make sure she was okay too.

He leaned against the metal barrier and called her number.

She answered after just a couple of rings.

"Hi Alex."

"Is it alright to talk?" he asked.

"Yes, I'm on my own in the firm's reading room. I'm trying to do some study while things are quiet but I'm struggling to concentrate on anything at the moment."

"Yeah, I can understand that. Listen, I just wanted to let you know that Jamie's asked me to go out to India for a few days to try to get to the bottom of this matter with Robrex. Just so you know what's happening. If there's anything that we uncover....., I mean anything that could be linked to Emma, ... well, we can involve the Police."

"You're going out there?"

"Yes, I talked it over with Jamie and we decided it's the only way we're really going to understand the company."

"Right......," she said. "Actually, I know you said not to get involved, but I did a bit of searching myself. I had a look through some of our old papers on Robrex. There was a note on the file from last year's audit saying that one of the Juniors was unable to verify a customer account."

"Really? Was it raised with the company?"

"Well, there was no correspondence that I could find, just an internal memo on the file saying that it had been resolved with them. It does seem a bit unusual."

"Yeah, nothing about this company feels quite right. I just hope I can make sense of it."

There was a brief pause, as though Leonna was weighing something up in her mind before coming to a decision.

"Why don't I help you?" she said.

"What do you mean?"

"Well, I could take a few days off and come with you. You said yourself that I should get away and have a change of scenery."

"Yes, but I.....," started Alex, before she interrupted him.

"Besides, it might be useful to have someone who can access information from the auditors, if you need it." That was certainly true, he thought. He didn't have much of a plan as it was, so having Leonna along with her contacts at the auditors did make sense.

"Alex, I need to feel like I'm doing something. If there's a way that I can help to understand what happened to Emma, then I have to do it." He thought for a moment.

"Okay, let me speak to Jamie, but Leonna, it's important that you don't tell anyone about this for the time being, right?"

"Of course. I'll just say I'm going to spend a few days with my sister. The firm's been encouraging staff to take time off if they need it."

"Oh, and there's something else," said Alex. "The Police contacted me yesterday. They want me to come in and answer a few questions having spoken to Emma on the day she died. I won't mention your name if I can avoid it."

"Don't worry about that. Are you going to say anything about the company?"

"I've got nothing of any substance to give them. I'd rather stay quiet about it until I really have an understanding of what's going on."

"When are you planning to speak to them?"

"I said I'd drop by this afternoon. Actually, I'd better get on my way. Listen, I'll call you later after I've spoken to Jamie and let you know what the arrangements are. Are you really sure you want to do this?"

"Yes, I want to do it."

"OK, I'll speak to you later," he said, before hanging up.

Alex stood for a moment by his bike while he pondered the latest situation. He couldn't say he wasn't happy at the idea of spending a few days with Leonna, but it did feel like a new layer of complication had been added to the trip. He tried to imagine how he was going to explain this to Jamie. There didn't seem a way that would be anything other than awkward. He'd leave that until later.

The Police Station was in Islington, only a short ride from where he was. He knew a good cycle route that took him along the canal, passed the long boats tied up alongside the path. It would be nice to get off the busy streets and follow the tow path along the water's edge. Another world where people with time on their hands pottered about on their boats.

As he approached the old stone bridge that marked the end of the tow path, he took the ramp up to street level and it was easy from there to work his way over to the main road. The Police Station was a large dour looking brick building, the entrance marked by the familiar old blue lamp above a brick archway.

Alex secured his bike to one of the metal barriers lining the pavement and went into the reception area. The drab interior was pretty much what he was expecting. Vinyl floor with metal bench seats fixed to the wall on one side and a line of window counters along the other. Low budget and minimal maintenance. He approached the only window that was manned and asked for D.S. Harris. The officer directed him to take a seat.

He had to wait about 10 minutes before D.S. Harris appeared in the reception. He was dressed in civilian clothes, about fifty something with short dark hair that was greying around the temples. He introduced himself and asked Alex to follow him through to the interview room.

They entered a small space fitted with dark brown carpet tiles and a small table fixed against one wall. D.S. Harris closed the door behind them and invited Alex to take a seat in one of the moulded plastic chairs before taking a seat opposite him.

"Thanks for coming in Mr. Samaras," he said. "This is what we call a voluntary interview, so you can choose to end the interview at any time. It's just a means for us to gather information about an investigation. We will need to record the interview and of course, I'll need to caution you that anything you say could be used in a court of law."

Alex nodded his head. Somehow, he'd just been expecting an informal chat, but the mention of recordings and courts of law suddenly brought it home to him. To the Police, he was a potential suspect; someone of interest in their investigation.

"So, you spoke to the deceased on the afternoon of the seventh?" said the detective.
"Yes, that's right."
"What was the reason for the call?"
"I was just clarifying some information about a company that Emma had knowledge of. I was doing some research on the company."
"Research? What kind of research?" he asked.
"Er, I'm a private investor. I was just gathering information on a company I'm invested in."
"So, you were asking an accountant for information on a company. Information that you couldn't otherwise access?" he said, raising an eyebrow.
"Well,....it's not like I was.....I just needed to get the names of their customers. It wasn't price sensitive information."
"I'm not suggesting anything Mr. Samaras. I just ask the questions," he said. Alex nodded. Not a good start.

"How well did you know the deceased?"
"Not at all," replied Alex. "It was the first time I'd spoken to her."
"And, how did you get her phone number?"
"It was through a mutual friend," he replied. The detective didn't quiz him on the mutual friend which seemed a little odd. Maybe they already knew.
"How did she strike you when you spoke to her?"
"She seemed perfectly normal, certainly not like she was about to commit suicide."

"Suicide, Mr. Samaras? Do you think she committed suicide?"

"Well no, but if you think she did, it didn't seem like she was anxious or depressed or anything."

"I didn't say anything about suicide," said the detective.

Oh God, this was going from bad to worse, he thought. D.S. Harris made some notes on the pad in front of him. Alex told himself to calm down a bit; just answer the questions and nothing more. Don't get drawn in to saying any more than you have to.

"Where were you when you made the call to the deceased?" he asked.

"I was in the reception of a company called Fast Lease, near Covent Garden."

"So, you were in the city centre at that time. Where did you go after that?"

"I went straight home."

"And where is home?"

"I live in Wood Green," answered Alex.

"How long did it take you to get home would you say?"

"Probably about an hour, door to door," said Alex.

"Did you meet anyone on the way?" he asked.

"No, nobody."

"And is there anyone at home who can verify your whereabouts during the rest of the day?"

"Well, no. I live in a flat on my own," said Alex, gradually realizing that he was minus an alibi on the night in question. D.S. Harris made some more notes, whilst Alex shifted uneasily on his chair.

The rest of the interview seemed to focus on Alex's background; why he didn't have a job and why he lived alone. By the end, Alex had the impression that the detective had him labelled as some sort of sociopath.

"Well, I think that's it for now," he said, and confirmed

the finish time before turning off the recording device. "You're not planning any trips are you, in case we need to get hold of you?"

"No, I've got nothing arranged," said Alex, which strictly speaking, was factually correct.

They got up from the table and he followed the detective back into the reception area.

"I've got your number," he said, looking Alex directly in the eye and offering his hand. "Your phone number," he added with a wry smile. "If I need to get hold of you again, I can call you."

"Oh yes, of course."

Alex walked out on to the pavement and headed over to his bike. *Well that could hardly have gone worse*, he thought. I guess when you deal with criminals all day, you can't help but see everyone in the same mould. Hopefully, that would be the last he'd see of D.S. Harris.

There was a park across the road and Alex rode his bike over there and found a bench that he could sit at for a while. He wanted to call Jamie to see if it was feasible to have Leonna join him on the trip to India. He was lucky to catch him between meetings.

"I think we're on for India," he said. "I met up with my friend Ravi and he's going to put me in touch with his cousin who's based in Mumbai. He should be able to help me with the practical stuff on the ground over there."

"Great, then I think we should fix for you to head out there as soon as possible. I'll get Stephanie to sort out the flights and accommodation."

"Yeah, about that.....," said Alex. "I was wondering if I could take someone else who'd be able to help me?"

"You mean Matt?"

"Er, no. It's Leonna," he said. There was a pause while Jamie made sense of it.

"What, you mean Stephen's Leonna?"

"Yes, she wants to help, after what happened to Emma, and I do think it could be useful to have someone from the auditors there."

"I take it that Stephen's not in the loop with this one," said Jamie.

"I imagine, probably not,' said Alex.

"Okay, but the budget only runs to 3 days, right? I need you to collect what information you can in that time and get back here asap."

"Right I understand. Let me know what the flight schedules are and I'll be ready to go."

That was it, he was going out there. It was a strange feeling now that it was all settled. On the one hand, he had no clear idea of how he was going to get the job done, but on the other, there was a sense of excitement; the thought that maybe at last he could get to the bottom of it all.

Chapter 18

Alex was a last minute packer. He could pack a bag from start to finish in around 10 minutes. It used to drive him crazy waiting for Lisa to finish filling a suitcase. He could never understand all that planning; the check lists and preparing for every imaginable scenario. The mid-sized sports bag sitting next to the door had more or less everything he'd need. The travel documents and other bits and pieces would go in his back pack with the laptop.

It felt like he was leaving with a few plates left spinning. The mortgage providers seemed to be dragging their feet over the re-mortgage application, but he expected a decision by the time he'd get back. He'd spoken to Jack to let him know that he'd be away and his Dad would cover his usual mid-week night at the restaurant.

He'd called a taxi to take him to the airport and he decided to head out to meet it in front of the house. One final check to be sure that he had everything, and he slung his backpack over his shoulder and went out of the door.

When he reached the hall at the bottom of the stairs, he took the chance to check his mail. Just a letter from an NPO that he'd supported. He put it in his pocket and reached to pick up his bag before something caught his eye. An A4 piece of paper had been pinned to the wall by the front door. It looked like it had been typed on a traditional typewriter and was headed, 'Notice to all Residents.' That was as far as he'd got before he heard a voice behind him.

"I thought we should nip it in the bud before things got out of hand."

"Sorry?" said Alex, turning to see Ms. Marks standing

behind him.

"I'm sure you've noticed the smell of fried food lingering in the stairwell," she said. "Well. I thought it was appropriate to highlight the nuisance that it represents to other residents. There's nothing that can't be grilled, boiled or steamed, and with far less inconvenience to one's neighbours. Wouldn't you agree, Mr. Samaras?" Alex was momentarily stuck for words.

"Er, I can't say I'd noticed," he said.

"You look like you're going on a trip," she said, noticing the bag he was carrying.

"Er, yes, just a few days. I should be back by the end of the week."

"Well, I'll keep an eye on things for you whist you're away," she said. *I bet you will*, he thought.

"That would be great, thanks," he said, forcing a smile. "Well, I better get on my way. I think there's a taxi waiting for me." He backed out of the front door and Ms. Marks closed the door behind him.

Did she really having nothing better to do? Probably not, he guessed, setting the bag down on the pavement at a spot where the taxi would be able to pull in. He didn't have long to wait before it showed up. The traffic was pretty clear and he still had plenty of time when it pulled up at the departure area at Heathrow.

He'd sent a text message to Leonna in the taxi. She was already at the airport and would meet him in front of the Check-in. He spotted her standing next to a smart aluminium-effect suitcase. She was casually dressed in jeans with a white T-shirt and a dark fitted blazer. Practical but stylish.

He gave her a wave to get her attention and she smiled when she saw him, lifting her sunglasses and setting them in her hair above her forehead.

"We've got plenty of time," she said, as he walked up.

"Shall we check in our bags?"

"Yeah, I checked us in online so let's just drop off the bags. The good news is that Jamie booked us on business class," he said, as he led them over to the free check-in counter.

"Oh great, that's music to my ears," said Leonna.

Relieved of their luggage, they made their way through Security and dropped in at the Business Class Lounge. Alex brought a couple of coffees over to where Leonna was sitting.

"This is my favourite time," she said. "The bit where you're checked in and there's nothing you can do but wait until you get to the other end. It's the totally free time. You don't feel like you have to do anything and no one can get to you."

"I take it you didn't bring your accountancy homework with you then?" said Alex, setting the coffees on the table.

"No, they think I'm staying up in Durham with my sister and I've even left my phone at home. No one can touch me." She leaned back and closed her eyes.

"How are you doing?" asked Alex, "....you know, with everything?"

"I suppose I'm beginning to come to terms with things. It's been difficult to think about anything else for the last few days. I think getting away for a while will really help."

"Well, I'm glad you're here. It'll certainly help to have two heads trying to make sense of this rather than just one."

"Thanks, I really want to make a difference if I can. Do you have some background stuff that I can read to get up to pace on the company?"

"Yeah, I can give you some financial documents when we get on the plane. That'll paint the overall picture for you, if it doesn't put you to sleep first."

"Alex, I'm an accountant," she said smiling. "We get off on stuff like that."

"Oh yeah, I forgot," he said.

"So, are you a big traveller?" asked Alex.

"Not as much as I'd like. I've been to the usual places in Europe; France, Spain and Greece, and I had a trip to the States after I graduated. How about you?"

"Well, I was born in Cyprus, so I guess you could say the first time I went overseas was when I came to London. After that we didn't go anywhere until I started University. There was never the free time, with the restaurant and everything. I travelled around Europe on a rail pass with a mate from University one summer and then just a few short trips here and there."

"I'd have thought Lisa would be dragging you off to exotic locations. I imagine her as a bit of a jet-setter," said Leonna. Alex laughed.

"Lisa's a City Break kind of a girl," he said. "We had a few long weekends. Paris, Barcelona and Copenhagen."

"I'll bet she's jealous that you're going to India." Alex wondered whether he should say anything or just keep up the pretence. In the end, he just said:

"She doesn't know."

"Oh,.....," said Leonna, inducing an awkward pause.

"Lisa and I had a break up a few weeks ago." He was glad to get it out in the end; to finally admit it, to himself as much as anyone else.

"Oh. I'm sorry to hear it," she said, looking up at him.

"Yeah, it's been difficult, but it's probably one of those decisions that we'll understand was right for both of us when we look back on it. That doesn't make it any easier though."

"Relationships can be complicated," said Leonna.

"I don't know, maybe they're not complicated at all," he said. "Maybe when you meet the right person, they're really simple."

"Hmm, perhaps you're right. Maybe it's just life that's complicated."

"Yeah, that could be it," said Alex. "I seem to have one of those complicated lives going on at the moment." She smiled and sipped her coffee.

"Will your friend be meeting us when we get to the airport in Mumbai?"

"No, he emailed me to say that he'll be able to meet us tomorrow morning at the hotel. He's actually the cousin of a friend. I don't know him at all, but he seems to want to help us out if he can. We only have three days so having someone local to help us get about will be a massive help."

"Having someone who can speak the local language will be a help too, I guess," added Leonna.

"Yeah, for sure. I read somewhere that they have around 30 official languages in India. Most people have either Hindi or English as their second language and that allows them to communicate with people from different regions."

"Well, India's somewhere I've always wanted to visit. I'm looking forward to discovering the real Indian food; the colours, tastes, smells. All of it"

"Yeah, just remember that we have a job to do whilst we're there. If there's anything to be uncovered, then we have three days to find it and document the evidence."

"Yes, but we have to eat, right?" she said.

"Yeah, that's true. Maybe we can get our Indian friend to show us some good places. Just try not to post it on social media, if you can avoid it," he said with a smile.

By the time they arrived at the gate, it was pretty crowded and the business class passengers had already been called to board the plane. They made their way on to the plane and found their seats.

"It's about an eight and a half hour flight and it'll be around midnight by the time we get there," said Alex, as he settled into his seat. "It's probably a good idea to stay awake on the flight and we can get on local time straight away."

"In that case, I'd better stay off the free drinks," said Leonna.

"That's probably a good idea." He passed her the Robrex admission document and the presentation for the placing.

"Here, get stuck into this."

"I might need to plug myself into the in-flight entertainment system to get through this," she said, connecting the headphones to the socket in her arm rest.

"Don't worry, I won't take it personally. I'm going to do some work on my laptop but let me know it you stumble across anything interesting."

"Okay, give me a nudge when we arrive," she said with a smile, as she put on her head phones and sank back into her seat.

As they emerged from the Arrivals Hall, it was the heat that hit them first, followed closely by the smell; a mix of sweet spice, car fumes and the sea. The unmistakeable message to the senses that they'd arrived in India.

A line of quirky looking taxis was there to greet them. Each taxi the same; a charmingly simple model with the appearance that it had been designed by a small child in the 1950s. All were painted black with a yellow roof. The driver of the first in line was standing by his taxi and opened the car door and beckoned them towards it.

"This looks like our ride," said Alex and approached the man and handed over his bag. He stored their luggage in the boot and Alex and Leonna climbed into the back of the taxi. They looked at each other and laughed. The interior had a luxuriant fitted carpet in a red and gold floral pattern. Apparently, there'd been a few left-overs, as the same material covered the inside of the doors and the roof as well.

The driver got in and Alex gave him the name of the hotel which he seemed familiar with. It was already 1 o-clock in the morning but the city streets were still alive with traffic and people strolling along the side walks or gathering around the street vendors. Traffic lights seemed to be discretionary rather than obligatory, and their driver took the opportunity to jump a few red lights as he wound his way through the city.

They passed through streets lined with ramshackle shops and shabby looking apartments before gradually the streets became wider and the buildings taller. The street vendors and canopies faded away and were replaced by more uniform shop fronts and tree-lined walkways. Eventually, their taxi pulled into a well lit entrance in front of the curved glass facade of their hotel. Alex settled the bill and they got out of the taxi to be greeted by a young man in a jacket and tie.

"Welcome to the Mumbai Raj," he said and signalled for a porter to take their bags into the lobby. Alex and Leonna followed him towards the entrance.

"Wow, this is a city of contrasts," said Leonna, looking around at the exotic gardens that surrounded the hotel.

"Yeah, I guess that's India for you," said Alex. "1.4 billion people and most of them just trying to make it through the day. Then you have places like this." They entered the lobby and made their way across the polished stone floor to an impressive marble reception desk.

"Hello, we have two rooms booked in the name of Redmead Capital," said Alex to the immaculately presented receptionist behind the desk.

"Yes,..... Mr. Samaras and Ms. May isn't it?" she replied, after consulting the computer screen in front of her. "We have you in two rooms on the 9th floor, overlooking the bay." Alex and Leonna handed over their passports and she completed their check-in. "Would you like us to take your bags up to your rooms?"

"Yes, can we have a look around before we go up?" asked Leonna.

"Of course. I'll have someone deliver the bags to your rooms just now." She handed over the key cards to their rooms.

"Shall we take a tour?" said Leonna.

"Sure," he said. "Sadly, it looks like the bar's closed for the night," he added, as they wandered into the lounge area. They carried on, and out through a pair of glass doors that led to an outdoor terrace. It overlooked the sea and the lights of the city below them.

"So beautiful," said Leonna, leaning against the glass balustrade that ran around the edge of the terrace. Alex couldn't help feeling exactly the same way, although he wasn't looking at the view. The warm light from the hotel illuminated the side of Leonna's face and a light breeze caused her hair to brush gently against her cheek.

Neither of them spoke for a while. Leonna was looking into the distance and seemed to be deep in thought.
"It's amazing to think of all the millions of people out there, isn't it?" she said. "Each of them at the centre of their own individual world, all with their own individual cares and dreams for a better life." Alex gazed out over the sprawling city and all the tiny lights that illuminated it.
"Yeah, every light has its own story," he said, "but I'm not sure we're really that much different from each other. We all basically want the same things I guess."
"And what is it you think we want?" she asked, tilting her head to one side and looking at him curiously.
"Ah, the eternal question," he replied. He thought he could get away with just leaving the question hanging but she wasn't about to let him off the hook.
"Well....?" she said.
"I guess we want to feel that things are getting better in some way."
"So we need to keep striving for more then?" she asked.
"Ah, you mean when is enough, enough?" said Alex. "Good question. I'm not exactly sure but it's probably around the time that you take up Yoga," he said jokingly. Leonna laughed.
"I thought I was going to get a serious answer out of you."

"Sorry, I'll think about it and get back to you. Hey, we better turn in and try to get some sleep. Yash sent me a message to say he'll meet us in the hotel lobby at 09:30.

"Okay, I think I'll just stay a bit longer," said Leonna. "You go on ahead."

"Right, I'll try to make it down for breakfast around 8:30. I'll maybe see you then." He headed inside and left her gazing out over the ocean.

Chapter 19

"The coffee's good. Can I pour you a cup?" said Alex, as Leonna took the seat opposite him.

"Mmm, I think I'm going to need more than just one cup though. I can feel the jet lag coming on," she said, with a bleary-eyed smile. Alex poured out a cup from the elaborate coffee pot that stood amongst the plates of food spread across the table. "Are we expecting guests?" she said, looking at the feast laid out before her.

"Yeah, maybe I did go a bit over the top. You did say you wanted to experience the Indian food didn't you?"

"It looks delicious," she said, and picked out a few delicacies and transferred them to a small plate.

"So, what's the plan for today?"

"Well, the plan, for want of a better word, is to visit the head office and take a look at things. Hopefully, we can speak to someone and understand what kind of work they're doing. Maybe take some photos and with Yash's help we can dig a little deeper into the company's background."

"So do we need to get into 'private detective' mode then?"

"Well, I don't think we'll be working under cover, if that's what you mean. I have a feeling we're going to stand out like a couple of tourists."

"Maybe that's not a bad thing," replied Leonna. "Nobody's going to be surprised that we're taking photos and looking around at everything."

"Yeah, that's true. I guess having Yash around will mean that there'll be nobody offering to be our guide for the day too."

"Have you tried these little potato cakes with the chutney? Just amazing," said Leonna, putting a bite-sized piece into her mouth.

"I made a point of trying everything before you arrived," said Alex, "and I can confirm that it's all amazing. If we had your little Tupperware box with us, I'd be filling it right now for our late morning snack."

"Do you think we should?" said Leonna with a laugh.

"No, but I've lifted a few bottles of mineral water," replied Alex, patting the back pack next to his chair. "It's going to be hot and pretty humid today so I think we'll need them."

They finished up breakfast and walked out into the lobby to await the arrival of Yash. It was only a few minutes before he came through the entrance door, held open by one of the hotel staff. He had that air of confidence that made people hold doors open for him. He looked the part too. Ralph Lauren polo shirt, designer jeans and loafers. Either a Bollywood actor or heir to a large fortune.

"Hey, you must be Alex," he said, holding out his hand. Alex shook his hand and introduced Leonna. "What a beautiful name," he said, seamlessly moving into charm mode.

"Thank you. It comes from Latin and means lion, but don't worry, I don't bite," she said.

"Oh, that's a pity," he said, flashing her a smile. Leonna laughed and Alex began to understand what Ravi meant when he described his cousin.

"Well, shall we get going?" said Yash, "I've got a taxi waiting outside and it should be a little easier on the roads now the rush hour is over." They walked outside into a muggy overcast morning. Yash took the front seat and Alex and Leonna got in the back. "Have you got the address of the company? he asked.

"Here, I've got it on Google Maps," replied Alex, handing him his mobile with the location marked on the city map. Yash had a brief word with the driver in the local dialect, who nodded his head in understanding and they set off.

As they drove towards the central part of the city, the traffic became heavier, despite the worst of the rush hour being behind them. Motor scooters weaved in and out of the lines of cars and pedestrians took their lives in their hands, spilling onto the road and crossing en masse when the opportunity arose. Yash took the opportunity to point out a few landmarks and tell them a little about the history of the city.

"You know Bombay was originally made up of seven islands," he said, casually leaning his arm against the back of the front seat. "The area we're in here used to be under water before the British started to reclaim it in the 19th century."

"Really? I didn't know that," said Alex. "I guess with the population, they needed the extra space."

"Actually, it was more the other way around. Create the land and the people will come to fill it. It's always been an important trading port and people came from the rural areas in search of work."

"Have your family lived here long?" asked Leonna.

"My grandfather was an engineer and he came to work at the docks in the 1950's. The family's been here ever since."

"It looks like an exciting place to live," she said.

"Oh, it is. This is the city that never sleeps. Maybe later I can show you both some of the night life," he said grinning.

"You know, Ravi warned us about you," said Alex. Yash laughed out loud.

"He did? Yeah, I could never get him to stop studying long enough to go on a proper night out."

"Well, if we can get to the bottom of this company research, we'll take you for a night out," said Alex.

"Right, I'll remember you said that," replied Yash, pointing a finger at Alex.

After a few minutes, they came to a down town area with a number of high rise towers and other purpose-built office buildings. Yash indicated that they were somewhere close to their destination. He got the driver to pull over alongside an old art deco building with a large bill board over the entrance. A beautiful girl from a Bollywood movie looked defiantly down on them, hands on hips, against a backdrop of dancers in colourful costumes.

"I think it's one block over from here, but it'll be easier to walk," said Yash. Alex and Leonna climbed out onto the wide pavement. They were immediately hit by the heat and the noise and bustle of the street. There was something organic about it all. The noise and smells and everybody on the move in a manner of organised chaos. Yash joined them and pointed down a side road.

"This way, I think," he said, and led them down a street lined with canopies over the first floor shops and eating establishments. They made their way along the busy road and came out into a small square with a large tree in the central space casting some welcome shade. "I suppose it's that building over there," said Yash, pointing to a five storey office building on the far side of the square. It was one of the more modern buildings that surrounded the square, concrete construction with lines of tinted windows running along each floor. Alex could just make out the Robrex logo above the entrance.

"Yes, that looks like it," he said. "Well, at least we know it exists now." They walked around to the building and stopped near the entrance, trying not to be too conspicuous. "Do you think they occupy the whole building?" asked Alex.

"Let me go in and ask someone," said Yash. "I can say I'm looking for office space in the area."

"Okay, we'll take a few photos in the meantime," said Alex. Yash walked confidently into the reception area whilst Alex and Leonna looked for the best locations to take photos of the building.

After they'd finished, there was still no sign of Yash near the building entrance. With the day getting hotter all the time, they retreated to the shade of the central part of the square. There were some old metal benches that ran along one side of the space and they sat down and shared a bottle of water.

"Do you think he's negotiating to buy the building?" asked Alex.

"You know, I wouldn't put it past him," said Leonna. "He doesn't lack confidence."

"Yeah, I think we really landed on our feet hooking up with Yash. He's going to be such a help."

Eventually, Leonna spotted him coming out of the building clutching some papers and looking around for them. She caught his attention with a wave and he came over to join them with a broad smile on his face. Alex smiled back at him.

"Well, this should be interesting," he said.

"Come on, let's go and get a cup of tea and I'll tell you what I've learned.

They found a small cafe just off the square. A couple of rotating ceiling fans provided some relief from the heat. They sat around one of the small tables that were randomly placed across the tiled floor and Yash organised three cups of Chai tea. With his audience waiting expectantly, he began to relate the events of the morning.

"Well, I found out they're using the bottom four floors. The top floor is mostly empty, and it was our lucky day. They're actually trying to find someone to rent it so I got the guided tour from the office manager."

"Great, what did he tell you?" asked Alex.

"He said they were sub-letting the whole of the fifth floor, but there'd be no problem with the landlord who'd agreed everything with them."

"Wait a minute. They said they were sub-letting it? They don't own the freehold?"

"No, they have a long term lease apparently," replied

Yash. Alex looked at Leonna.

"Didn't it say they own the freehold in the documents for Robrex's reverse takeover?"

"Yes, I'm sure it did. The freehold property was a major part of the net asset value of the company," she said.

"Well, that'll be something of interest to Jamie," said Alex. "Did you find out the name of the landlord?" he asked.

"No, I didn't. I asked him, but he didn't want to give me that information. I got the impression they have quite a close relationship."

"The manager gave me these copies of the office plans with dimensions of the floor space, and this is his business card," said Yash, placing them on the table. Alex picked up the business card. It had the familiar Robrex logo in one corner and the office manager's name, *Anil R. Prasad*, printed across the card. The address and contact details were underneath and then in fine print along the bottom of the card was written, *'Mumbai Techcom Group Ltd.'*

"What's this company at the bottom?" asked Alex. Leonna took the card from him and examined it herself.

"Isn't that the name of the original company that took over Robrex?" she said, looking up at him.

"Yes, I think you're right, but why would they still be using the old name when they've become Robrex?"

"Yes, my understanding of a reverse takeover is that the private company merges into the public company and so no longer exists as a legal entity," she said.

"Yeah, I could understand if they were using the old private company name as a trading name, but this is a limited company name."

"Yash, you've done a brilliant job. It feels like we've got something to work on here," said Alex. "I'd still like to try to talk to someone myself in the company if I can. Do you think I'd be able to get in to see someone if I presented myself as looking for IT work?" Yash looked a little sceptical.

"It might be better to let them think you're a potential customer. Indian companies are always interested in new overseas customers. They usually pay better," he said.

"Okay, I'll say I'm looking to outsource some IT work. I still have some of my trusty old business cards that'll do the job. Yash, why don't you take Leonna over to the company's other office in Mumbai this afternoon and find out what you can. We can meet up in the square later and have a debrief." They nodded in agreement.

They took the chance to grab a light lunch in the cafe. Yash ordered some chapattis with a lentil curry and various pickles and chutneys that they could all help themselves to. Suitably refreshed, they ventured outside again into the midday heat. The streets had become busy with office workers taking their lunch breaks and the spicy smells from the street vendors filled the air. They walked over to a shady part of the square.

"Well, wish me luck," said Alex.

"We'll give you five minutes shall we?" said Leonna. "If you don't come out, we'll know you've managed to see someone." Alex nodded and headed over to the building.

There was a welcome rush of cool air from the air conditioning that greeted Alex as he entered the building. The reception area was off to one side and a young woman stood up from behind the reception desk and smiled as he approached. Alex handed her one of his business cards.

"Hello, I work for a British software company, based in London. I'm trying to make contact with companies in the IT sector here in India that we might be able to use for outsourcing. Is there somebody I could speak to?"

"I see, Mr. Samaras Sir," she said looking at his card. "Do you mean for your Call Centre Sir?"

"Well, that's one possibility," replied Alex.

"Please wait one moment Sir," she said and picked up the

phone. After a brief discussion, she replaced the phone and invited Alex to take a seat in one of the chairs along the side wall.

A few minutes later, a young man in a suit and tie emerged from the lift. Alex rose from his seat to greet him and they shook hands.

"My name is Chandra," he said, handing Alex a business card with a bow of his head. "I'm the call centre assistant manager. I'm afraid the manager is not in the office right now, but I hope I will be able to assist you."

"Well, thank you for giving me your time," replied Alex and passed him his own business card, trying to replicate the same level of respect and formality.

"Shall we go to my office?" said Mr. Chandra, and he led them to the lift.

They came out on the 4th floor to a pretty typical open plan office space. Lines of desks back-to-back, each with it's own young occupant wearing a head set and with a foot firmly on the first rung of the corporate ladder. The assistant manager showed Alex into his office and offered him a seat next to a small coffee table. He brought another chair from behind his desk and placed it opposite. "Would you like a cup of tea Mr. Samaras?"

After he'd poured out two cups of chai tea from a small pot next to his desk, Alex asked him to outline the kind of services that the company could provide. He gave a pretty thorough explanation of their technology and telecommunications and laid a lot of emphasis on their recruitment and training of staff. They only employed university graduates with high levels of English. This was what differentiated their company from the rest.

"So, your company is predominantly a call centre specialist. Are there any other IT services that you provide?" asked Alex.

"We have an IT centre that supports all our customers. That's based in our office in Chennai," said Mr. Chandra.

"And do they develop your own software?", asked Alex. The Assistant manager was a little hesitant.

"That's not really my area of expertise but I could have someone contact you when we have a better idea of your requirements."

"Right, sure," said Alex.

They talked a little longer and then the assistant manager offered to give Alex a tour of the office. He showed him the various teams that they'd established to support each of their major customers. Clusters of monitors were hung from the ceiling, each showing a flag to denote the customer's country and the local time and weather details underneath.

"This is one of our customers in London," said Mr. Chandra. "They're supported by our London office."

"Right, that's been operating since your UK stockmarket listing, hasn't it?" Mr. Chandra seemed a little confused.

"No, we don't have a stockmarket listing in the UK, just an overseas branch office," he said.

"What? You don't have a UK listing?" he said.

"No, we're a private company here in India," replied Mr. Chandra, matter-of-factly.

"Oh right. I.....er, guess I must have misunderstood."

Alex was completely thrown by it for a moment. Was it even possible that they didn't know they were a UK public listed company? It just didn't make sense. Could he just be unaware of it; such a fundamental aspect of the company's structure? He hadn't shown the slightest doubt in his understanding. He just calmly walked on ahead, continuing their tour of the office.

Alex followed on behind him, thankful for the chance to regain a little of his composure. Had he misheard him? No, he was quite clear that they were a private company. That could only mean one thing; that the directors were keeping the reality from the rest of the staff; but for what reason?

They went through the remaining parts of the organization but Alex was barely listening to what his guide was saying by then. He just couldn't shake off this latest revelation. Eventually, Mr Chandra accompanied him to the first floor and they shook hands at the entrance. Alex promised to get back in touch after speaking to his director and thanked him for his time. There was a twinge of guilt at the deception, but he was here to get answers. It had been a useful meeting.

As he left the building, it seemed that he had another piece of the jigsaw; one that, in time, would reveal a little more of the picture. It felt like he'd moved a step closer.

Chapter 20

Alex had been sitting for about half an hour on the bench in the shade of the square. He'd already been through another bottle of water and was contemplating going back to the cafe to get out of the heat for a while when his phone rang. It was Leonna.

"Hi Alex. How did it go?"
"Well, I had a good chat with one of the managers and he gave me the guided tour of their Call Centre. Strangely, he didn't seem to be aware that he worked for a UK listed company. There's definitely something going on here."
"Yes, and I think we may be getting closer to understanding exactly what it is," she replied.
"Really? Tell me more," said Alex.
"Well, we went to the other office and Yash managed to chat up a couple of the call centre girls when they were outside on a break. He asked them about the company name and why it was different from Robrex. They said that the company started using Robrex as a trading name at the same time they changed their name from Mumbai Techcom Ltd to Mumbai Techcom Group Ltd."
"They changed the name?" said Alex.
"I'm not sure they did," she said. "I had another look through the Robrex takeover document and the company that merged with Robrex was Mumbai Techcom Ltd. So if they're continuing to trade under this 'Group' name, then what exactly does Robrex do?"

Alex was silent for a few seconds whilst he took in the significance of this latest news.
"I think this is beginning to make sense," he said. "How do we find out the details of this name change or whatever it is?"

"We're on our way to Yash's office. He's going to look into the details from the Companies Register that he can access from work. Can you get a taxi and meet us there?"

"Sure. Can you get Yash to send me a link with the location and I'll get there as soon as I can."

Alex only had to wait a moment before the tone on his phone announced that he'd got the link from Yash. He walked back up to the main road that they'd come in on and hailed a taxi. Not all the taxis in Mumbai boasted air conditioning and this one relied on a couple of open windows to generate some kind of ventilation. Alex had full exposure to the sounds and smells of the roads as they made their way through the city to the government office where Yash worked. Cars and motorcycles honked at each other at every opportunity and the smell of exhaust fumes filled the air.

They arrived at a wide avenue and the driver pointed to a large modernist building that was set back from the road. Alex asked him to drop him off near the entrance. The driver carried out a deft U-turn manoeuvre to pull alongside two white pillars that marked the main approach to the building.

Alex paid the driver and got out of the taxi. He looked around but there was no sign of Leonna and Yash so he walked up to the large revolving doors at the entrance to the building. They led into a substantial reception space with a high ceiling. He heard Leonna call his name. She was sitting on a bench seat alongside one wall and he walked over to join her.

"Where's Yash?" he asked.

"He's just gone to get us a couple of visitor passes," she replied. "Here he comes." Yash came through the security gate holding the two passes, each contained within a plastic case.

"Here, you'll need these to get through to my department, I told my boss you're the founders of a Start-up that's opening an overseas office here. He thinks I'm talking you through the regulations and set-up process."

"And all this on your day off?" quipped Alex.

"Well, he knows how dedicated I am to my job," replied Yash with a grin.

They followed him past the reception desk and took the lift to the fifth floor. The building had that rather tired and unloved feel that's familiar to most government buildings. Everything looked like it could do with a make-over, or more likely, another coat of off-white paint to keep it going.

They walked down a narrow corridor to a pair of swing doors at the end with a sign marked, *'Development Planning.'* They entered into a large open plan office with rows of desks, each piled high with files surrounding its over-worked incumbent.

"Wow, that's what I call a lot of paperwork," said Leonna, looking around at the heaving desks.

Yash led them over to his desk by the window, slapping a couple of backs on the way, and exchanging greetings with colleagues. Everybody seemed glad to see him. He borrowed two chairs from a meeting table close by and set them in front of his uniquely clear desk and the flat screen monitor.

"So, what's your secret?", asked Alex. "You seem to be the only one on top of the work here." Yash tapped the side of his nose with his finger, knowingly.

"Delegation," he said. Alex cracked a smile. Yes, it wouldn't be long before he was running this place, he thought.

They all sat around the monitor and Yash logged on to the government intranet.

"We can access the Companies Register. That will give us the information about when the company was set up and any name changes. Then we can look at the annual financial statements."

"Right, shall we start with the company that merged into

Robrex," suggested Alex.

Yash entered the name, *Mumbai Techcom Ltd* into the search window.

"Have you got the Robrex takeover document Leonna?" asked Alex. "We can check the details against what they submitted in the document." She retrieved it from the folder in her bag. Yash started to read out the key details from the screen. It all matched with the takeover document. Yash accessed the financial statements that had been submitted on an annual basis. The final full year of trading matched exactly what was included in the take over document.

"Well, that all seems to check out," said Alex. "Now, how about this group company?" Yash entered the name and the registration details came up on his screen. The company was formed in the same year as Mumbai Techcom Ltd and the directors and shareholders were the same.

"If it's a holding company, there should be consolidated accounts showing the relationship with any subsidiaries," said Leonna.

"Okay, let me check the financial statements," said Yash and he opened the documents in a separate window. There was a balance sheet noting the share capital of the company and some minor cash elements but no apparent trading income or consolidated accounts.

"So, it's not actually a holding company then," said Alex.

"I suppose it's not," replied Yash. "No, wait a minute, the law changed a few years ago. Before that, private company accounts didn't have to show related parties. Let me check the later statements."

"Can you pull up the last three years?" asked Alex. "That'll show us before and after the Robrex takeover."

Yash opened the first of the documents and nodded his head with a smile.

"There it is," he said. Mumbai Techcom Group Ltd was

listed as the holding company and Mumbai Techcom Ltd as its subsidiary. The consolidated accounts included the property ownership in the balance sheet and a full profit and loss statement for the subsidiary's trading.

"So, how about the next year, after the Robrex takeover," asked Alex. Yash pulled up the relevant documents and, on the face of it, everything looked pretty similar. Except the difference was, these were not consolidated accounts. They were the financial statements for the holding company which had now taken on all the trading activity of its subsidiary.

"Well, that's it then," said Alex. "They restructured the company. Judging from the balance sheet, they stripped out the assets from the subsidiary and transferred everything to the 'Group' company. Which means of course, that they took over the Robrex shell company with another worthless shell company." Alex shook his head and laughed. "You know what the really funny thing is? That worthless public listed company is currently my biggest holding."

"I think it might be a good time to sell, Alex," said Yash.

"Yeah, I'm working on it," replied Alex with a wry smile.

"You know, it looks like the property's been sold," said Leonna, who'd been looking at the balance sheet in more detail. "Here, there's a figure that roughly matches the book value of the property but it's under receivables."

"Shouldn't it be a cash item if they've sold it?" said Alex.

"Well, not if they haven't received payment yet. It's possible that it's being paid for in instalments," she said.

"We could really do with getting the details of the property ownership," said Alex. "We can see pretty clearly what's going on here, but from a legal perspective it's still circumstantial. The property is specifically mentioned in the takeover document. If we can follow the ownership trail, we can prove absolutely that it's a fraud. Is there a way we can check it Yash?"

"We need to search the Land Registry," he said. "I don't have access to it on this computer. I'd need to speak to someone I know in another department. Wait, let me see if I can reach him."

Yash flicked through his contacts on his phone and leaned back in his chair. After a few seconds, his face broke into a broad grin as the phone connected.

"Hey Qasim," he said. There then followed one of those strange conversations in the local Indian dialect, but punctuated with words or short phrases in English. From what Alex could gather, it seemed to be mostly about partying and night clubs. Nevertheless, by the time he'd finished, Yash seemed to have reached some sort of agreement.

He returned his phone to his pocket and looked over to Alex and Leonna who were waiting expectantly.

"Well, I can't do it today. He's dealing with something urgent, but he said I can use his desk tomorrow afternoon for an hour or so." Alex looked at Leonna and shrugged.

"That should be okay. We still have another day," he said.

"Yes, thanks Yash. I'm not sure how we'd have done this without your help," added Leonna.

"Well, he owes me a favour, and I said I'd introduce him to a couple of girls I know." Leonna and Alex looked at each other and exchanged a smile.

"Hey Yash, do you think you'd be able to print off copies of the documents we've looked through today? We need to take back something that confirms all that we've uncovered."

"How about if I export them as pdf files and you can have them on a USB drive. Will that do?".

"That would be ideal," said Alex.

Yash quickly pulled everything together and transferred it to a spare drive that he had in a drawer of his desk.

"Thanks a lot Yash. Now, how about if we treat you to dinner somewhere? Leonna really wants to discover the authentic Indian food." Yash raised his eyebrows.

"Really? I know the perfect little place that serves the best vada pav in Bombay," he said. "It's the Indian burger. When you taste this with their chutneys, you'll never eat anything else."

"Well, what are we waiting for?" said Leonna.

When they came out of the building, the sun was lower in the sky and the fierce heat of the day had relented. There was a warm glow over the street but the traffic seemed as busy as ever. Alex turned the USB drive over in his fingers in his trouser pocket. There was a sense of relief that they finally had something that amounted to evidence. It felt like some of the pressure of the trip had abated. If they could just confirm the property ownership tomorrow, they'd be able to go back with a feeling that it was job done.

Yash hailed a taxi and Alex and Leonna got into the back seats.

"I'm suddenly feeling hungry," said Alex.

"Me too," she said.

Chapter 21

Alex found Leonna reading a book on a lounger by the hotel pool. She wore a pair of loose cotton pants that looked like a long summer skirt as she reclined back in the seat. A slim arm stretched out from the sleeveless top to hold the book open in front of her face. Her other arm supported her head as she absently wound the end of her hair around her fingers. She hadn't seen him approach and he stood there for a moment just looking at her. If he was a painter or a sculptor, he'd have captured that moment, he thought to himself.

Eventually, she seemed to sense his presence and she looked up from her book, shading her eyes from the morning sun.
"Oh, good morning," she said with a warm smile. "Did you get some breakfast?"
"Just a cup of tea and some toast. How about you?"
"I just couldn't face it this morning, We ate so much last night, I feel like I need a day off to recover."
"Yeah, I know what you mean, but it was amazing food wasn't it. Yash wasn't kidding about that place."

Alex sat down on the edge of a recliner next to her and placed the laptop he was holding on the seat.
"What are you reading?" he asked.
"Oh, it's just some trashy romantic thriller," she said, turning the book to show him the cover.
"Has she got her man yet?" Leonna laughed.
"No, not yet, but there's a certain inevitability about it. Are you doing some work on your laptop?"
"I've just been checking up on a few things," he replied. "Our favourite share seems to be oblivious to the fact that it's a worthless pile of garbage and made a new all-time high yesterday."
"Can you not sell up?"

"I'd like to, but Jamie's company hold mine and Matt's shares until the next trading update in a week or so. That's the earliest we can sell."

"That must be a bit nerve wracking," she said.

"Yeah, it is, especially as I might need the money pretty soon. I got an email from the lender I was hoping would refinance the restaurant and they're offering less than we need."

Leonna closed her book and sat up facing Alex.

"I hope things work out, I know how much the restaurant means to you Alex."

"It's not so much for me, but for my Dad and my brother, Jack. They're the ones who have invested all the time and energy. It would crush my Dad if the restaurant went under."

"Can't you negotiate over whatever debts are outstanding; give yourself some more time?"

"No, that's not really feasible. I didn't tell you the full story before. The truth is, my Dad borrowed some money from the wrong kind of people and they're looking for their pound of flesh. If we don't find a way out of it now, then he'll probably lose everything."

"That's so unfair," she said.

"Yeah, it is isn't it," replied Alex, pursing his lips. "People like my Dad, they don't understand the complexities of financing and accountancy. They just start a small business, work hard and trust people. Then they end up trusting the wrong people."

Leonna stood up and gave him her best smile.

"Come on, let's not dwell on it. These things have a way of working out. We've got a free morning and the receptionist told me there's a nice walk along the edge of the bay."

Not for the first time, Alex felt glad she was there with him. They packed up their stuff and dropped off Alex's laptop in the hotel.

"I agreed with Yash that we'd meet him at his office

around 3pm," said Alex, as they headed out of the main entrance. A man in a spotless white uniform held the door open for them.

"Great, I made a note of a few interesting sights that we can take in nearby."

"Show me the way," he said, and they headed out into the hazy sunshine.

It was good to have some time to take in a bit of the city; to be tourists for just a morning. They visited a memorial garden dedicated to Gandhi and walked along the wide esplanade that followed the edge of the bay. It felt like the front window of Mumbai, the city skyline stretching out before them and the palm trees giving it that tropical feel. They stopped for an iced tea and just spent time people watching whilst sitting under the shade of the palms.

They still had some time to spare when the taxi pulled up alongside Yash's office building. Alex called to tell him they'd arrived and they walked up to the front of the building. Unlike the previous day, the reception area was crowded and bustling, almost like a street market. Whole families seemed to have come together and were huddled around the bench seating or queuing at each of the reception windows.

"Lucky we have a direct line to our man on the inside," said Alex, leading them over to a place where they could be seen near the security gate.

"People don't seem very happy about something," said Leonna, looking over at the animated conversations taking place with the officials at the front of the queues.

After a couple of minutes, they spotted Yash and he beckoned them over to the gate. Before they could move though, several people pushed forward and demanded his attention. He did his best to calm them down, but in the end he had to summon a security guard to hold them back from the gate to allow Alex and Leonna to slip through.

"What's that all about?" asked Alex as they made their way to the lift.

"Oh, they just announced that they're planning to clear an area of the slums for re-development. As usual, the people who live there are the last to be consulted."

"Yeah, I guess if my home was about to be bulldozed, I'd probably be at the front of that queue," replied Alex.

"We need to go to the Land Survey office. It's on the third floor," said Yash. The lift doors opened to the same nondescript interior as Yash's floor and they made their way along a corridor to a similar pair of swing doors. These ones were marked, *'Land and Property Management.'*

They entered into a space that resembled a particularly untidy library. Metal-frame bookshelves were lined up in rows, heaving with a mix of binders, box files and large manilla envelopes.

"It's this way," said Yash, leading them through a gap in the shelving. It led to an open plan office beyond. Yash waved to a young guy in a light blue shirt who was talking on the phone and he nodded his acknowledgement After a couple of minutes, he finished the call and came over.

"Hey Qasim, my friend, I owe you one," said Yash, putting his hand on his shoulder. Qasim laughed.

"What only one? I thought you said you were going to introduce me to two girls." Alex and Leonna laughed too. They introduced themselves and Qasim led them over to a secluded desk that was screened from the main office.

"I think it's better if you use this other terminal. We use this for research and it's a bit more private," he said.

He booted up the terminal and logged in to give them access to the database.

"The boss is in a meeting for the rest of the afternoon, so nobody's going to bother you. If anyone asks, Yash, just tell them you're doing some research for me." Yash gave him a friendly slap on the back and Qasim left them to it and headed back to his desk.

Yash sat down in front of the monitor. There were a couple of stools that Alex and Leonna pulled up to sit either side of him. "Okay, give me the address of the head office," he said. Leonna had the takeover document ready and she flicked through the appendices to find the list of properties purported to be owned by Mumbai Techcom Ltd.
"Here it is," she said, and placed it on the desk indicating the address with her finger. He entered the postcode and a list of coordinates appeared on the screen.
"This is a crazy system. I have to copy the coordinates and then find the plan for that area. That will give me a reference number to search for the ownership. Designed by idiots," he said.

Yash worked his way through a series of unconnected plans before he found what he was looking for.
"That's it, isn't it," he said, sitting back in the chair.
"Yes, we walked down this road to the square, didn't we. So, it should be this building here, right?" said Alex.
"That's right, there was a building on the corner and it was the one next to it, wasn't it," added Leonna.

Yash copied the reference number that was typed over the footprint of the building and exited the application.
"Okay, now maybe we can get somewhere," he said. He opened up another window and entered the reference number. A page opened listing a description of the property and identifying the tenure as, freehold.

"It says the current owners are a company called, S.I. Holdings Ltd. Ownership was transferred from their subsidiary, K.P. Digital Ltd, earlier this year." Alex and Leonna looked at each other.
"Well, the plot thickens," said Alex.

"Do you know this company?" asked Yash.

"K.P. Digital was the company that was recently bought by Robrex," said Leonna. "I think we're beginning to see a pattern here."

"Can we trace the ownership back to Mumbai Techcom Ltd?" asked Alex. "We need to know the dates and parties of each transfer of title."

"Okay, let me see. This is totally crazy. I have to go back out now and find the reference numbers for the earlier transfers of title."

After a few minutes, Yash had located the relevant pages.

"Right, here it is. Ownership was transferred from Mumbai Techcom to the 'Group' company about 3 years ago."

"Yes, right before the takeover of Robrex," added Alex.

"Then, just a month later, the property was sold to K.P. Digital for about 250 million rupees."

"How much is that in UK pounds?" asked Leonna.

"It's about £2.5 million," he replied.

"That's roughly the book value that was shown in the takeover document," she said. "Did they pay in full?"

"No, it says here a 10% deposit was paid at the time of sale."

"So, it was a sale and lease-back," said Alex, "and what's the betting the instalments on the purchase match the lease payments for the rental. That way, they just transfer the ownership and shuffle the money backwards and forwards between the two companies."

"I can check the accounts later and see," said Leonna.

"So, it seems they pulled the same trick twice then," said Alex. "First, they stripped the property from Mumbai Techcom and reversed it into the Robrex listed company, with the assets still shown on the balance sheet. Then they did the same with K.P. Digital before selling it to Robrex."

"We need to check the beneficial shareholders of S.I. Holdings Ltd," said Leonna. "That seems to be where the money ends up."

"Yes, you're right," said Alex. "Could we copy those land registry pages onto the USB drive, Yash? And, is there any chance we could do the same for the other freehold properties?" he said, hopefully.

"I was afraid you were going to say that," said Yash with a wry smile. "This is going to take a bit of time. Do you want to get a drink or something? There's a drinks machine near the elevator."

Alex and Leonna made their way back to the lift and found the drinks machine tucked into a small space by the window. They bought a couple of bottles of iced tea and sat down on the wide window sill that improvised as an informal seat. Alex took a long drink from the bottle and exhaled slowly.

"Well, I think we know the whole story now," said Leonna.

"Yeah, I don't think even Jamie will be expecting more from this trip than we've achieved. We've got pretty much all that we need to demonstrate this whole thing is a fraud." Leonna took a sip from her bottle.

"What amazes me is that, if we've been able to uncover all this, then why has nobody else done the same?" Alex shrugged his shoulders.

"I think most people just make the assumption that they don't need to bother. They expect that if a company's listed on a major stock exchange, there must be checks in place that prevent this sort of fraud. Investors always want to believe a good story. You'd be amazed at what people will turn a blind eye to."

"Well, I doubt we would have got this far without Yash," she said.

"That's for sure. I guess we owe him a night out. What do you think? Are you up for it?" She gave him a sideways glance and smiled.

"Well, I suppose it is our last night. Okay, let's see what this city has to offer."

They finished off their drinks and made their way back to see how Yash was getting on.

"Find anything interesting?" asked Alex, as they came back to the terminal. Yash was leaning forward at the desk, busy copying documents onto the USB drive. He stopped and sat back in the chair stretching the stiffness out of his arms.

"Well, it's as we expected with the other properties. They all changed ownership along with the head office on the same dates. No surprise there. After that, I had a look at this company, S.I. Holdings Ltd. The directors are different from those at Mumbai Techcom, but I did a search on the names. They came up on a couple of old companies that went into liquidation. And guess what? The Mumbai Techcom CEO was a fellow director of both companies." Alex clapped him on the shoulder.

"That's brilliant Yash. He's now the CEO of the UK-listed Robrex company. We've got evidence that ties him right the way back to the money."

Yash finished transferring image files of the relevant documents onto the USB drive and removed it from the computer port.

"Don't lose this," he said, as he passed it to Alex. "I'd hate to have to go through all that again." Alex gratefully took it from him and slipped into his pocket.

"Thanks Yash. You're an absolute star," he said. "We were just saying how we could never have uncovered all this without you." Yash gave a shrug to make light of it, but the smile on his face revealed the sense of satisfaction he was feeling.

"Hey, it's our last night," said Leonna. "Alex and I were wondering if we could take you for a night out. Would you be able to make it?" Yash laughed.

"I can always make it. It might be better though, if I take you. This is my city and I know all the best places."

"That sounds like a better idea, but we'll pay, right?" said

Alex.

"Sure," he said. "I'll give you a night to remember."

Yash got up and touched base with Qasim before joining Alex and Leonna and leading them back to the lift.

"I need to deal with a few things in the office, but why don't I meet you somewhere later? There's a fun place near your hotel. I can send you a link. Is 7pm OK?" Alex and Leonna looked at each other and nodded.

"Yeah, that'd be great," said Alex.

They said their goodbyes at the lift and Alex and Leonna made their way back to the reception.

The sun was just setting by the time they left for the venue Yash had suggested. It was an easy walk from the hotel and they were able to enjoy the sight of the sun going down over the city skyline. The hazy orange ball casting golden rippling reflections across the bay.

The place was a couple of blocks back from the ocean front and had a quirky ramshackle frontage. It was designed to look like it had somehow emerged from the city slums, rather than the more upmarket neighbourhood where it was located. A security guard dressed all in black opened the door for them.

Yash was already there when they walked in. He'd installed himself at the bar and was in animated conversation with one of the the barmen. He greeted them with open arms and introduced them to his friends behind the bar. They ordered some cocktails and clinked glasses to toast the success of the past two days.

"Are you working tomorrow?" asked Leonna. Yash nodded as he took a sip of his rum cocktail. "I don't know how you do it," she said.

"Oh, I just start with two cocktails and then it's mocktails all the way," he said, with a grin.

"Ah, non-alcoholic. That's a smart idea. I might join you."

"Great, someone to carry me home," said Alex. Leonna laughed.

"No, I'll just dump you in a taxi," she said.

"Okay, I promise to go easy."

"So, what's the plan for tonight, Yash?" asked Alex. Yash put his glass down on the bar and raised his hands as though asking for his audience's attention.

"Okay, what I thought is, first we can have a couple of drinks here, just to get in the mood. Then I'll take you to another bar near here. They have pool tables, good music and lots of cute girls." Alex and Leonna caught each other's eye and suppressed a smile. "After that, we can take a taxi to a live music place I know and then we'll finish off at a night club on the bay. They have the best D.J.s in town. What do you think?"

"Wow, that's not my average Thursday night," said Alex, "but you're the boss." They all raised their glasses again and toasted Yash's epic plan.

By the time they'd reached the night club, with the ceiling lights pulsating to the music, Alex had that Bollywood dance beat reverberating through his whole body. The place was packed and they joined the throng of humanity that moved as one on the dance floor. It was just a total release for Alex. It felt like all the stresses that he seemed to be carrying with him were just melting away as he lost himself in the music.

Eventually, Leonna tapped him on the shoulder and pointed over towards the area that they'd come in. Alex followed her and they squeezed their way off the dance floor. She turned around and smiled, her face flushed and strands of her hair matted against her temples. She cupped her hand against his ear.

"I think I'm done. Do you want to get some air?"

"Yeah, let's find Yash and tell him we're making a move," he said.

They found him entertaining a couple of girls up near the bar. He greeted them like long lost friends. Alex had to stop him from getting in another round of drinks.

"Yash, I think we're going to head back to the hotel. We can walk back along the sea front," he said.

"I was going to show you some great street food," he said, in one last effort to keep the party alive. Alex and Leonna laughed.

"We don't have your stamina Yash," said Leonna, "but it's been a night to remember."

They managed to finally say their goodbyes and thank him for everything, amid promises to entertain him in London whenever he came over. They left him to his two latest admirers and headed out of the hotel.

It was still warm but there was a welcome breeze coming off the bay as they joined the esplanade that would lead them back to their hotel. In spite of the late hour, there were still groups of people clustered around the street vendors and couples walking along the sea front. Some were sitting on the wide concrete sea wall that lined the edge of the bay and Leonna suggested they sit for a while and take it all in. They could hear the sound of the water lapping against the shore and could make out the distant lights of passing ships in the deep blackness. Behind them the city that never sleeps and in front, a vast emptiness.

"I really needed this trip. I'm glad I came," she said, turning her head and smiling at him.

"I'm glad you came," said Alex, holding her gaze. The alcohol and the euphoria of the music had wiped away any inhibitions. In that moment, he didn't care about having the wrong idea or misreading the situation. He just wanted to let her know how he felt. The smile slowly ebbed away from her face.

"Are you?" she asked. He didn't need to reply. They just kissed. Slowly at first and gradually with more urgency. Leonna had to stop it from going too far. They climbed down from the wall and headed back towards the hotel. All of a sudden, it seemed like the city and the ocean had faded away and all Alex could see was the girl who's hand he was holding.

Chapter 22

Alex slipped carefully out of the bed so as not to wake her. The room was a mirror image of his own, but with a subtly different colour palette to the walls and furnishings. He found his boxer shorts and T-shirt amongst the clothes strewn across the floor. He put them on before picking up the rest of the clothes and placing them on the chair by the bed. Leonna stirred and half opened her eyes. A smile crept into the corners of her mouth and she slowly stretched out an arm from under the duvet towards him. Alex took her long slender fingers in his hand and smiled back at her.

"Is it time to get up?" she asked.
"We've got a bit of time yet," he said. She gave him a contented smile.
"Well, I think we should make the most of it then." Alex laughed and sat on the edge of the bed. He leant down and kissed her mouth, gently at first. As each kiss became longer and deeper, she wrapped an arm around his neck and drew him forward. They made love again. This time, slower than before, with less hunger and more desire to savour the moment.

They both lay back in the bed, their heads side by side on the pillow. They lay there for a while, motionless, with the quiet hum of the air conditioning the only sound. Eventually, Leonna turned her head towards him.

"I wish we could stay here."
"Yeah, shall I text Jamie and tell him we need another week?"
"No, I mean stay here much longer. Go backpacking around the country and head back in about a year or so. By then, everyone will have forgotten about me." Alex shifted his head on the pillow to look at her but she was now looking

up at the ceiling. He knew what she meant. It was the elephant in the room. The fact that she was in a relationship with somebody else.

"Leonna, I don't know anything about your relationship with Stephen, I just know what I feel for you," he said. She turned onto her side and buried her face into the side of his chest. He put his arm around her and they lay there without speaking for a while.
"I don't think he'll take it well," she said eventually. "Stephen's someone who usually gets what he wants. It's difficult to say no to him."
"Well, I understand it's not what he wants to hear, but there needs to be two people on board to make a relationship work." She nodded her head.
"I know. I'm just not looking forward to having to deal with it, that's all."

They remained in bed for a while longer, both of them deep in their own thoughts. Alex glanced at the digital clock below the TV screen.
"We have to check out in about 40 minutes. I better go and sort my stuff out."
"I guess we've missed breakfast then," said Leonna, stretching her arms above her head.
"Yeah, we can grab a coffee at the bar once we've checked out," he replied.

Alex summoned the energy to get out of bed and found his clothes from the previous night. He quickly got dressed and turned to see Leonna watching him, her head propped up by one arm.
"Okay, I'm going to get a shower. I'll give you a knock in half an hour or so," he said. She smiled and nodded. "Are you going to get up?" he asked.
"Just five more minutes," she said, and sank back into the duvet. He went over to her and gave her a kiss, one of those long ones where you both end up smiling before it's

finished. Finally, it felt like something in his life was on the right track.

They checked out and left the bags with the front desk. They still had more than an hour before they needed to take a taxi to the airport. They wandered through to the hotel lounge and ordered coffee and pastries which were served to them at one of the tables overlooking the terrace.

"I'm going to give Matt a call," said Alex. "I just want to let him know what's going on with the Robrex investment. I got a text message from him earlier and it sounded like he was getting a bit anxious." Alex dialled his number and strolled out onto the terrace.

The sun was already high in the sky and it was another warm day. He walked over to the side of the terrace that was shaded by a group of palm trees and leaned against the balustrade. After a few rings, the call connected to Matt's familiar voice.
"Well, hello stranger."
"Have you missed me?" replied Alex.
"No, but I was beginning to think you'd run off with my money," Alex laughed.
"Do you want the good news or the bad news?" he asked.
"Go on, give me the bad news and let's get it out of the way,"
"Well, the bad news is that Robrex is worthless."
"So what's the good news?"
"The good news is, we're the only ones who know it." There was a brief pause as he took it in.
"And we're stuck in this turkey of a share until when?" he asked.
"Jamie thinks there'll be a trading update in the next week or so and that's the earliest we can exit."

"You know, I think we should at least give the heads up

to Carlo and Seb, and maybe the other guys on the conference call," said Matt. Alex interrupted him.

"Wait. Jamie was pretty clear that he didn't want us to share anything with anybody at this stage. It only takes one person to let it slip and the news will be around the whole market."

"Yeah, but I think we owe it to those guys," said Matt. "We were the ones who got them into this investment and they've got an easy opportunity to get out, and with a really nice profit." Alex thought about it for a few seconds.

"I just don't think we can take the chance."

"Look, how about if I speak to each of them in person?" said Matt. "I'll stress to all of them that it goes no further under any circumstances. They're all experienced investors and they know how things work." Alex knew them all well, and trusted them too. In the end, he gave way but insisted that Matt impress absolute discretion on all of them.

"How did you get to the bottom of all this anyway?" asked Matt.

"Well I'd be lying if I told you I worked it all out myself. A friend from University hooked me up with his cousin here in Mumbai and he was a fantastic help." Alex wondered if he should tell him about Leonna, but decided it was best to say nothing. "I'll come over after I get back and I can walk you through the whole thing. We've got all the documentary evidence to prove it's a total fraud."

"Well, you were right to be sceptical of the company. Remind me to take note in the future when your sixth sense kicks in."

"Yeah, but we still have to find a way out of this mess," said Alex. "I haven't spoken to Jamie yet but I'll give him a call later, once the morning trading has settled down."

They swapped news on their other investments for a while before agreeing to catch up when Alex got back home.

Alex slipped his phone into his back pocket and paused for a while to look out over the bay. The hazy skyline stretched out along the edge of the ocean. A city of 20 million souls looking out to sea. He'd grown attached to this place over the last few days. It felt like a new frontier, somewhere with infinite possibilities that was about to make its mark on the world. He took in the view one last time, building a mental picture to take with him, and then turned to head back inside.

Leonna was reading her book but she closed it when she saw him approaching.

"Everything OK?" she asked.

"Yeah, I brought Matt up to date with the grim reality of our investment," he replied. He decided not to mention the bit about bringing the others into the loop, as deep down, he still felt uncomfortable with it. He took the seat next to her and poured himself a coffee from the pot on the table.

"I'll give Jamie a call from the airport. I'm not sure he's going to be happy with the news."

"Well, it's better that he knows than not, I guess," said Leonna.

"Yeah, he manages a hedge fund so he can go short as well as long. He can effectively take a sell position that balances the shares that he owns. That way he'll probably come out of it pretty much unscathed. I'm just not sure where that leaves Matt and I," he said ruefully.

"Surely, he won't allow you to lose money after you've uncovered the very fraud that he's shorting."

"No, if there's anyone I would trust to do the right thing, it's Jamie. He's a smart guy. I'm sure he'll figure something out."

"We better make a move pretty soon," he said, finishing off his coffee. Are you going to stay over at my place tonight when we get back?" Leonna put an elbow on the arm of the chair and rested her chin on the palm of her hand.

"Do I get my own room?" she asked. Alex laughed.

"Only if you want to sleep in the bathroom."

"Oh well, I suppose I could make an exception," she said, smiling.

The taxi pulled up under the impressive canopy that spanned the departure area of the airport. They stepped out and retrieved their luggage from the driver as he unloaded it and made their way into the departure hall. It was a chaotic scene that greeted them. Lines of passengers in disorganized queues inching their way to the check-in gates. They were grateful that they didn't need a baggage trolley and they could weave their way towards their gate and tag on to the end of a mercifully shorter queue for business class passengers.

Finally, they were able to check in their bags and make their way through to Security. Sadly, that marked the end of the preferential treatment and they joined the back of an even longer queue that wound its way at glacial speed towards the departure lounge.

By the time they'd made their way through Security, their flight had been called and it was time to go to the departure gate. There was still a few minutes before they started boarding, so Alex took the opportunity to call Jamie.
"I'll just see if I can get through to Jamie before we board," he said. He gestured towards the windows where there were fewer passengers and it was a little quieter.

He dialled his number and stood looking out onto the tarmac and the shimmering runway beyond. After a couple of rings, Jamie answered.
"Alex, how's it going?"
"About as well as we could have hoped," he replied. "We've got a very clear picture, but I'm afraid it's not good news"
"Okay, so give me the condensed version."
"Well basically, the whole thing's a fraud. They shifted the assets out of the company that they used for the reverse

takeover, so Robrex is still just a shell company. They seem to be continuing the operations of the business under an Indian registered private company. The recent takeover of K.P Digital appears to be a fraud too. They stripped out the assets before the sale and there's no evidence that the company has any operational value. I think we have to assume that Robrex is pretty much worthless."

There was a long pause as Jamie took it all in.

"Have you got the evidence to prove all this?" he asked.

"Yes, we followed the transfer of title of the property portfolio that's supposed to be owned by Robrex. It's now registered in the name of a company called S.I. Holdings Ltd. The shareholders of that company are associated with the Robrex CEO."

"Okay, well, ordinarily I'd call this a complete disaster. However, in this business, information is power and right now we're the only ones who have that information. Alex, it's vital that we keep this completely confidential whilst I figure out how to play it."

"Er yeah ...., I'll make sure it goes no further," said Alex, already regretting that he'd caved in to Matt's idea to tip off their fellow investors.

"Can you come into the office tomorrow? We'll go through everything and work out the best way forward."

"Yeah sure. I've got everything on a USB drive. I'll bring that with me."

"Is Leonna with you?"

"Yes, we're at the airport. We're just waiting to board."

"You need to make sure she understands that this is all confidential. The last thing we need is for the company auditors to get wind of it."

"Yeah, she understands how sensitive this all is, but I'll ask her to say nothing until the story breaks." He didn't like to put her in this position but it was difficult to see any other way.

"Okay, we'll catch up tomorrow," said Jamie, "and by the way Alex, you've done more than I could have expected here.

If we can find a way out of this mess, it'll be largely down to you. I won't forget that."

"Thanks, it's been a team effort at this end," said Alex. He instinctively looked over towards Leonna. She was searching through her bag for something. When she caught his eye, she pointed over to the gate where the first passengers were beginning to board. "I think we've started boarding, Jamie. I better get going."

"Right, give me a call tomorrow before you come over and we'll thrash this thing out." They finished the call and Alex walked over to join Leonna.

"How did he take it?" she asked, retrieving her passport and boarding card from her bag.

"He was okay, but obviously he wants to make sure that nothing gets out before he's had chance to minimise their losses. He er...., mentioned you specifically." Leonna paused for a second.

"Well, I suppose I've already compromised myself by coming on this trip. What's another week?" she said with a shrug of her shoulders. "Come on let's go and find our seats."

Chapter 23

Alex got off the bus and walked up towards Jamie's office. The financial district at the weekend had a quite different feel to the mid-week hustle and bustle. People were walking along the waterside footpaths and enjoying the morning sunshine, but the office buildings stood quietly waiting for the next week's market opening. There was a strangely eerie feeling walking alongside the monolithic glass structures without the usual throng of people. Something unreal, like he'd somehow found himself transported onto the set of a virtual computer game.

He'd left Leonna in the flat after a lazy start to the day. They'd got up late and sat around drinking tea, chatting and listening to his eclectic music collection. He smiled to himself, thinking how easy it had felt just being with her. He imagined what it would be like to get home to find her still there, but he knew that she wouldn't be. She was going to make her way home. There were things that she needed to sort out.

He arrived at the entrance to Jamie's office and gave him a call.

"Hi Jamie, I've just arrived. I'm waiting in the lobby downstairs."

"Right, well just stay there and I'll be with you in a couple of minutes," he replied. "We'll go around the corner to the new Tapas restaurant and get some lunch."

Jamie emerged from the lift and came over, smiling. He had that look of someone with a plan; someone with confidence in his ability to navigate whatever the fates put in front of him. He slapped Alex on the shoulder. "Come on let's go," he said.

The restaurant was on the second floor of another high rise just a few minutes walk away. It was a modern and stylish informal space. The kind where the galvanized service ducts are exposed in a black painted ceiling space. Jamie asked for somewhere with a little privacy and they were shown to a table next to a large pillar by the window.

"So, show me what you've got," said Jamie. Alex had taken prints of all the files they'd saved. He retrieved them from his bag and handed them over.

"These are the photos of the head office, and these are the records from the Company and the Land Registry." Jamie took a few minutes to leaf through everything, nodding his head as he went through each document.

"This is ideal Alex. I think we have everything we need."

"So, what's the plan? Are you going to take out a short position?" asked Alex. The waitress came over to take their order and placed a basket of Spanish breads on the table. They ordered a selection of small dishes and a carafe of red wine.

Jamie leaned back in his chair.

"Well yes, the ultimate strategy will be to go short, but it's a matter of timing. I got wind yesterday that Robrex are planning to make a trading update next Thursday. The great thing about knowing that the company is a fraud, is that we know with absolute certainty that it will be a positive update. It can't be anything else." Alex smiled. *This is what separates the men from the boys*, he thought.

"So, there'll be plenty of liquidity to sell into and at a rising price?" he said.

"That's what we're hoping," replied Jamie.

He poured them both a glass of wine.

"The company's brokers are going to make an announcement on Monday about the trading update. They'll also announce that there'll be a presentation to Institutional shareholders on the Thursday morning. I want to break the story at the presentation." Alex raised his eyebrows.

"Wow, that should create a bit of dramatic effect," he said. "Yeah, it won't be dull," said Jamie. "It's not going to be easy to get the shorts in place in such a brief window. If it turns out we can't manage it, we'll just have to hold off a day or two. I've got one of our best traders on the job. I can trust him to keep it quiet until we're over the line."

Alex helped himself to some of the dishes spread out on the table.

"How are you planning to distribute the research we've done then? Are you going to put something on your website?"

"Yes, we'll do that, but I want to have a document that we can hand out at the presentation. A shorting thesis, that sets out in simple terms, the evidence we have and the basis for our short position." Jamie looked up at Alex. "I was hoping you might be able to pull something together from the research you've done. You'll be on the payroll of course, at full consultant's rates."

Alex hadn't been expecting it, but he realized that it was an opportunity. If he could put his name to this document, and if everything went to plan, it was the sort of thing that would open doors. Besides, it felt like he would be seeing things through to the end.

"Yeah, I could do that. Do you have anything that I could use as a template?"

"We've got a couple of documents that you could use for a check list, but it needs to be short and punchy. I want the other fund managers to be able to get the full story from a quick scan read." Alex nodded.

"I understand. I'll get started on it straight away," he said.

"Do you need anything else?"

"No, I should be OK with what I've got. Well...., actually there is something else," he said. "Er,....Matt and I were wondering what would happen with our shareholdings in Robrex. You know, given that we're locked in with you guys."

"Well, we'll aim to sell all that we can on the day of the trading update. I'll make sure both of you get the best price we trade at. After that, it's up to you if you want to participate in the short."

"Wow, that's great. We've both got quite a bit of profit tied up in this. If we can realize it, that would be a big result. I don't normally short stuff myself but I'll talk to Matt and we can decide what we want to do there."

Jamie took a drink from his wine glass.

"Whatever you make from this Alex, will be well deserved. You really did an amazing job over in India."

"Well, I don't want to take all the plaudits," he said. "Leonna and Yash deserve just as much credit."

"Yeah, it seems like you made a good team," said Jamie, looking at him over the rim of his glass. Alex knew what he was thinking. He looked down at his plate while he decided how to put it.

"Jamie, Leonna and I have become quite close," he said. "I mean....., I know that Stephen's an old friend of yours, but it just happened, you know." Jamie smiled and put his glass down on the table.

"Listen Alex, you don't have to explain it to me. She's a really nice girl and I don't blame you. Besides, Stephen's really not an old friend. We went to the same school but I'd never say we were close friends; more like acquaintances. I do know him well enough though, to be sure he won't just accept it and move on with no bad feelings."

"Yeah, I got that impression from Leonna. It probably doesn't help that they work at the same company either," said Alex. Jamie shrugged his shoulders.

"It's never going to be easy. You just have to give it time

and let everyone get used to the new reality," he said. Alex wasn't sure himself what the new reality was, but he couldn't imagine it now without Leonna.

They finished off the food and drained the last of the wine before heading back to Jamie's office. He had some documents that might help Alex with his shorting thesis.

The office was pretty quiet; just a few of the hard core employees working their Saturday. Jamie dug out a couple of files and passed them over to Alex. They were the sort of thing he was expecting. Enough to give him some ideas on how to structure his own report. It was agreed that Alex would work to a deadline of Tuesday to finish the report and they parted ways at the lift outside Jamie's office.

Alex decided to drop in on Matt on the way home. He wanted to update him on the India trip and they could start to map out the shorting report together. It was easy to take the underground from Canary Wharf to Islington and just a short walk from there to Matt's house. As he came out of Islington station and set off down the high street, it felt like he was back in the real London. No glass towers in meticulously planned geometric blocks, just busy pavements alongside small shop fronts and people going about their business.

When he arrived at Matt's house, he could see the curtains at the front were closed, but there was a faint glow from the lights that were on inside. He rang the bell and waited. No response. He tapped on the bay window and cupped his hands against the glass to try to catch a glimpse inside. He cursed to himself that he hadn't called to make sure he was in. He took out his phone and rang Matt's number. After a few rings it went through to answer phone. He's probably hooked up to some game or other, he thought. Head phones on and deaf to the world.

Alex turned around and walked reluctantly back on to the street. That was when he remembered it; the key that was hidden under the window sill. He smiled to himself. *This'll give him a shock*, he thought. He returned to the house and bent down to run his fingers under the sill. He could feel a small crevice at the top of the brickwork and crouching down, he could make out the corner of a small plastic envelope wedged into the space. He pulled it out and grinned in triumph as he saw that it contained the key for a Yale lock.

He turned the key in the lock and the front door opened. The usual pile of newspapers and unsolicited mail had been collected from the floor in the hall. It was piled up on the window sill next to the door. Alex stepped inside and closed the door behind him.

"Matt, it's Alex," he called out. There was no response, so he slowly opened the door to the living room and peered inside. The usual mess on the floor had been cleared up but there was no sign of Matt. He opened the door fully and walked into the room. No obvious signs that he'd even got up yet. He walked into the dining area and as far as the entrance to the kitchen. Well, he must be out, he concluded. Probably he was visiting his Mum, he thought. He couldn't see any point in hanging around and waiting for him to come back, so he decided to head off.

He walked back into the living room and was heading to the hallway when he noticed something. It was at the bottom of the open plan staircase that led into the living area. A set of small steps. The kind that can be folded up and stored away in a cupboard. They were lying on their side and Alex reached down to pick them up and set them upright at the bottom of the stairs. He was wondering to himself what they were doing there, when he noticed in the edge of his vision, an almost imperceptible movement of the shadow on the wall. It made him look up.

It felt like time stood still while his mind tried to make sense of what he was seeing. Two feet in white sports socks were suspended above the stairs. The upper half of the body was obscured by the bulk head of the staircase. The whole scene just seemed unreal. It took a second or two for Alex to come to terms with what he was looking at. When the realization dawned, his mind began to race. Suddenly, he was searching for some rational explanation; some explanation that wouldn't end in the inescapable conclusion that it was Matt's body. He forced himself agonizingly to climb the stairs, to brush past the suspended limbs and to look up and face the horrendous truth. He knelt down on the stairs and wept.

Chapter 24

Alex just sat on the sofa, numb and almost unable to move, whilst the emergency services moved around him. The ambulance staff had called the Police, as they were required to do in the event of an unnatural death. A police forensics specialist was taking pictures of the scene. Alex stared straight ahead, not focusing on anything and feeling detached from everything that was going on around him. A voice to the side of him said something and he turned his head to see a uniformed police officer.

"Sir?" he said. Alex focused on the face that was addressing him. "I'd like to ask you a few questions if that's alright."
"Er, yes of course," said Alex, trying to pull himself together.
The officer sat on the sofa next to him and pulled out a notebook.
"Are you related to the diseased?" he asked. *'The diseased'*, thought Alex. Is that what Matt had become? It just didn't feel real.
"No, I'm a friend of Matt's," he said.
"And you live in the property, do you Sir?"
"No, I was just visiting." There was a brief pause whilst the officer recognized the obvious inconsistency here.
"Can I ask you how you found the body?" he asked.
"The spare key," said Alex. "There's a spare key hidden outside the house. I thought maybe he was playing a computer game with headphones on and couldn't hear the door bell. Matt said it was OK to use it if I needed to get in." The officer wrote something in his book and then took down details of Alex's name and address.

"I'd like to ask you to come down to the station if you

wouldn't mind. Just to go through some of the background to what's happened. It shouldn't take very long." Alex nodded his head absently.

"Do you have any contact details for the next of kin?" asked the officer.

"He has his Mum, but she's in a nursing home. She has Alzheimer's," said Alex. "He's an only child but I know he has a cousin who lives not far away. I don't have any details, I'm sorry."

"Okay, we'll look into that," he replied. "Shall we go? I'll run you down to the station in the patrol car." Alex hesitated. He was still in shock, barely making sense of what was going on.

"What's going to happen with....., I mean where will they take the body?" he asked.

"We'll arrange for it to be taken to the Coroner. It's standard procedure where we need to ascertain cause of death and rule out the possibility of foul play."

The Police Station was just a few minutes drive away. It was only as they drew up alongside the brick building that Alex recognized it as the place he'd come to be interviewed about Emma's death. The officer parked the car in a designated area with the other patrol cars and opened the rear door to allow Alex to step out. They went inside through the main entrance to the reception and the officer had a brief word with the Desk Sergeant who allowed them access.

They walked down the same corridor that Alex had come along for the previous interview, but this time he was shown into a bigger room. A large wooden table stood in the centre of the room with two seats on either side. Tinted glass extended across one wall of the room, presumably to allow observation from an adjoining space. Alex was invited to sit opposite the glass wall.

The officer excused himself and left Alex alone in the room.

Sat there, looking at his reflection in the tinted glass, Alex felt very alone. His best friend was dead and he hadn't even had the chance to tell anyone. The first person he was going to talk to about it would be an anonymous Police Officer. Someone who didn't know Matt; didn't know how smart and funny he could be; someone who would fill in the forms, go through the process and close the file on him. Alex had a deep empty feeling in the core of his body.

He waited for about 20 minutes before the door opened and a plain clothed officer walked into the room. Alex recognized him immediately. It was D.S. Harris, who'd interviewed him before. Alex's presence in the room didn't seem to surprise him.

"Good afternoon Mr. Samaras," he said, as he took the seat opposite. "I wasn't expecting to see you again so soon." Alex said nothing. D.S. Harris opened his notebook on the table in front of him. "Two friends dying in unnatural circumstances within a couple of weeks, that's.....well, unfortunate." Alex felt his jaw tighten in annoyance before he let the feeling subside.

"Emma wasn't a friend, she was someone that I spoke to just once, and it isn't unfortunate, it's heartbreaking." The officer showed no emotion. He was looking to provoke a reaction and he'd got one.

D.S. Harris went through the usual process. He read out the official caution and started the recording device before beginning the interview.

"So, can you tell me what your relationship was with the deceased, Mathew Saunders?" he asked.

"He's a friend," replied Alex.

"And, how long had you known him?"

"About six or seven years. We met through our interest in stock market investing."

"Oh yes, you're a private investor aren't you," said D.S. Harris. "Now, can you explain how you came to find the body? As completely as possible, please." Alex went through everything again, trying not to re-live the experience but just keeping to the facts and trying to stay as detached as possible. When he'd finished, D.S. Harris nodded.

"So, what was the purpose of your visit to the house?"

"I wanted to share some research I'd been doing on a company that we were both interested in. We'd often meet up to talk about shares," replied Alex.

"Now, you contacted the emergency services at 3:10pm, as soon as you discovered the body, you say. We have a record of the time. Can you tell me what you were doing earlier today, before you came to the house?"

"I had lunch with another friend. I met him at his office in Canary Wharf."

"Another investor friend?" asked D.S. Harris.

"Yes, that's right."

"And what's the name of this friend?"

"His name's Jamie Sinclair." D.S. Harris took a note of the name.

"Could you give me a contact number so we can confirm everything with him?" Alex hesitated.

"Er, Jamie's a friend of Matt's and he doesn't know anything about what's happened. I'd like to speak to him first. I'd like him to hear it from me." D.S. Harris thought for a moment and then checked his watch. He announced the time and added that the interview would be temporarily paused, before switching off the recording device.

"Okay, you've got a few minutes to make a call," he said. "I'm going to have to be present in the room whilst you make the call and I'd appreciate it if you'd keep it as short as possible." Alex took out his mobile phone from his back pocket. He had no idea what he was going to say or how he was going to break the news. He just made the call automatically. Jamie answered almost immediately.

"Hey Alex, finished it already?" he said.

"No, it's....... Listen Jamie, I've got some really bad news." There was a pause whilst neither of them said anything.

"Go on," said Jamie.

"When I left your office today, I called round to Matt's house. I found him......," Alex swallowed and looked up at the ceiling to try to compose himself. "He's dead," he said. Jamie said nothing for a few seconds and then asked simply,

"How?"

"He committed suicide," said Alex. Jamie sounded incredulous. "Suicide? Was he depressed? Did he say anything?"

"No, he never gave any indication anything was wrong. His Mum's health was a worry for him, but he'd made sure she was getting the right care. I just can't believe things could have got this bad."

"Where are you now?" asked Jamie.

"I'm at Islington Police Station in one of the interview rooms," he replied.

"Right, listen to me very carefully Alex. Just answer yes or no. Is there a police officer in the room with you?"

"Yes."

"And do you have a solicitor with you?"

"No," he replied.

"Okay Alex, it's important that you say nothing more to the police without a solicitor present. I'm going to call a guy I know. His name's Jeremy Philips. He's a solicitor and he'll tell you what to do. Tell the police officer that you want to exercise your right to a solicitor, and they can't question you further until he arrives. Have you got that?"

"Er yeah, I understand."

"Right, I'm going to get straight on it," said Jamie.

Alex ended the call and looked up at D.S. Harris.

"After talking to my friend, I'd like to exercise my right to a solicitor before continuing the interview," he said. The officer was expressionless, although a slight twitch in the corner of his mouth seemed to give away a feeling of annoyance.

"Do you have a solicitor, or would you like to use the Duty Solicitor?" he asked.

"My friend's arranged for a solicitor to represent me. His name's Jeremy Philips."

"Well, I suppose we'll just have to wait for Mr. Philips then." With that, he got up from the table. "We'll let you know when he arrives," he said, before leaving the room.

Alex was left waiting for about an hour before the door to the interview room opened and an officer came in. He held the door open for a man wearing a suit and tie and carrying a slim briefcase. He looked about 40, with short red hair that was beginning to recede at the front. The man had a word with the officer, who then left the two of them alone in the room and closed the door behind him.

"My name's Jeremy Philips," he said, offering his hand to Alex. "Jamie's asked me to advise you over this matter." He took a seat next to Alex and pulled out a business card from his top pocket.

"Now, if I can just very briefly confirm the situation. You were invited by the Police to attend a voluntary interview. As the name suggests, this is voluntary on your part and you're free to leave at any stage. The police are required to disclose any evidence or basis for compulsory questioning and they have confirmed that they have no such evidence. In the circumstances, it's my recommendation that we cease the interview now."

"Well, if that's your recommendation," said Alex. "I mean, I don't have anything to hide."

"Yes, I understand that," replied Mr. Philips. "The problem from my experience is that the police force is full of over-zealous officers who have a habit of putting two and two together to make five. It's usually best not to give them the chance to jump to the wrong conclusion. We can always arrange a suitable time for a later interview. I've asked that they contact me if they believe it's necessary." Mr. Philips stood up. "Shall we go?" he said.

"Is that it?" asked Alex. "Can I just leave now?"

"Yes, I'll deal with the paperwork, but you're free to go."

The solicitor walked over to the door and knocked on it. The police officer who was waiting outside opened the door and they followed him down the corridor to the reception. Jamie was there waiting and he came over and shook hands with Mr. Philips before the solicitor excused himself to deal with the formalities. Jamie put his hand on Alex's shoulder.

"Come on, let's get out of here," he said.

Jamie led them over the road to where his Range Rover was parked.
"Alex, I thought you could maybe come over and stay with us tonight. Just to give yourself a chance to come to terms with everything. Have someone to talk to about it, you know." Alex stopped on the pavement next to the car whilst he thought about it.

"Thanks Jamie. I really appreciate the offer and everything you've done, but I think I'd like to go over to my Dad's place tonight. I just feel like I need to get away from everything for a bit and process it all."

"Sure, I understand," said Jamie. "Well, let me give you a ride over there, okay?"

They talked in the car, trying to rationalize what had happened, but unable to make sense of any of it.

"I guess you never real know what people are going through on the inside," said Jamie. "People put on a public face and that's the only side you're ever allowed to see."

"I just feel that I would have known if something was really wrong," said Alex. "Matt was such an open guy, you know. What you see is what you get. I just can't imagine he was hiding any dark secrets."

"Well, I'm not sure we'll ever the know the answer. He didn't leave a note did he?" said Jamie.

"No, there was nothing. I'm not sure who he'd have been writing it to anyway," said Alex.

Jamie pulled up alongside the restaurant.

"By the way Alex, you don't have to do the shorting thesis, you know. I can get someone in the office to pull it together from the documents that you brought back."

"No, I want to do it. I want to finish it," replied Alex.

"Okay, but if it ends up being too much, don't feel like you have push yourself." Alex nodded and clasped hands with Jamie before getting out.

He watched the car pull away and then walked down the passage to the back of the restaurant. The day was just beginning to fade into dusk and the light was on in the kitchen window. He could see Jack in his white apron moving around the island counter and gesturing to someone. It had that warm inviting feel; somewhere where there were people that you cared about, and that would be happy to see you. For the first time in so long, it felt like home.

Chapter 25

Detective sergeant Harris parked up next to the makeshift stall, just off the main road. It was the house at the end of the cul-de-sac. He'd checked it against the address he had for Alex Samaras. Flat 3A would be the top floor, he guessed.

He didn't usually go to these lengths on the basis of a hunch, but it just felt there was more to this guy than he'd let on. He'd have liked the chance for a proper interrogation but the solicitor had put paid to that, at least for the time being. Still, there was nothing stopping him from keeping him under observation. Maybe he could grab a word with a neighbour; get a feel for what was going on here.

He screwed up the paper bag that had contained his lunch and brushed the crumbs off the passenger seat into the foot well. He was about to get out of the car when he noticed someone approaching the front door of the house. He stopped for a second. There was something familiar in the way he walked; the unhurried stride, the long overcoat and slicked-back hair.

The man stopped in front of the house and studied the names on the panel next to the intercom. He pressed a button and stepped back onto the pavement. After waiting for a while, he glanced up towards the top floor and then back towards the main road, before flicking the remains of a cigarette onto the pavement. D.S. Harris narrowed his eyes to get a good look at him.
"Denny McCabe," he said to himself under his breath. It sounded almost like a question, although he knew for sure it was him. He just couldn't make the connection of why he would be here. The McCabe family were well known to the Met. police. They had a finger in most of the underworld operations in north London. Any time they showed up, you

could be sure that serious crime wasn't far behind. So why turn up here, at this house?

McCabe leaned forward to press the intercom once more before stopping himself as he heard a voice address him from the street.

"Can I help you? I'm the owner of the house," said Ms. Marks, holding a shopping bag and looking pointedly at the discarded cigarette butt on the pavement.

"Er, yeah. I'm looking for a Mr. Samaras. He lives here."

"And, may I ask what this is about?" inquired Ms. Marks.

"It's business," he said, with a fixed smile on his face.

She hadn't liked the look of him from the moment she'd seen him standing outside the house. He wasn't the usual cold caller or tradesman. He just looked a bit too sure of himself.

"I'm afraid Mr. Samaras is away for a while."

"Oh, right. Do we know when he'll be back?" he asked, the smile still fixed on his face.

"We're not exactly sure when that might be. Perhaps you'd like to leave a business card and I'll pass it to Mr. Samaras when he returns."

"That's OK, I have his phone number. We'll just have to make it another time," he said. He remained standing there, looking her in the eye, for longer than felt comfortable. Eventually, he turned away, without saying more, and walked off towards the main road.

D.S. Harris watched him go until he turned on to the high street and moved out of sight. He remained looking vaguely in that direction while he considered this turn of events. It was putting a totally new complexion on the investigation. A renowned criminal just turns up at the house of a possible suspect in an unexplained death case. His experience told him that there had to be a connection. He'd been right to have his suspicions. Another case of the cop's instinct paying dividends. He guessed from the scene that had just played out, that Samaras wasn't in. Maybe he could have a word with the old lady. She'd gone inside after talking to McCabe, so presumably she had a flat in the house.

He got out of the car and walked over. He pressed the button with Alex's name printed next to it, just to confirm that he was indeed out. He then looked down the other names on the panel. One name stood out, 'Miss E. Marks,' not least because it was hand written using a calligraphy pen. *That must be the old girl,* he thought. He pressed the button to Ms. Marks flat and she answered promptly.

"Yes, hello?"

He could tell from the clipped and formal tone of her voice that he'd hit the mark.

"Hello, my name's Detective Sergeant Harris. I'm an officer with the Metropolitan Police. Could I have a brief word Ms. Marks?"

She came to the front door with a look of apprehension on her face but D.S. Harris was quick to put her mind at rest.

"It's nothing for you to worry about," he said. "It's only that I witnessed you just now talking to a man at the front of the house. He's someone that may be of interest to us in one of our inquiries. I'd be interested to know what business he had coming to the house. Perhaps I could....." He gestured towards the hall as he was showing her his warrant card.

"Oh yes, of course. Come in Sergeant." Ms Marks air of concern had changed to a sense of intense curiosity. She ushered him into the hall and suggested they discuss the matter in her flat.

She brought out two cups of tea on a tray and placed them on a low table next to the armchair that D.S. Harris was now occupying. The room was quite dark, despite it being the middle of the day. Heavy curtains framed the windows and the deep maroon curtain fabric was matched by the cushions that were lined along the sofa that Ms. Marks was perched upon. It had the feeling of somewhere from another era; somewhere that hadn't changed in decades.

"The man you met outside the house, Ms. Marks; do you know who he came to see?"

"Oh yes. He was looking for one of my tenants, Mr. Samaras. He rents a flat on the top floor."

"Can you tell me anything about this Mr. Samaras?" He didn't want to give away the fact that he'd already met and questioned Alex. He'd just give her the chance to tell him everything she knew.

"Well, he seems quite a pleasant young man," she said, before leaning forward as though she were about to impart something of significance. "I really don't know what he gets up to during the day. He's always up early in the mornings and he spends a lot of time in his room on his own. I see him from time to time on his way to somewhere or other, but it all seems a bit odd to me."

D.S. Harris nodded his understanding.

"How about the man that called round today. Have you seen him before?"

"No, I'd have remembered seeing him, that's for sure. I consider myself a good judge of character Sergeant, and I didn't like the look of that one the moment I set eyes on him."

"I can't say I blame you Ms. Marks. He's not someone you'd want to get mixed up with." D.S. Harris tapped his pen against the small notebook he was holding. This wasn't getting him very far.

"So, anyone else that visits the flat that you may have noticed; anyone at all?"

"Well, we don't have many visitors Sergeant. We like to maintain a sense of privacy here in the house. Although......," a frown crept across Ms. Marks face. "I do believe Mr Samaras may have had a couple of lady friends stay over." This was definitely getting him nowhere but he let her ramble on for a bit longer. "I didn't care much for the first one. She was here for about two weeks. I almost thought she'd moved in. She walked around like she owned the place and hardly gave you the time of day. I wasn't sorry to see her go."

The frown on Ms. Marks face softened a little, before she went on.
"He came back to the flat a couple of days ago with a different young lady, just for a night. I haven't seen them since. I bumped into her at the bottom of the stairs as she was going out; a lovely girl. She told me her name. What was it? It was an unusual name, Lowena ....., no that wasn't it. Leonna, that was it."

D.S. Harris looked up in surprise.
    "Leonna, you said?"
    "Yes, her name was Leonna."
That was the name of the girl's flatmate. They both worked at the same accountancy firm. So now Samaras was involved with the dead girl's flatmate. He needed to pull this guy in and get some straight answers.

    "Ms. Marks, you say that your tenant isn't currently staying in the flat?"
    "No, he went away for a few days and then just came back for a night. That was two or three days ago. I haven't seen him since."
D.S. Harris pulled a card from his top pocket.
    "Perhaps I could give you my contact number? When you see Mr. Samaras again, maybe you could give me a call; just to let me know that he's back in the flat." She took the card and after putting on the glasses that were hanging around her neck, she examined it closely.
    "You don't suspect Mr Samaras of anything improper do you?

"Well, we always like to keep an open mind Ms. Marks. You can never be sure what people get up to. We just want to be careful."

"I'll be sure to keep an eye open, Sergeant," she said.

As D.S. Harris came out of the house, he rubbed his chin thoughtfully. It felt like he was beginning to piece together what was going on here. He didn't have the complete storyline but he had a better idea of the cast now. He just needed to find the connections that linked the characters together.

The old girl would keep an eye on things for him here. It would have been a stretch to get authorization for an officer to watch over the property, but now he didn't need to. A nosey landlady would be better than any officer he could put on the case and she had the perfect cover too. All he had to do was wait for the suspect to return and pull him in.

Chapter 26

Alex was at at one of the tables in the restaurant next to the window, his laptop in front of him. They wouldn't open for lunch, so the place was empty and quiet. It gave him time to focus on finishing off the document for Jamie.

It had been three days now. Three days since his world had been shaken to its core. He'd gone over things relentlessly in his mind, reliving the experience, somehow hoping that it would end in less pain or some kind of closure. It wouldn't. It helped that he'd had the chance to work in the restaurant. They'd been busy over the weekend, so an extra pair of hands had made a difference. Keeping himself busy had allowed his subconscious to begin to work through the grief he was feeling.

It was a couple of days before he'd felt able to call any of Matt's friends, or to answer Leonna's messages. Every time he broke the news, it felt like he was reopening the wound. He'd talked on the phone to Leonna for the first time the previous evening and she'd wanted to come over. In the end, they agreed to meet for dinner later in the week. Carlo and Seb both met the news with complete disbelief. They told him that Matt had called them individually to tell them about the fraud and there'd been nothing to indicate there was anything wrong. There seemed to be no answers, nothing to make sense of an inexplicable tragedy.

Alex could hear the sound of someone moving about in the kitchen. A moment later, Maya put her head around the door.
"Do you want a coffee Alex?" she asked.
"Yeah, I'm pretty much done here," he said. "I'll come through to the kitchen." He just needed to format the document and append the image files and he could send it off

to Jamie. He decided he'd finish it off back at the flat. It was time to get back there anyway.

He walked through to the kitchen as Maya was pouring out the coffee. She brought two cups over to the island counter and they sat down.

"Are you sure you don't want to stay another night?" she asked. "Yeah, I need to get back and find my old rhythm, but thanks for putting me up," he replied.

"It's us that should be thanking you. It made such a difference with you working in the restaurant."

"Yeah, we were a good team weren't we," said Alex, with a smile. They both took a sip of the hot coffee.

"Are you doing okay?" asked Maya.

"Yeah, a little better I think. Being able to come over here and work in the restaurant just feels like it's grounded me. It's given me a chance to reset, you know." Maya nodded her head.

"Sometimes it's good to have somewhere you can just go back to," she said. Alex wondered to himself just how long there'd be somewhere to come back to. He didn't know what she knew about the restaurant's financial problems. Jack wasn't the sort to share his troubles and he wouldn't want to burden her with money worries.

"Maya, I don't know how much Jack's told you about the restaurant finances, but my Dad got into a bit of a mess. I've been looking at how we can straighten things out. Hopefully, by the end of the week I may have a solution. I just don't want you to think that nothing's being done about it, you know." She looked down at her coffee.

"Jack doesn't talk about it, but I had an idea that something wasn't right." She looked up and forced a smile. "I know you'll do your best for the restaurant," she said.

"Yes, I will," he replied. It was only as he said the words that he realized just how much he meant it. He would find a way, no matter what, to make sure the restaurant survived.

He swilled the last of his coffee around the cup before downing it and getting up from the counter.

"I better get on my way," he said.

He could take a bus back home. There were plenty running along the main road. Maya saw him off at the back door and gave him a hug before he headed down the steps.

When he arrived home and entered the flat, he could see that Leonna had tidied things up before she'd left. The bed was neatly made and the cups and plates had been stored away in the kitchen cupboards. So much had happened in the few days since they'd spent the night here and suddenly coming back, the flat felt empty without her.

He walked over to his desk and switched on the computer. He retrieved the files that he needed to complete the presentation and it only took a few minutes to do the formatting and incorporate all the image files that were required. With everything finished, he emailed the document to Jamie and sat back in the chair. That was it; everything he'd learned over the last few weeks. It was going to be a bombshell when it went public. Investors of all kinds would lose money; some who could probably ill afford it, but that was the stock market. Risk and reward. Sometimes you only understand the risks you've been running after it's too late.

The news would break on Thursday morning, the day after tomorrow. He knew that he should already be looking for the next investment opportunity, but it was difficult to focus on anything else until things had played out. Besides, he felt responsible for sorting out Matt's affairs. He needed to make contact with someone in his family and make sure that his Mum's situation was secure. He'd spoken to Carlo and Seb, but there were many others within the investment community who would want to know too. He'd send a message to Phil Carmen and ask him to send something out to the community, but there were a few people that he should phone in person first.

He picked up his phone and flicked through his contacts. He'd start with Jeremy and David. They'd been on the conference call with him and Matt. He called Jeremy's number and after a few rings it went through to his answer phone. He didn't want to leave a message, so he ended the call and tried David. This time he had more luck. Alex took a deep breath.

"David, it's Alex Samaras."

"Alex, you're back. I think I owe you a large drink my friend," he said.

"I take it you spoke to Matt a few days ago then?"

"Yes, I've sold up and grateful for the early warning," he replied.

"Er, David, I'm afraid I have some very bad news. It's nothing to do with the investment. It's Matt. He took his own life sometime before Saturday evening."

"Oh my God. I'm so sorry," said David. "I only spoke to him the day before."

"How did he seem?"

"Just the normal Matt. Nothing that would have made me think....., anything like this."

"Yeah, that's what Carlo and Seb said. I haven't spoken to Jeremy yet," said Alex.

"Well, Matt told me he'd just spoken to Jeremy when he called me, so I think you'll get the same story. Have you spoken to Noel?"

"Noel?" asked Alex.

"Yeah, 'Ya Man Noel.' Matt was going to speak to him later. He couldn't make the conference call but Matt said he was going to give him the heads up anyway."

"Oh right, I'd forgotten about that. Do you have a contact number for him?"

"No, I only ever contacted him direct through the bulletin board message service."

"Yeah, me too. I'll send him a message to let him know."

"Listen David, I'm going to talk to Phil to see what we can do in Matt's name. Maybe some sort of fund raiser or a charitable portfolio. I don't mind managing it."

"Sure, you can rely on my full support."

"Thanks. I'll let you know when something's been decided and when I have any details of the funeral arrangements."

"Okay Alex. I'm really sorry about everything. You just take care of yourself, right."

"Yeah, thanks David, I'll speak to you again soon."

Alex put his mobile phone on the desk. It felt emotionally draining to keep breaking the news, to keep feeling the other person's shock and disbelief and reliving his own painful memories. There was nothing he could do other than keep pushing on.

He thought he might as well send a message to Noel, so he logged onto the bulletin board site. He opened the search window and entered Noel's user name into the profile search. A message came up on the screen,

'No match found.'

Odd, he thought. Maybe he'd made a mistake with the case sensitivity. It would be quicker to pick his name from the bulletin board. Alex opened the Robrex board and scrolled through the messages to find one of Noel's posts. He right clicked on the name and selected 'Profile' from the drop down menu. Another message appeared on the screen,

'This Profile is no longer available.'

Without a current profile, he'd be unable to message him. He right clicked again on the name and selected 'Recent Posts.' It listed his posts. All were to the Robrex board. The last post was a week ago, Wednesday. He'd been a regular poster since the board was established then suddenly he'd disappeared from the site. Maybe, if he'd sold up after speaking to Matt, he'd just decided to move on, but then why delete your profile? It left Alex puzzled but there was nothing else he could do. He closed down the site and decided to go round the corner to pick up something for lunch.

Alex passed the rest of the day in the flat. He called Phil Carmen and they talked about what kind of announcement should be made, and what might be a fitting remembrance. Phil was a guy who made things happen and having him alongside him gave Alex the support that he needed. He called a few other people that he thought should know first hand and after that, it felt like he'd done as much as he could for the time being.

Still though, there was something that he just couldn't shake off. The mysterious Noel. When he thought about it, he realized how little he knew about him. They'd never met, or even talked, although he'd been a regular poster on the site. Then, he'd suddenly vanished. Well, there was no way to reach him now, he thought......, but then, maybe there was. If Matt didn't have a contact number for him, he would probably have used the bulletin board message service. There would be a record of Matt's messages on his account. Alex still had the key to Matt's house. It was in his pocket. He could at least give it a try. He could bike over to Matt's house and see if he could access his computer.

He looked out of the window and it was still light. An orange glow from the setting sun was reflected in the windows of the building across the street. Alex picked up his phone and keys and headed out.

The light was beginning to fade as he came down the road to Matt's house. He got off his bike and opened the gate as quietly as he could manage. He didn't want to draw attention to himself. He wheeled the bike down the side of the house to make sure it couldn't be seen from the road. There was nobody about on the street outside the house, so he was able to slip in through the front door without being seen.

It felt cold in the house and eerily quiet. Alex opened the door to the living room and stepped inside. It was gloomy with the curtains still closed. He didn't want to look up at the staircase but he felt drawn to do so. He stood there for a moment just staring into the shadows. Eventually, he made himself look away and walked over to the computer that was stationed on a desk in the corner of the room. There was a small angle poise lamp on the desk and Alex switched it on. He booted up the computer and waited.

His heart sank a little when a box appeared in the centre of the screen with a request for a PIN number. He'd been hoping it wouldn't be password protected. Alex typed in *1111* and then the year of Matt's birth, but no luck. There was one more option that he could try. He changed the login from PIN to Password. A new box appeared on the screen. He clicked on the option 'Re-set password.' A question appeared,
'The name of your childhood pet?'

Alex remembered Matt talking about the family dog. He'd used the name. It felt like it was on the tip of his tongue. What was it? 'Jasper?' No that wasn't it. It was......., he smiled to himself and typed in the letters, C,A,S,P,E,R. The screen changed and he was able to re-set the password. A moment later and Matt's desktop appeared on the screen. He was in.

He opened the browser and typed in the address for the bulletin board. Matt had saved the username and password so they came up automatically when he logged in. Great, he had access to Matt's account. He selected 'My Account' from the drop down menu. From there, he could open all his previous messages. As soon as he opened the folder, the latest messages popped up.

The last message was between Matt and Noel. It was part of a series of messages that were threaded together. Alex hovered the cursor over the message and clicked to open.

Re: Robrex
Noel,
I have some information on the company that I'd like to share with you. It's highly confidential so I need to speak to you in person. Do you have a contact phone number I can reach you on?
Matt.

Re: Robrex
Matt,
I've been having trouble with my phone and I took it in for repair yesterday. Can you not just give me an idea of what it's about? I'll treat it as confidential.
Noel

Re: Robrex
Sorry, I need to pass over any information in person. Is there not a land line you can use? Believe me when I say you'll want to hear this. It has major implications for the investment case.
Matt

Re: Robrex
You're in north London, right? Why don't I drop round and we can talk about it. Are you free sometime this evening?
Noel

Re: Robrex
Yeah, I should be around all evening. The address is, 79, Meredith Road, Islington, N1 3BH
Knock on the window. I may be on the X box!
Matt

Re: Robrex
Right I should be there around 8pm.
Noel

Alex stared at the screen and re-read the messages several times in almost disbelief. He was here. He came to the house. This was way beyond coincidence. A stranger comes to the house and the next day Matt is found dead. He took some deep breaths to calm himself and tried to think rationally about it.

Okay, this has to have something to do with Robrex, he thought. There are too many things that tie back to the company. The fraud, the apparent suicide of Emma who was part of the audit team and now Matt who was passing information about the company to Noel. So, who is Noel?

There had to be a link between Noel and the company, other than just someone with an interest in the investment board. As that thought went through his mind, he suddenly realized that there was someone from the company who also had an interest in the investment board. The CEO. Alex had seen him in the restaurant. He'd been looking at the Robrex bulletin board. Could he possibly be Noel? It seemed almost unbelievable but when he thought about it, this was the guy who was orchestrating a major fraud in a listed company. Who knows what lengths he might go to to cover that up.

Alex opened up the Robrex board and flicked through the posts. He'd read just about everything that had ever been written on the site but he scrolled back to find Noel's posts. Noel had been a true believer in the company right from the start and his posts always came across as well thought out and knowledgeable. Someone who knew the company inside out, you might say.

Then something occurred to Alex. That night in the

restaurant, when he saw him. He was sending a message on his phone. Alex had a clear memory of walking up to the table and seeing the man tapping into his phone. What if he was posting onto the bulletin board? He was logged into the site, so that would make perfect sense. *What was the date?* he thought. It was the day after Jack went into the hospital; the first day he'd covered for him in the restaurant. He flicked through the calendar on his mobile and found the date. It was the Monday. The CEO came in late. Alex scrolled back through the bulletin board posts to the same date, and there it was, YaManNoel's post at 09:53pm. That seemed like the time he'd been there in the restaurant. It all tied up.

Alex could feel his heart pounding in his chest. Up to now, it had all been about a fraud, getting to the bottom of the financial irregularities, but this changed everything. Two people were dead and he had a prime suspect. His mind was racing with what to do. Should he call the police straight away? Would they even take seriously what he was telling them? *No, slow down,* he thought. He needed to talk to Jamie. He'd know what to do and how to handle this. Alex picked up his phone, his hand shaking, and called him.

Alex took a couple of long slow breaths to calm himself whilst he was waiting for the call to connect.
"Hi Alex," said Jamie. "I got the report and it all looks good. I just changed the wording a little in the conclusion."
"Jamie, forget the report," said Alex. "It's the CEO."
"What do you mean?" he said.
"I'm at Matt's house. I managed to get into his home computer. He came round to the house, the day Matt died."
"Who did?"
"The CEO. He was posting on the Robrex bulletin board."
"Alex, you're not making any sense," said Jamie. "Now start from the beginning and walk me through it."

Alex realized he'd have to give Jamie the full story. He'd need to tell him about the agreement with Matt to warn off their close associates, against his express instructions. He went through everything. When he'd finished, Jamie took a while to respond.

"Okay, this is how I see it," he said, eventually. "We could take this to the police and they might bring him in for questioning, but I doubt there's sufficient evidence for him to be detained. Alternatively, we could expose the fraud, as planned, and have him arrested. Then when we give our evidence to the police they have time to investigate it whilst he's in custody. I just think that's the smart thing to do." As always, everything Jamie said seemed to make sense. It wasn't lost on Alex though that it also made perfect sense for Jamie in terms of salvaging his investment position in Robrex.

"For this to work Alex, we can't afford any further leaks. Do you understand?"

"Yeah, I know it was a mistake, but it's not going to happen again."

"Right, now you need to be at my office Thursday morning at 8am and we'll go over to the presentation together. You've done everything you can Alex, so just get some rest and we'll soon be able to hand this over to the police, okay?" Alex agreed. He knew that Jamie was right. He was too emotionally involved to think straight at the moment. He thanked him and they ended the call.

Alex sat there for a while just staring at the computer screen in front of him. The harmless chat between two fellow investors laid out on the page. He'd had countless such interactions with people he'd never set eyes on or spoken to. They could tell you things about themselves; you could kid yourself that you know them or that you had some kind of relationship with them. The truth is, most of the time, you don't have the first clue who you're dealing with.

Chapter 27

It was light when Alex finally woke up. A shaft of bright sunlight pierced the top of the curtains where they didn't quite meet in the middle of the rail and illuminated a narrow strip across the ceiling. Like the inverse of a sun dial, It told him the morning was already late. He forced himself out of bed and walked over to the window to peer out into the street. He had to squint to be able to make out the people passing up and down the road in the bright sunlight. He kept the curtains drawn and walked back to the sofa.

It had been a restless night. He'd called Leonna when he got home and they'd talked for over an hour. She seemed the only person who really knew how he was feeling. The only person who could understand what it was like to be so deeply connected in all this. She'd said they should involve the police straight away, but Alex had persuaded her that Jamie's idea made more sense. He wasn't even sure himself now whether they were doing the right thing or whether he'd just succumbed to Jamie's persuasive powers.

The Robrex trading update was tomorrow morning and it couldn't come soon enough. After that, they'd be able to hand everything over to the police. There was the debt owed by the restaurant too. He was over due on the deadline set by the loan sharks and he'd had to ignore a couple of calls to buy a bit of time. If everything went to plan tomorrow, he'd have enough to settle it once and for all.

He'd decided to join Jamie in the short trade. It wasn't something that he usually liked to do. Betting against a stock, there was theoretically no limit to the potential losses you could incur, but this time felt different. He had all the evidence and the backing of an institutional investor. There would be an avalanche of selling pressure. What ultimately convinced him though, wasn't the opportunity to bag a profit, it was the desire to help take the company down. He'd begun to hate everything that it stood for. It felt like his only means of hitting back. He'd speak to Jamie tomorrow morning and give him his decision.

Leonna was going to come round after work and he'd make dinner for them. It seemed like he was just killing time until then. He sat down at the computer and went through the latest announcements. There was a trading update on one of his holdings but nothing much of interest. The Robrex share price had consolidated a little over the last week and seemed to be waiting for more news. Well, they'd certainly be getting it tomorrow morning, he thought.

He struggled to fill the rest of the day. His head wasn't in it. With tomorrow's showdown hanging over him, he just couldn't move on to any new ideas He found himself making regular cups of strong coffee and becoming side tracked by half-interesting TED talks. By the time it reached late afternoon, he'd given up. He'd go and pick something up from the deli around the corner. He had some bits and pieces that he'd brought back from the restaurant so he'd be able to knock something up.

He'd started to do some of the preparation and was thinking it would be fun to do the cooking together, when there was a knock at the door. He was surprised that she'd arrived this early.
    "Hey, perfect timing," he said, as he opened the door. That was as far as he got.
    "You've been ignoring my calls," said McCabe. Alex was momentarily stunned into silence. Before he was able to regain his senses, the loan shark had walked passed him into the room.
    "Wait....., er how did you.....?" he started to say.

"One of your neighbours let me in," said McCabe, looking around the room. "Cosy little place you've got here."

"Look....., you're going to have to leave," said Alex. He seemed taller and thicker set than he remembered but there was the same languid demeanour.

"I suggest you close the door if you don't want this to get ugly," he said, fixing Alex with a penetrating stare. There was something in the eyes that contradicted the outwardly relaxed manner. It gave you the sense of someone who would be capable of almost anything. Alex closed the door.

McCabe walked nonchalantly over to the window, his back to Alex. He stood there for a moment looking out onto the street.

"When I make an agreement with someone, I expect them to keep their side of the bargain. I don't want to go chasing after them, listening to their crappy excuses and promises. I just want them to do what they say they'll do." He turned around and looked over at Alex.

"I just need one more day," he said. McCabe laughed.

"Yeah, they always need one more day. How exactly is one more day going to change anything?"

"It's an investment, said Alex. If I sell tomorrow morning, I'll have enough to add to what we can borrow from the mortgage lender. You'll get all your money. I just need one more day to put everything in place."

"Yeah, and what kind of investment is going to miraculously pay off in 24 hours?"

"It's a stock market investment. I own shares in a company and if I sell them first thing tomorrow morning, I can raise the rest of the money."

"So you're just going to pull off a deal on the stock market and all your troubles will be over, right?" McCabe scoffed. "You might be better off taking a trip down to the bookies." He reached into his pocket and took out some dice or similar objects and began turning them around in his fist. They made a light clicking sound as they moved around in his hand. He casually walked over to the sofa and sat down.

It felt like some of the tension in the room had abated a little and Alex cautiously walked over to the kitchen and leaned with his back against the bar counter. *If he could just get him out of here believing that he was going to get his pay off.*

"I should be able to raise around half the money tomorrow and I can get that to you within two or three days. The rest, we'll get from the mortgage lender which will take a bit longer. I'd guess we should have a cheque from them within a couple of weeks."

"I told you. There's an easy way to solve this problem. Give us the guarantee against the property and we can cut you some slack. We'll sort out a new repayment plan and you'll have plenty of time to work things out."

Yeah, that would suit you just fine, thought Alex. He looked down at the floor and shook his head.

"No, that's not necessary. We want to settle this matter as soon as possible and make a fresh start. I'll get you the first half of what's outstanding as soon as I can. It shouldn't be more than a couple of days. The rest will follow within a week or so."

McCabe's mouth noticeably tightened and he looked away from Alex, barely concealing his annoyance.

"I don't think you understand what I'm saying. All I'm hearing here is, 'as soon as possible......, just as soon as we can.....' I gave you a deadline and you couldn't meet it. Now you want another deadline. Well, maybe you're not the person I need to talk to. Maybe I should go and see one of the other members of the clan. The old man maybe?" He placed one of the objects he'd been holding on the table in front of him. It was a bullet, about 2cms long standing on it's end, the copper casing catching the sunlight from the window. "Or the chef maybe?" he said, putting another bullet next to the first. "Or maybe the waitress?" he added, before placing a third one in the line.

Alex swallowed. He could feel his heart beating up in his throat. McCabe reached into his jacket pocket and withdrew a black semi automatic pistol which he placed on the low table next to the bullets. He looked slowly up at Alex. He didn't say anything. He didn't need to.

Leonna came around the corner into the cul-de-sac and walked up to the house. She'd been able to get off work a little earlier than usual and it would be nice for them to spend some time together. With everything that had happened over the last few weeks, it felt like they needed each other.

She walked up to the front door and was about to press the intercom button when the door suddenly opened. She was surprised to see the landlady, Ms. Marks. She didn't come out through the doorway but stood there for a moment, the palms of both hands together as though she was praying or thinking of what she was about to say.
"Oh hello. We meet again," said Leonna with a smile. "He's expecting me."
"I don't think you should go up there right now," said Ms Marks.
"You don't?" replied Leonna.
"No I don't."
Leonna stood there for a second, puzzled by the earnest expression on Ms. Marks face and unsure of exactly how she should respond. "Come in. I think we should have a word in my flat," said Ms Marks.

She ushered Leonna into the living room and motioned for her to take a seat on the sofa whilst she took one of the armchairs opposite. Leonna reluctantly lowered herself onto the edge of the sofa.
"There was a man who came in to the house earlier. I have reason to believe he may be up in Mr. Samaras's flat."
"A man?" said Leonna.
"A policeman was looking for your friend here the other

day. I don't know what any of this is about, but the policeman told me this man is dangerous. I don't think you should get involved."

Leonna was struggling to understand any of it. She knew that Alex had been questioned by the Police. It was possible that they'd been round to the flat to speak to him again, but this other man, *who was he?*
Then it hit her. Alex had told her about the loan shark. *Was this the man?* She looked up at Ms. Marks.

"I don't know if this has anything to do with it, but Alex's family have a restaurant and they borrowed money from someone. Alex has been trying to negotiate a settlement with them. That might be it. I got the impression they weren't the kind of people you'd want to deal with."

"Well I don't imagine Mr. Samaras will have been expecting a visit. He talked his way in at the front door. I saw that half wit on the second floor let him in."

"Do you think we should call the Police? I mean, if he's come in uninvited."

"Let me try something else first," said Ms. Marks. "You stay here." She got up from the armchair and brushed the creases out of her skirt. Maybe it was a way of giving herself a few seconds to steel herself.

Alex was unable to take his eyes off the gun on the table. He was running through all the permutations in his head. *What was the quickest way to raise the money? Who could he borrow it from?* Whatever it would take to get them out of this nightmare.

There was a knock on the door. McCabe instinctively reached for the pistol.
"Who's that?" he said under his breath.
"It'll be my girlfriend."
"Get rid of her," he said, standing up and moving to a position by the bathroom that would be out of sight when the

door was opened. All Alex could think about was getting Leonna as far away as possible. He gave himself a second to come up with a story and then walked over and opened the door.

"Oh, I'm sorry to disturb you Mr. Samaras. There was something that I'd forgotten to tell you," said Ms. Marks. Probably for the first time that he could remember, Alex actually felt glad to see her.
"There was a policeman who came round earlier when you were out; a detective sergeant Harris. He said he needed to speak to you about something and that he'd come back at six o-clock. Well, I suppose he should be back any time now," she said, glancing at her watch.

Alex had only been out briefly to pick up some things for dinner and that was barely an hour ago. Had he missed him? Whatever the case, it was a stroke of good fortune.
"Ah right, D.S. Harris," he said, making sure it was loud enough for his unwelcome guest to hear. "Thanks for letting me know. It's just a routine matter." Ms.Marks nodded her head and smiled. She seemed unusually accommodating, given that a police officer was about to pay a visit to one of her tenants. Alex closed the door.

He looked over at McCabe who was nonchalantly running his fingers along the barrel of the pistol.
"If you think getting the cops involved is going to do you any favours, you really don't understand how these things work," he said.
"It's got nothing to do with this. They want to speak to me about an unexplained death; someone I knew."
"Well, well. It looks like we may have underestimated you. I'm going to have to keep a close eye on you."
"It has nothing to do with me. I found the body and contacted the Police. They think it was suicide."
"Well, let's just keep our business dealings out of it then shall we. Now you need to have a serious chat with the old

man and make him understand what's in his best interests. I'm going to be calling on you again real soon and next time, D.S. Harris won't come riding to the rescue. You better be ready to tell me what I want to hear." He slipped the pistol back into his jacket pocket and walked over to the door. He paused for a second with his hand on the door handle and turned to look back over his shoulder. "Maybe you can introduce me to your girlfriend next time, eh?"

Alex could hear his footsteps receding down the staircase, then the dull impact of the front door closing. He'd gone, at least for the time being. If he didn't understand what was at stake before, Alex surely did now. He needed to find a way out of this mess and it didn't feel like he had too many options. He sat down on the sofa and leaned his head back against the cushion, closing his eyes for a second.

There was a light knock on the door. Just for a moment he wondered if he'd come back, but just as quickly he dismissed the thought. It wasn't his kind of knock. He got up and walked to the door expecting to find Ms. Marks again. He was surprised to see Leonna standing there.

"Is everything okay?" she said, with an anxious look on her face. He ushered her into the flat and closed the door behind her.

"Well, better for seeing you. I just had an unwelcome visitor. The loan shark I told you about. Did you see him coming out of the house just now?"

"No, I was in the landlady's flat."

"What? Ms. Mark's flat?"

"Yes. She told me not to go up after she saw him come into the house." Alex looked confused.

"She saw him come in? I mean....., how does she know who he is?"

"It seems the police have been keeping an eye on you. They saw him come by the house the other day and warned her to stay clear of him. They asked her to let them know when you came back to the flat."

"Yeah, the guy who interviewed me is coming over tonight. Any time now I'd guess." Leonna smiled and shook her head.

"No, that was just something Ms. Marks made up. She thought it might scare off the loan shark."

"She did that?" said Alex with a look of surprise. He began to think that maybe he'd misjudged her. "Come on, grab a seat and I'll get us a drink. I feel like I need one."

Alex kept a bottle of Jack Daniels in the cupboard and he brought it over and poured out a couple of glasses. He drained his glass and poured himself another.

"You know, this loan business is getting pretty heavy. She got me out of a difficult spot there. I don't know how much of it is bluff, but I wouldn't want to take my chances with this guy."

"Is there not a way to settle things with them and get out of this? They're bound to come back and you shouldn't be the one they come looking for Alex."

"I don't have much choice. Hopefully, after tomorrow, things will look a lot better. It just feels like everything's hanging on Jamie's big plan working out."

"It does seem like tomorrow's the day, doesn't it. What time's the presentation?"

"It starts at nine."

"You know, I'd like to go with you if I can."

"Don't you have to be at work?"

"I can use flexitime. If I can get in for around ten, it should be OK. I just want to see it through to the end; be there with you when the truth comes out, I guess."

"Yeah, of course. You should be there. I'll need to speak to Jamie, but I imagine he'll be able to arrange it." He'd become so wrapped up in his own problems that he'd lost sight of the fact that she needed some sort of closure too.

"Is everything okay at work? I mean, with all that's gone on and Stephen working there?"

"It's been okay so far. Stephen seems to be busy at the moment so I've not seen much of him. A lot of what we do is out of the office so you can go for weeks without seeing people." She smiled and reached out to hold his hand. "I know it's not ideal, but if we give it time, things will work out." He took her hand and held it against his lips for a moment. He was glad she was there; glad there was someone who wanted to stand by him through it all.

"Did I tell you, you were making dinner?" he said with a smile. She raised her eyebrows in mock surprise. "Come on. I've done the hard work. I'll leave you to work your magic."

Chapter 28

Walking along the High Street as the morning traffic began to build up, Alex could feel a nervous sense of anticipation. A tightness in his stomach, knowing that things were all suddenly coming to a head. Leonna seemed to sense his unease and gave his hand a squeeze. He was glad she was coming with him and that Jamie had been able to arrange access to the presentation for her. They'd take a bus into the city and meet up with Jamie at his office.

When the bus arrived, they were able to find a couple of free seats on the top deck and settled down for the ride. Alex took out his phone and did a quick search for the morning announcements on the stock exchange.

"Right, let's have a look at this update," he said. It had come out first thing, as expected. He clicked the link to open it and quickly read through the contents. Leonna sat and waited for him to finish, studying his face for hints as to the contents. Long before he'd reached the end, Alex began to slowly shake his head, an ironic smile playing across his face. When he'd finished, he looked up at her. "Higher margins expected to transform future profitability," he said.

"Well, of course they are," she replied, and took the phone off him to read it for herself.

After she'd finished, Alex had a look at the bulletin board site to check the early morning chatter. It was no surprise to find a few posts spreading unbridled enthusiasm and anticipating a sharp move up in price at the open. *Lambs to the slaughter*, he thought.

"It's going to be a blood bath when this story breaks," he said.

"I suppose this is why you need to use a stop loss," said

Leonna.

"Well, yes to some extent. It might get you out earlier if you're lucky, but remember, it's just a trigger for a sell order to be generated. You need to fill that order, and with so many sell orders all coming at once, it's just going to accelerate the crash in the share price. A lot of ordinary people are going to lose a lot of money."

"It makes you wonder why people invest at all," she said. "If you can't rely on what the company itself tells you, what chance have you got?" Alex shrugged his shoulders.

"I guess it's one of the risks that you have to accept. Ultimately, the only defence you have is to manage those risks by diversifying your investments. That knowledge usually comes from bitter experience though."

It was a little after 8am by the time the bus came into Canary Wharf. The office commuters spilled out onto the pavement and purposefully began to make their way towards the imposing glass towers in the financial district. Alex and Leonna followed them towards Jamie's office. They looked like just two more young and ambitious city types heading in to the trading floor of some global financial giant in pursuit of the dream. It felt strange for Alex as he tried to imagine himself making this commute every day. Somehow, he felt unconnected from it all, like he was observing rather than participating in it. Maybe it was the knowledge of what was to come later that morning that set them apart from all the other commuters.

They came into the lobby at Jamie's office and Alex spoke to one of the receptionists. She made a call to the company to confirm they were expected and then asked them to go straight up. As they entered the reception area of Jamie's office, the receptionist came out from behind her desk and greeted them with a smile.

"He's in the trading suite, I'll take you down," she said. They followed her down a hallway that went passed Jamie's office and she pushed open a pair of swing doors that led into a large bright office space. In spite of the early hour, there was an unmistakable energy in the room. Three lines of desks went the length of the room, each line comprising back-to-back desks and three monitors to each desk. There was no shouting or calling across the room at this stage of the trading day, but there was a palpable tension in the air.

Jamie was standing behind a trader seated at one of the desks on the far side of the room. They were both focused on the screens in front of them. Jamie caught sight of them and motioned for them to come over.

"Well, it's game on," he said. "There's a lot of buying strength out there and we're letting them have everything they want." The daily share price graph was displayed on one of the screens and Alex could recognize clearly the story that it told. The share price was pushing against a ceiling. It wanted to move higher but Jamie's relentless selling was keeping a lid on it. On the right hand screen, there was a multi-coloured table showing the bid and ask prices for the stock. The difference between the two figures represented the price spread and Alex could see it was remarkably narrow. That meant there was a lot of demand out there for the stock, and so long as it remained, they'd be able to offload all the stock they cared to sell.

"When do you aim to put the shorts on?" asked Alex.
"We've already got some of the shorts placed, but we need to be careful," replied Jamie. "We'll wait until we're largely out of the stock before we put the remainder on. I don't want to announce it to the market too early. Are you coming along for the ride?"
"Yes, I've decided that I'll join you," said Alex.
"What about Matt's share?" he said. Alex realized that he hadn't considered that question. The share holding would form part of Matt's estate and he couldn't take investment decisions that would put that at risk.

"If he was here, I know he'd want in, but I can't take that decision for him," he said. Jamie paused for a second.

"You know what, he would want to be part of this, wouldn't he? I'll tell you what, I'll guarantee that he doesn't lose anything from the short and we'll add his holding to the mix." Alex didn't need any more proof of Jamie's integrity and generosity. It was the kind of gesture that he'd come to expect from him. "Come on, we'd better get moving," said Jamie.

On the way out of the trading area, Jamie stopped at one of the desks and a young woman with a dark bob hairstyle stood up. He introduced her to Alex and Leonna.

"This is Harriet," he said. "She'll be joining us for the presentation." He said something to her in a low voice that they couldn't catch and she nodded her head in agreement. She picked up a large manilla envelope from her desk and transferred it into a brief case. The four of them then went out to the reception area together. "There's a taxi waiting for us outside," said Jamie as they entered the reception. They took the lift down to the ground floor and a black cab was parked close to the entrance.

It wasn't a long drive over to the broker's office. For the duration of the journey, Jamie had one eye on his phone which displayed the current Robrex share price chart. Harriet was receiving messages from their trader and shortly before they reached their destination, she confirmed to Jamie that they were half way through their sales.

"Now, I appreciate what you guys have to do," said Alex. "It's a whole different ball game when you're trading in big volumes."

"Yeah, you're dead right," said Jamie. "You have to realize a profit when the opportunity arises, and you can't be too picky, either."

They got out of the taxi alongside the stockbroker's office; the narrow street with the tall Georgian architecture pressing in on both sides. It took Alex back to the first time they'd come here; he, Jamie and Matt on that rainy day a couple of months back. It seemed like a lifetime ago. He could remember the sense of excitement at the possibility of unearthing a hidden gem. The next big thing, perhaps. He and Matt feeling like they were part of the in-crowd for a day; privy to information that just wasn't available to the small investor. As they walked into the reception, Alex knew for sure that this time, they had information that nobody else had even dreamed of.

They were met in the lobby by a receptionist who confirmed their attendance and escorted them to the lift.

"You're in the main auditorium today," she said.

"Are you expecting a big crowd?" said Jamie with a good-natured smile. She smiled back.

"Nothing we can't handle. There'll probably be around thirty five people today so we thought it was best to use the auditorium. It's on the basement floor," she said, leaning forward to press the elevator button.

The lift doors opened onto a small hallway that led towards the auditorium. The double doors at the entrance were open and they could see one or two people milling around near the front, by a low podium. The receptionist led them through the entrance and into what looked like a small lecture theatre. Several rows of seats stepped up on one side and overlooked the stage area.

It was about half full and she invited them to take a row of seats near to the front. Jamie suggested instead that they sit higher up near the back and she was happy to let them find there own way. It occurred to Alex, as they took their seats, that Jamie was carefully staging things for dramatic effect. When he dropped his bombshell, he wanted to be addressing the whole room. It would be better to have everyone in front of him when the time came.

There was a lectern and microphone set up at the front, but no sign of the company directors who would be making the presentation. Leonna leaned over towards Alex.

"What time are they starting?" she asked in a low voice. "I don't want to miss anything, but I need to be in work by 10am."

"They're due to get under way in a few minutes," Alex replied, glancing at his watch.

He looked over towards the entrance but there was just the girl who greeted them, standing by the doorway, next to a small table with bottles of mineral water lined up in neat little rows. It felt like they were awaiting the start of a stage production, with the actors in the wings somewhere, ready to begin the tale. In reality, that wasn't far from the truth and at that moment, as if on cue, the CEO appeared at the entrance.

It was a strange feeling seeing him in the flesh once again. The same smart suit and grooming, and that air of confidence that he seemed to carry with him. Only this time, Alex could see right through it all. Through all the lies and deceit, through the veneer of respectability to the rotten core, the ruthless greed and murderous means. He could feel a sense of anger welling up inside him and took a deep breath to clear his head and maintain his composure.

It took a few minutes before the representatives were seated on the stage area and the presentation could get underway. It started with the CEO going through the trading update that had been released earlier that morning. Alex had to admit he was good. Nothing that could be considered overly optimistic or selling the story. He was pitching it as a company with a clear strategy and a measured approach. The listener was left reassured, but with an unmistakable sense that a bright and profitable future lay ahead for the company. If Alex hadn't known it was complete fiction, he might have been taken in.

The company finance director then followed on with his summary of the accounts figures. As he was working his way through the fictitious numbers, Harriet leaned over and whispered something in Jamie's ear. Jamie nodded. Alex had the Robrex share price chart open on his mobile and he could see that the share price, which had been trading sideways within a tight range, had suddenly spiked up a little. That was all the confirmation he needed, to know that Jamie's selling phase was complete. He would now start to place the remaining shorts.

By the time the directors came to invite questions from the audience, the share price had risen well above its all time high. Alex could see that he wasn't the only one monitoring the share price reaction to the mornings news and this added to a sense of quiet satisfaction amongst those present.

The questions that followed were all focussed on the scale of the upside potential and it seemed like the only way was up for the company. The directors for their part had an easy time of it. They were preaching to the converted, and all they had to do was confirm their expectations. There's nothing more comforting for an investor than being amongst a group of their peers and with everyone on the same page. Sadly, that page was about to be re-written.

Jamie had been getting regular updates from Harriet, but there came a point when they both sat back in their chairs and no longer focussed on their phones. Alex looked over at Jamie and caught his eye. Jamie gave a slight nod of his head. He didn't need to say anything. It was all set up. Alex leaned over to Leonna and whispered,
  "It looks like show time's about to begin."

The CEO had just wrapped up another satisfactory response to a question from the floor and the facilitator was looking around the room for any further questions. Jamie slowly raised a hand and the young woman with the microphone hurried over to hand it to him. Jamie made a point of standing up to deliver his question.

"I have a question for the CEO," he said. "Mr. Gupta, the company recently raised an amount of £11.2 million through a placing. I wonder if you could tell us what the net asset value of Robrex was immediately prior to that cash raise?" The CEO looked a little bemused.
"Well, that information was presented in the placing document, I believe," he said. He looked over at his finance director who was leafing through a document he'd pulled from his briefcase.

The FD nodded to indicate that he'd found what he was looking for. "I think my colleague has the figure," said the CEO. The FD confirmed a figure of £12.9 million and the CEO smiled his appreciation. "I hope that answers your question," he said to Jamie.
"Well, yes it does, but it leaves me a little confused," he replied. "You see, my firm paid a visit to Mumbai recently to carry out some research of our own." The smile on the CEO's face began to fade a little. "According to our research, the net asset value of the company was precisely zero, the same amount as when Mumbai Technology Ltd completed the reverse takeover of Robrex 3 years ago. We have evidence that indicates that the assets and operations of the business were transferred to a holding company in India, and I suspect the money raised in the recent placing has headed in the same direction. In short Mr. Gupta, my firm believes that Robrex plc is a complete fraud and totally worthless."

There it was, the bomb shell had landed. Almost everyone in the audience turned their heads to look up at Jamie. The shock was writ large across their faces. Some turned back to look towards the CEO, perhaps expecting some rational explanation to make sense of this misunderstanding. Jamie didn't give him the chance to dig himself out of the hole.

"We've prepared a brief summary of our findings and the rationale for currently shorting the stock," he said. "My colleague will distribute a copy to anyone who'd be interested to read it." Harriet stood up and began to pass the copies around the audience. One or two more experienced brokers had already taken to their phones and it wouldn't take long before the panic selling would begin.

The focus of the audience had turned to the document that was being passed around and the meeting came to something of a halt. Leonna tapped Alex on the arm.

"I would so love to stick around but I'm going to have to dash," she said. "If I take a taxi, I can just about make it, I think. I guess I should take a copy of this too," she added, holding a copy of the shorting thesis. "It's probably time my employer understood exactly the kind of accounts they've been signing off." Alex nodded.

"I'll give you a call later when the dust has settled," he said. Leonna got up and made her way down to the exit.

Jamie was leaning forward, talking to someone he knew in the row in front of them. The CEO and FD were now in huddled consultation on the stage with someone from the Brokerage firm, no doubt in search of some last minute damage limitation. It felt like things had moved way beyond that. Most of the audience seemed more interested in scanning through the report that had been passed around or talking animatedly on their phones. Alex pulled up the latest Robrex share price chart. It was no surprise to see that the price had gone into free fall. Each time the site refreshed, the chart took another leg down; another chunk of illusory value evaporating into the ether.

Eventually, a rather flustered representative from the brokerage firm took to the microphone and made an announcement. As they had completed the formal part of the trading update, they would draw the meeting to a close. An announcement would be made to the market in due course to clarify the company's response to the claims made by Jamie's firm. Some of the audience had already taken their leave and the announcement prompted those remaining to quickly make their way out of the auditorium.

The CEO wisely held back to allow those waiting for the lift to clear. Alex felt a sense of frustration in the end. The CEO was going to walk out of there. Yes, Jamie's solicitor would make sure charges were pressed against him, but Alex wanted him to answer for everything here and now, in public. He wanted to tell him just what it meant; just what the cost was in terms of people's futures; the cost in terms of people's lives.

Alex felt a hand on his shoulder. It was Jamie. He seemed to know what he was thinking.
"You've done everything you can Alex It's only because of you that we've exposed them, and now we need to leave it to the Police. I've got Jeremy on it already. He's going to make sure charges are filed straight away." Alex nodded. "I've just got to make a call to the office and then we'll get on our way," he said, and stood up to find some space to make the call in private.

Alex looked straight ahead. The CEO was talking on his phone. As he ended the call, he glanced around and seemed to decide the time was right to slip away. He said something to the FD before quickly making his way to the exit.

Alex couldn't help himself. He had to confront him. He got up and walked quickly to the aisle and down to the exit. He could see him standing alone by the lift doors. His back was to Alex and he periodically glanced up to check the progress of the lift. Alex walked slowly towards him.

"Why did you do it?" he said. The CEO turned around in surprise. He hesitated for a second before turning away and ignoring the question. "I get the bit about the money. You can never have enough of that, right? Even though you were born with opportunities that 99% of people could only dream of, you couldn't resist taking the short cut, could you?"

The CEO seemed to shift uncomfortably in his tailored suit. "We're all mugs for a good story aren't we. All you have to do is promise us a multi-bagger and we'll line up to hand over our money. Yes, I understand all that. What I don't understand is why people have to die so you can get a bit richer than you already are." The CEO turned around.

"I really don't know what you're talking about," he said.

"Sure you do," said Alex. "I was there at the restaurant. I saw you posting on the site." The CEO's eyes narrowed and he turned his head slightly as though he was remembering something.

"The Greek restaurant. You were the waiter," he said. "I rarely forget a face."

Alex pulled out his phone and opened the bulletin board app. He flicked through the Robrex site to find an old message to the board.

"So, you'll remember that you were logged into the Robrex bulletin board site Mr. Gupta........., or should I call you Noel?" he said, thrusting his phone towards the CEO.

He didn't say anything for a few seconds and then it was as though he'd taken a decision.

"I know what you're thinking," he said. "You're thinking, these foreigners, they come over here to our financial centres, our great institutions, built on trust and ethical standards, and they introduce their immoral practices. You think we're not good enough, not made of the right stuff to be allowed into your financial club. Well, let me ask you. Do you seriously think we could have pulled off something like this without help from one of your great British auditors?"

Alex was speechless for a moment as it sank in. *'The Auditors?'* he said to himself, incredulously. He looked down at his mobile, at the post from YaManNoel. Perhaps it was because he was reading it upside down. It was like he was seeing it for the first time. He read it backwards, 'leoNna MaY.' Something triggered in his mind, a recollection of something he'd read somewhere. Around half of people use a password or username which has some reference to their partner. It was Stephen.

Alex stood there almost unable to believe it, before a sharp ping sound brought him back to his senses. It was the lift. The doors opened. Alex pushed past the CEO and punched the button for the ground floor. The CEO took a step backwards. He wasn't about to join him.

Chapter 29

Alex ran out on to the street, desperately looking up and down the road, somehow hoping there'd be a passing taxi he could flag down. There was nothing. It was a quiet street tucked away in the financial district. He'd need to get back to the main road.

Wait, he thought. Why not just call her? He took out his phone and stopped on the pavement. He needed to calm down and think straight. He found Leonna's number and pressed the call button. It connected to an automatic message,
"The number you have called is unavailable."
Alex cursed. She'd turned off her phone when the presentation started and hadn't switched it back on yet. There was nothing he could do but get over there as soon as possible.

He jogged to the end of the street and it was two blocks over from there. It was a warm morning and he could feel his shirt sticking to his back as he reached the main road. A taxi came towards him almost immediately and he stepped forward to the edge of the pavement to hail it. The taxi was occupied and sailed right passed. He could see a black cab on the other side of the road that had stopped to drop someone off. He didn't hesitate. No time for pedestrian crossings, he just dodged his way to the centre of the road and ignoring the horns, ran through a narrow gap between two cars to reach the other side.

As Alex jogged up to the taxi. An elderly lady was struggling with two carrier bags whilst trying to shut the rear door.
    "I'll help you with that," he said, but instead of closing

the door, he hopped inside and closed it behind him.

"Hey, I've got another fare to pick up," said the driver over his shoulder.

"Could you drop me off near the British Museum on the way? It's an emergency," said Alex. The driver hesitated whilst he weighed up the inconvenience.

"Okay, it's a bit out of my way, though," he said.

"Thanks. I'd really appreciate it if you could go as quickly as possible."

"Yeah, that's the name of the game in this business," replied the driver.

Sitting in the back of the taxi, Alex had nothing to do but wait. Nothing to do but urge the taxi to go faster and replay everything over in his head. It all made sense now. He could see how Emma would have gone to her superiors with her suspicions, someone she could trust, like Stephen. It would have blown the whole thing wide open. He had to silence her. Then, he must have been risking it all. He was following the Robrex share price. He was probably betting big on a re-rating and what better place to ramp the stock than on the bulletin board. If he was still invested this morning, he could have lost everything. Leonna was the one who was about to break the bad news to him.

The taxi had become stuck in a queue at some roadworks and Alex began to shift uneasily on the back seat. Maybe he should call the police and get them to go straight to Leonna's office. How would he explain it though? Would they take him seriously or understand the urgency? Unlikely, he thought. It would sound like a far fetched theory to anyone hearing it for the first time. Then it occurred to him. There was someone who knew the background to the case, someone who knew there were two questionable deaths. Did he still have D.S. Harris's card? Alex had it somewhere. He pulled out his wallet and flicked through the receipts and scraps of paper. Finally, there it was.

There was a mobile number on the card and Alex punched it into his phone. After a couple of rings he answered.

"D.S. Harris speaking," he said.

"Detective sergeant, this is Alex Samaras. Do you remember me?"

"Oh yes I remember you Mr. Samaras. You're not going to tell me you've got another body for me are you?"

"No, no, but I know who did it now. It was the Auditors. I mean, one of the Junior Partners. He was covering up for a fraud."

"The Auditors?"

"Yes, it's the firm that Emma worked for. I'm on my way there now. I don't have time to explain, but trust me when I say I know it for sure. His name's Stephen Westbrook and there's someone in danger right now."

There was a pause on the other end of the line.

"Give me the address, and you better hope you're not wasting my time," said D.S. Harris. Alex read out the address from Leonna's card. "Wait for me there. If this is what you say it is then you need to leave it up to us."

"Right, but just get there as quick as you can," said Alex. He hung up and Alex caught a glimpse of the driver looking at him in the rear view mirror.

"There's a detour that might save us some time," said the driver. He turned down a side road and it was a welcome relief to be moving again. After another five minutes, they'd made good time and were closing in on their destination. They turned onto a street that was lined with ground floor shops and restaurants and what looked like apartments above.

"This is your address mate," said the driver. There was a 1960s style office building above a cafe and a furniture store that looked a likely candidate. Looking up, Alex could just make out the name of the firm etched into the 1st floor window.

"This is it," he said. He couldn't immediately see the entrance to the office but he wasn't about to waste any more time. "Just drop me here, thanks," he said, and handed the driver a £20 note. He didn't stick around for the change.

Alex ran around the corner and discovered the entrance at the other side of the block, facing onto a small square. He took a couple of deep breaths and smoothed the creases from his suit before going into the reception. A woman of middle age and wearing half-rimmed glasses looked up from behind the reception desk.

"Hello, I have an appointment with Ms. Leonna May. My name's Alex Samaras," he said.

"Just one moment," said the receptionist. She spoke to someone on the phone and replaced the receiver. "Ms. May's just in a meeting with one of the Junior Partners. Would you like to wait?" Alex felt his heart miss a beat.

"Er......yes," he said. He couldn't wait for D.S. Harris, he thought. He had to do something. "Is she.....er, still on the second floor?" he asked.

"Well no, she's in the audit department on the fourth," said the receptionist. "If you'd like to take a seat Mr. Samaras, I'll let you know when she's free." Alex walked towards a low sofa before turning and asking:

"Is there a toilet I could use?"

"Yes, there's one just through the double doors, on the right."

Alex walked through the double doors and his prayers were answered. The toilet was next to the stairwell. He went quickly up the stairs, taking two at a time and was breathing hard by the time he got to the fourth floor. He pushed open the swing doors and they led through to a large open plan office space. Nobody seemed to take any notice of him, other than a young woman who was using the photocopier on that side of the office. She looked up, a little surprised to see a breathless Alex emerge through the doors.

"I'm.... er, looking for Stephen Westbrook's office," he said.

"It's one of the rooms along the far side of the office," she said, pointing the way. Alex nodded and headed in that direction.

The offices were all the same; a heavy hardwood door next to a full height glass wall, the upper part of which was opaque glass. A small plaque next to the door revealed Stephen's office. Alex wasted no time, he just opened the door and walked in.

Stephen had his back to the door and was facing the window reading something, whilst Leonna was standing off to one side of the room.

"Alex!" she exclaimed with astonishment. Stephen turned around but barely seemed phased.

"Close the door Alex," he said. "Well, it seems you're quite the detective," he added, holding up the report that Leonna had brought back from the meeting. "This is going to be very embarrassing for us, but I suppose we owe you a debt of gratitude for doing our job for us." Alex could just make out the screen of Stephen's desktop monitor reflected in the window behind him. It looked very much like a share price chart with an unmistakable downward trend.

"And what exactly is your job Stephen?" asked Alex. "Is it your job to aid and abet fraud? To cover up for false accounting that you're supposed to be there to prevent?" The wry smile on Stephen's face faded.

"You should be very careful about making accusations like that," he said.

"Oh, I'm just getting started," replied Alex, barely able to conceal the emotion in his voice. "You killed her didn't you?" he said. He heard Leonna's sharp intake of breath but he didn't take his eyes off Stephen. "Emma came to you with her suspicions didn't she? The blank headed paper that they were using to forge the bank statements. She trusted you to do the right thing and she paid with her life."

Stephen tossed the document he was holding onto the desk.

"This is ridiculous," he said. "I think you've taken the detective thing a little too far Alex. You're in the realms of fantasy now." Alex's expression didn't change and his eyes never left Stephen's face.

"You killed Matt too didn't you."

"I don't know who you're talking about," he replied. "Look, you need to leave right now or I'm going to have you removed."

"I know who you are," said Alex.

"Yeah, and who am I?" said Stephen leaning forward across the desk, looking directly at him.

"You're Noel," said Alex.

It felt like time had momentarily stopped. Stephen remained motionless, but Alex could read it in his eyes; the shock, the gradual realization of what it meant. Alex helped him understand it a little more clearly.

"The Police will be able to track the IP address of your computer. They'll link it to your bulletin board account and from there they'll access your messages to Matt. It will place you at his house on the evening he died," he said. "The Police are on their way here right now. It's over Stephen."

Alex glanced over towards Leonna. She was staring at Stephen, with a look of almost total disbelief. He was looking down at the desk. He let out a short laugh, as though he was somehow amused at the absurdity of his situation. He slowly took the document that he'd tossed aside from the desk and opened the desk draw to place it inside. When his hand re-emerged from the drawer, he was holding something. At first, it looked like a stapler or some other office device. As he turned it around in his hands though, Alex could see it was some kind of pistol, the kind they use for sports events.

Stephen slowly looked up at Alex. He'd regained his composure.

"You don't tell me when it's over, I tell **you** when it's

over," he said.

"Stephen, please. You're scaring me," said Leonna.

"Shut up," he said, without moving his eyes from Alex. "You've got it all worked out haven't you? Just tie up the loose ends and wander off into the sunset. Well, that's not going to happen." Stephen was pointing the pistol directly at Alex's chest. "Now get down on your knees," he said.

"What?" said Alex.

"I said, get down on your knees."

"Look Stephen, it doesn't have to be like this," said Alex. He'd moved the aim of the pistol to Alex's head.

"Stephen, please stop this," cried Leonna. He rapidly switched the aim of the gun towards her.

"I told you to shut up," he said, through gritted teeth. "Now, get down," he said to Alex. Alex slowly lowered himself down to his knees. He was looking directly down the silver barrel of the pistol, the trained hand completely motionless. He wasn't going to miss.

So, this was how it was going to end, he thought. He felt strangely calm, almost accepting of it. He closed his eyes and waited for the inevitable conclusion.

It was the light that was so different. So bright and clear. The sun shining between the white sheets as she attached them to the line. She was smiling at him as he sat on the stone step at the entrance, his bare feet drawing pictures in the dust. He looked up and she was reaching out her hand towards him. The sun was so bright, he had to hold his hand over his eyes. There was a sharp crack sound and the light became blindingly white. He could no longer see her, no longer see anything, but he could hear her calling his name. "Alex...., Alex...."

It was a few seconds before he realized that it was Leonna's voice. He could feel her head in his lap and the shudder of her crying. He opened his eyes. Stephen was gone. Alex could make out a slowly moving dark patch that was creeping outwards from under the desk. The sticky liquid matting the fibres of the carpet tiles. *It was over*, he thought. It was over for Stephen and it was over for Matt and Emma. The senseless waste of it cut a scar deep inside him. Nothing was ever going to be the same.

He could hear voices outside the office, closely followed by a sharp knock on the door. The door opened almost immediately and someone let out a sudden exclamation before he heard D.S. Harris's voice.

"Out of the way," he said, and entered the room. He walked around to the other side of the desk and looked down at Stephen's body. He glanced back at Alex, and Leonna, all the time getting an impression of the scene, piecing together what had happened.

"Everybody stay out of the room," he said. "Watkins, get a record of everyone on this floor and call CSI." He walked back around the desk and looked down at Alex and Leonna. There was a look on his face that Alex hadn't seen before. It was something close to compassion. "I'll clear the office next door. When you're ready, you can tell me what happened," he said.

Chapter 30

It felt like midsummer, walking along the tree-lined roads. The tall trees casting dappled shade across the pavement and the sweet scent of the lime blossom in the air. It had been about a week and this was the first time he'd really been anywhere. After all the interviews with the police and everything, he'd called Leonna. They'd talked for a bit but it felt like there was a shadow hanging over them; like something had fallen between them. They both needed time to be alone, time to process it all.

Jamie had asked Alex to come over to the house. There was something that he wanted to discuss and it seemed like it might be a chance to start to close the chapter; to begin to move on. He came up to the house and climbed the steps to the front door. He rang the bell and Jamie opened the door dressed casually in a pair of jeans and a t-shirt.

"Hey, come in," he said. "Are you doing OK?" Alex shrugged.

"About as well as I've been in a week," he said.

"Right. Well, come on through. We'll sit out at the back after I pick up a couple of beers."

They went down the stone steps that connected the kitchen to the terrace overlooking a walled garden. There was a long metal table with hardwood boards inlaid into the top and Jamie placed the beers at one end. They both took a seat on either side.

"Jeremy tells me the police have pretty much everything they need from you now. You shouldn't be troubled by them, at least until things come to trial," said Jamie.

"When's that likely to be?" asked Alex.

"Well, it looks like it may take longer than we were

expecting. The CEO managed to get on a flight back to India before the police had chance to issue an arrest warrant. I'm afraid they'll have to try to extradite him. It's not a straight forward process." Alex nodded. He'd read about these cases. They could drag on for years and then just get forgotten. White collar fraud wasn't high on the agenda unless it had some political angle to it. *Would he ever be held to account?* he thought.

"On a more positive note," said Jamie, "we've closed our positions in Robrex now and it's been a very profitable venture, for all of us." Alex hadn't even given it a thought, with everything that had been going on. He guessed it would make a significant difference to the value of his portfolio. It would likely plug the gap in the re-mortgage plan for the restaurant, which would be one positive thing to come out of all this.

"We managed to sell at an average price of 575p and then shorted it all the way down," said Jamie. Alex did the maths in his head. He'd roughly 4-bagged on the way up. That would have realized around £60,000, and then with the Robrex share price having fallen to near worthless, he'd have doubled that capital on the way down.

"So, I end up with about £120K then? I'll drink to that," he said with a satisfied smile and picked up his beer.

"Well, not exactly," replied Jamie. "I should have explained it in more detail, but we were using derivatives to short the stock. For something as sure fire as this we always use leverage." Alex paused with the bottle at his mouth.

"So, exactly how much leverage?" he asked. Jamie grinned.

"Your take is about £750K," he said. Alex said nothing at first. It was a bit of a surreal moment. With his other holdings, he'd have a portfolio of over a million. It was the magical number, the target that he'd always have in mind when he projected forward his portfolio growth. Now, suddenly, it had arrived, just like that.

"Well, I guess that's nice," he said. Jamie laughed.

"Listen Alex, there's another reason I asked you to come over. Everything you did to uncover this fraud, it's just reinforced what I already knew about you. You don't have to give me an answer right now, but I'd like you to come and work for me." Alex hadn't been expecting it and he looked up at Jamie as if to confirm that he was serious. Jamie nodded. "You're as good as anyone I've come across in this business and you deserve to be given every opportunity to make the most of yourself," he said. Alex needed a moment to take it all in.

"Wow, you just told me I'm wealthy and now you're offering me a ticket to the big league. This is turning into quite a morning." he said. Jamie smiled.

"Alex, you're not wealthy. Not by the standards in the City. If you join me at Redmead Capital, the bonuses can take you to a whole different level. Think about it. You don't have to decide straight away."

Alex took a drink from his bottle and gazed out over the garden.

"Why do you think he did it?" he asked. "I mean Stephen. He had everything going for him and then he risked it all, and for what?" Jamie shrugged and took a deep breath.

"I don't know. Greed? Ego? I think people like Stephen need to feel they're in control. They believe they're untouchable and if things don't work out the way they should, they feel they have the right to change them."

"Yeah, and God help anyone who gets in the way," added Alex.

They talked for a while and then went back up to the kitchen to fetch a couple more beers. Jamie got some left overs out of the fridge and they had a casual lunch at the kitchen table. He talked about the firm, the plans they had and what Alex's role could be. It was the opportunity of a lifetime and it was his for the taking. By the time they'd finished and Jamie was seeing him off at the door, Alex had a completely new vision of his future. Jamie had painted it for him, showed him the direction his career was going to take and all he had to do was grasp it.

Alex walked back towards the station feeling that he was on the brink of something; that he was about to start on something that would completely change the course of his life.

As they crossed the road, the last of the daylight was fading away into a dark blue-gray sky.
"It looks lovely; so pretty," said Leonna. The lights from the restaurant illuminated the corner of the street and Alex had to admit, it did have a certain charm at this time of the evening. It felt strange to be entering through the front door for once, viewing it from the customer's perspective.

Alex opened the door and Maya came over to welcome them. She gave Alex a hug and he introduced her to Leonna.
"It's so nice to see you," she said, giving her a hug too. "Alex has told us a lot about you."
"Only the good stuff, I hope," said Leonna.
"Well, he did say you were a bit of a foodie, so we're doing our best to impress you tonight," she replied with a smile. "Here, we saved you a table by the window." She led them over to their seats.

The restaurant was busy, with most of the tables occupied. Maya brought some drinks over and they gave her their orders.

"I got a call from the solicitor," said Alex. "The restaurant is now officially debt free."

"Oh, that's great," said Leonna. "Ready for a fresh start then."

"Yeah, they weren't too happy with the settlement offer but Jeremy suggested we take it to arbitration and they suddenly became more amenable. It's all been agreed in writing."

"Have you spoken to Jamie?" asked Leonna.

"Yeah, we met up for a drink. He thinks I'm crazy," said Alex, with a laugh.

"I don't think you're crazy. I think you're at the beginning of something. Something that could be amazing."

"That's what I like to think," he said. "I'm meeting the architect next week to go over some ideas for the restaurant. Jack suggested opening it up so you can see into the kitchen which I think would be a great idea. It would make it more of an experience and we could run a bar along that side for people to sit and have drinks or eat snacks at lunch time. I want to create somewhere memorable, and if we get it right here, then maybe we can roll it out in other locations." Leonna laughed.

"Hey, slow down. You haven't even started yet." Alex laughed too.

"Yeah, maybe I'm getting ahead of myself."

Maya arrived with a platter of appetizers for them and laid it on the table.

"Oh, that looks delicious," said Leonna.

"Leave some room for the souvlaki, it's Jack's speciality," said Maya. "Kali Oreksi." They helped themselves to the food: zucchini balls, tzatziki, olives and a delicious tahini dip.

"This is fabulous," said Leonna, as they both eagerly got stuck into the food.

Alex looked over at her.

"Do you mind if I don't become a financial hot shot?" he

said. Leonna smiled and reached out across the table to put her hand in his.

"Alex, I would mind if you didn't follow your dream, if you didn't have passion for what you do. You told me once that you wanted to build something real, to create something that lasts. Well, this is it. You're at the beginning of that journey."

"Yeah, that's the way I feel about it. You've got to have something in your life that gives you purpose. Then, if you can do it with people that you care about, I guess you can't ask for much more.

"You know, I used to think that being a professional investor was the end goal; that that was what it was all about. I think I realize now that it's more of a means to an end. I'm not about to quit the investment game. I love it too much. I just have the feeling I'm going to be more of a 'long term buy and hold' kind of a guy, going forward." She squeezed his hand and smiled.

"That's okay. There's a lot to be said for a long term hold you know." He laughed and looked at her across the table, her deep green eyes sparkling in the candle light. It felt like things would work out.

The End

Acknowledgments

I started writing this book during the COVID epidemic. I imagine I wasn't alone in choosing that time to embark on writing a debut novel. Stuck inside the house with no one for company but a would-be novelist, deep in his own thoughts, was a lot to ask of anyone. I should firstly therefore, thank my wife *Naomi* for allowing me the time to complete this reckless endeavour.

There are many things that you come to learn when writing a book for the first time. Completing a first draft does not mean that you're on the home stretch. It does not mean either that your friends and acquaintances will be lining up to pass judgement on your masterpiece. It takes a certain type of person. Someone who is generous enough with their time and is prepared to look through the imperfections to see what the book could be, rather than what it currently is.

I was fortunate early on to come across the people at *Writersservices*. They opened my eyes to the world of editing and what it takes to elevate a draft to something that could be worthy of publishing. I was truly amazed at their ability to read my manuscript over the course of just a few days and put together the most insightful and educated feedback. Thank you for putting me on the right road.

My good friends, *Nils Salgeback, Ian White and Tim Barry;* you were my sounding boards. Nils, it feels like I should put you in with the professionals. You always tell it the way it is, even when you're delivering the truth to a friend. Somehow, you find a way to make it inspiring. Ian, I couldn't have found anyone more qualified to run the rule over my work and Tim, you gave me the belief and encouragement to keep going when I needed it most.

Finally, I must acknowledge the Investing Community. The people who write the blogs and create the content; the people who actively participate every day to maintain the community that we can all feel a part of. You were the inspiration for this novel.

About the Author

Andrew Vaughan was born and brought up in the north of England, but now lives with his wife and two children in Tokyo, Japan.

He first came to Japan on a government scholarship before becoming a landscape designer and some years later returned there to make it his home. It was a long and winding road that led from one small island country off the European continent to another off the eastern edge of Asia, but like all the best adventurers, he followed his heart.

His fascination with the world of private investing began more than twenty years ago and he has been an active investor ever since. Investing is one of the few disciplines where the amateur has some real advantages over the professionals. You're just not supposed to know it.

Printed in Great Britain
by Amazon